Daughter of Magic

Karen Eisenbrey

For Kerit

Karen Eisenbrey

Dedication

For Keith,
who saw a story in a dream and a book in a draft;
and who sets a daily example
of doing the creative work that is yours to do.

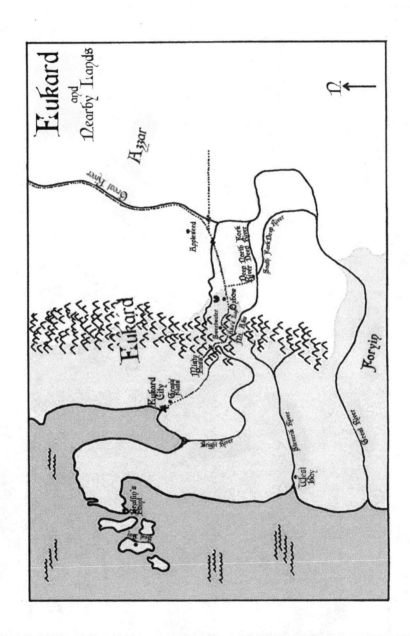

Daughter of Magic

Chapter I

Luskell walked at twilight on a country road she didn't know. She wasn't lost; she was on her way to Deep River. It was the town that was lost, and she had to find it.

She could make out silhouettes of scattered trees in the distance, but no lighted windows or darkened houses. Yet she knew she was near, the way she knew things in dreams. Oh. A dream. Of course. She kept walking.

But not alone. Luskell sensed a presence at her side, keeping pace with her. She didn't dare look but stopped in the road and whispered, "Who are you?"

"Don't you know me, Luskell?"

Her fear fled, and she turned to face her companion. He was a tall young man, rail thin, with Mamam's pale skin. It should have been too dim to see clearly, but a light from somewhere else showed his hair to be as red as Mamam's, too.

"Ketwyn?"

He grinned. "You do know me! I knew you would! I told him you would."

"But you're a baby. You're dead."

"Had I lived, I would be eighteen now. Almost nineteen."

Luskell struggled to make sense of this. She couldn't remember a time when she didn't know about her only sibling, a half-brother who died at birth. She had visited his grave, but she had never seen him; he died years before she was born. In her mind, he was both her big brother and her baby brother. She thought about him sometimes when she was lonely but had never expected to speak to him. What did one say to a ghost-brother?

"You don't have any freckles." That sounded rude as soon as it was out of her mouth. "I guess you wouldn't. You've never seen the sun." Even worse! "I mean, you haven't, have you? Is there a sun where you are?" That radiance from somewhere else...

"No, but...there is light." He looked up at the darkening sky. "Not like here."

"Where are we?"

"Your dreams."

"Oh." She swallowed bitter disappointment. Only a dream, as she'd suspected. "Then you're not real."

"I'm not?" He made a face of such exaggerated confusion that she had to laugh.

"You're teasing me!"

"I'm your brother, after all. So I *am* real. See?" He laid his hand on her shoulder.

His touch was cool and almost weightless, a tingling energy all the way to her fingertips. "You are." She wanted to touch him, but her own hand was too heavy to lift. "What are you doing in my dream?"

"Grandfather Knot has taught me many things. Visiting dreams is one of them."

"He's not *your* grandfather!" Luskell didn't mean to sound jealous, but if there were anyone she would have wished to meet more than Ketwyn, it was Knot. Everyone she knew told stories about the great wizard, a man who lived and died by his own rules. He died the spring before she was born. She never knew him, either.

Ketwyn made a slight bow. "I thank you for sharing him with me."

"Why haven't I dreamed of you before?"

"I think you have."

That sense of an unknown presence—she had felt it before in dreams but had never put a name to it. "That was you? But I couldn't see anyone."

"You weren't ready."

"Ready for what?"

"To see."

That was no answer, but he didn't seem likely to give a better one. "Do you go into Mamam's dreams?"

"I used to, but it made her sad. I go to Crane sometimes."

"Dadad? Why not your own father?"

He laughed at that. He had a wonderful laugh, the kind that tickled. She wished she could hear it every day. "Walgyn has no power."

"What do you mean?"

"We will meet again, Luskell, but now I must go."

"No, Ketwyn, wait! I—"

The dream faded as she rose from the depths of sleep. She could hear other voices now, but feigned sleep a moment longer. She hated to lose such a good dream. It had seemed so real.

Chapter 2

"Wake up, Luskell. We're here."

Luskell rubbed her eyes and rolled onto her back. She lay in the box of Uncle Jagree's wagon, starry sky overhead. "Ketwyn has no freckles," she murmured.

Where had *that* come from? No one responded, so maybe she hadn't said it aloud. She felt muddled from a day on the road. Although she usually dozed off when traveling by coach or wagon, she always woke groggy and unrested. She climbed down from the wagon box and stumbled inside the inn. Not even the good supper her grandmother had waiting for them could tempt her; Luskell was soon asleep in Klamamam's own bed.

Luskell woke in the morning to the sound of the adults talking in the next room. She didn't get up right away but lay back and listened.

"You're sure it's not a problem?" Dadad asked.

"You know I'm thrilled to have Luskell for the summer," Klamamam replied. "It'll be good for both of us. Before, you've always kept her with you."

Dadad sighed. "If only we *could* keep her with us. We used to leave her with our friend Ellys when we were on Embassy business, but—"

"But what?"

"Ellys has a son, a few years older than Luskell," Mamam explained.

"He's starting to *notice* her," Dadad said. "You saw how pretty she's getting—who wouldn't? But what if *she* starts to notice *him*? She needs a more watchful eye on her this time."

Klamamam chuckled. "I'm honored. But what about your Aklaka friends?"

"Same problem," Dadad growled.

Luskell's face burned. She was not getting pretty and she didn't *notice* boys! Not Ellys's boy Ambug, and certainly not Laki, who was like a brother to her. It was because of him that she called her parents by the Aklaka terms. Only one boy interested Luskell right now, and that was her real brother. Her dead brother.

Why did she wake with his name on her tongue? And what was that about freckles?

"There's something else." Mamam spoke so quietly, Luskell had to strain to hear her. "I'm not sure what it is, but things have...changed in Eukard City."

"Because of the new governor, you mean?"

"I hope that's all it is. It just seemed better to bring Luskell here. You'll keep her safe."

There was that word again—safe. It didn't sound like they were worried only about boys. But what danger could there be? Whatever it was, her parents would take care of it. They could do anything. That was the problem. How could she hope to measure up to people like that? It was probably just as well she had no magic of her own, but she didn't look forward to spending the whole summer in Deep River, where Dadad was the hometown hero.

Luskell's stomach rumbled. The good sleep had been worth the empty stomach, but it was time to get up. She rose, dressed, and joined her family for breakfast. Old Uncle Jelf had the same idea, entering the kitchen ahead of her.

"I hear Crane and Ketty, but where's the baby?"

"Right behind you." Luskell hugged him as he turned. Klamamam's uncle had never been a big man; now Luskell looked down at the top of his bald head. Blind as long as Luskell had known him, he still had his hearing. "But I'm not a baby, you know."

"I can tell." He reached up to touch the top of her head. "When did you grow so tall?"

She frowned, but Dadad laughed. "Get used to it, Luskell. Once I leave, you won't be looking up much."

"There's my sleepyhead!" Klamamam gave Luskell a warm smile. Luskell hadn't seen her grandmother in a few years. How tiny she appeared! But she hadn't lost any energy. Her silver braid swung as she set out food and stirred a big pot over the fire. "So, Crane, how long can you stay?"

Dadad sighed. "Not long. Only today, to get Luskell settled, but we have to leave early tomorrow."

"So soon? We'll barely see you at all!"

"I'll go around and greet everyone today. And we'll be able to stay awhile when we come back at the end of the summer."

"Be sure you let Sulika know. She says she's delaying her wedding especially so you and Ketty can be there."

"Sulika's getting married? We'd love to be there," Mamam said. "Who to?"

"Do you remember Foli?"

"The miller's youngest? Is he still sharing Keeper duties with Myn?" Dadad asked.

Jelf snorted. "No, he had to take charge of the mill when his brother Rynk left town. Myn's more suited to the job, anyway."

Dadad chuckled. "I'm not sure I'll ever get used to that—people leaving Deep River."

Mamam kissed his cheek. "It's been over twenty years, Crane! And all thanks to you." She turned to Klamamam. "I hope it's not an inconvenience to delay the wedding for us."

Klamamam shook her head. "If you ask me, Sulika's looking for reasons to put it off."

"What makes you say that, Mama?" Dadad asked.

"I'm not sure. Just a feeling."

Luskell only half-listened to the conversation as she ate. Mamam and Dadad seemed interested in this hometown gossip, but they knew these people better than she did. She was familiar with Sulika, who had often looked after her when she was small, but Foli and Myn were two of many interchangeable adults.

Klamamam got her attention by addressing her directly. "Luskell, I'm happy to share my room with you, but how would you like to move upstairs after your parents leave?"

"To the best room? I'd love it!" The last time they'd come to Deep River for a long stay, she'd been a little girl, sleeping on a pallet on the floor of her parents' room. But now she was fourteen, practically grown. If she had to stay here, it would be nice to have a room and a bed all to herself.

"Just—keep her safe." It was hard to tell whether the gruffness in Dadad's voice was real or put on. "No boys, Mama. Promise?"

Klamamam laughed. "I'll do what I can. I'm sure Luskell won't be any trouble."

The kitchen was cozier than the big, empty common room, but it was near the front door if anyone came looking for Klamamam. As they were finishing their meal, the door burst open. "Are they here, Auntie Stell?"

"Yes, Jagryn, they're here."

A dark-haired, freckle-faced youth came into the kitchen. Jagryn was Sulika's brother, and more than a year older than Luskell. She was taller now. She liked how he was named for his Uncle Jagree and Auntie

Brynnit, similar to how Luskell was named for her two grandmothers. It seemed more creative than being named for one's parents as so many people were. He gave Luskell a brief glance, but all his attention was on Dadad. "Papa sent me. He didn't want to miss you this time."

"I was just on my way to see him. Tell him I'll be along soon."

"Good. Oh, and Mama says you're all invited to lunch." Jagryn grinned, glanced at Luskell again, and hurried away.

Mamam watched him go. "I was right, Crane. He has it."

"You always know. I'll talk to Elic right now. It's time." He got up from the table and followed Jagryn before Luskell could ask what they were talking about.

Mamam began to clear the table. "Let's help Stell, and then we'll go see Brynnit."

Luskell wished she could have gone with Dadad. Why did she have to work, and he could go visiting without a second thought? But she liked Auntie Brynnit, and maybe the twins would be there.

It didn't take long to clear and wash the breakfast dishes. There were no other guests at the inn this morning, though Klamamam expected a crowd in a few days time because of the summer dance. "I'm sorry you'll miss it. Are you sure you won't stay?"

Mamam shook her head. "We can't, but I'm sure Luskell will enjoy it."

"I thought Dadad said to keep me *away* from boys."

Both women laughed. "You'll be well supervised," Klamamam said.

Luskell frowned. "I can take care of myself."

Mamam patted her shoulder. "We worry."

Luskell shrugged her off. "Let's go."

It was a bright, clear morning, already growing warm. The summer sky seemed huge without the city's crowd of buildings or the forest's dense canopy. The houses were relatively close together, but they weren't big, and there weren't many. The wide, rolling prairie beyond added to the sense of openness.

Luskell and Mamam headed to the house on the other side of the inn's stable. Unlike most of the houses in Deep River that were made of river rock and field stones, it was built of wood. It was solid, though—as solid as Uncle Jagree, who built it.

Auntie Brynnit greeted them with a bright smile and hugs. She was smaller than Mamam, if that was possible, still young and pretty with her pink cheeks and long brown braid down her back. "Look at this girl! Jagree told me she'd grown up, but I didn't believe him. I guess she got her pa's height."

"I'm not that big," Luskell objected.

"No—not among the Aklaka," Mamam said with a smile. "Enjoy it. I've always wished I was taller."

Auntie Brynnit and Uncle Jagree weren't blood kin to Luskell, but like everyone she called "aunt" or "uncle," they were such long-standing friends of her parents that they might as well be family.

They went inside and sat at the square table.

"Where are Greelit and Grynni?" Luskell asked.

"They went with Jagree to look at a horse," Auntie Brynnit said. "If I'd known you were coming so early, I would have had them wait."

"That's all right. I'll be here all summer, so I'll see them another time." Luskell wasn't that disappointed. She liked the twin girls, but they were three years younger than she was. She wasn't sure they would have much in common anymore.

Auntie Brynnit poured three cups of tea. "I had a letter from Kiat, so I knew you were on your way. She says they'll keep your rooms for you."

"I hope it's no trouble. We won't need them this summer, but it's nice to have a familiar place when we're not at Embassy House."

"Maybe we'll come and stay again, now that the girls are bigger."

"Your sister would love that. She misses you."

Luskell half-listened as she stole glances around the room to see if anything had changed. The house was small but seemed spacious. Uncle Jagree had designed the three rooms cleverly with many shelves and hooks so all needed items were close at hand but out of the way. This main room had a row of five windows with a broad sill where Auntie Brynnit grew herbs and flowers in pots. It was summer, so the iron cookstove stood in a lean-to outside the back door where it wouldn't overheat the house. This opened up the main room even more.

She began to fidget as Mamam and Brynnit left off sharing news and began to talk shop. They were both healers and were soon speaking of things Luskell didn't understand at all. Mamam must have noticed because she broke off with a chuckle. "I'm sorry, Luskell. Why don't you go out and find your friends?"

Luskell leaped up. "Thank you!" She hurried out the back door to visit the only friend she had really missed.

Chapter 3

The river winked in the sunlight, and Luskell felt at home.

She reached a set of steps cut into the steep riverbank and climbed down to the pebbly shore. The air was warm and still, noticeably moister, with an indescribable green smell. A few cottonwoods grew on the bank and cast islands of shade on the water and the damp, rocky shore.

In her going-on-fifteen years, Luskell had lived in small towns, a big city, and the forest, but if she had a home, it was Deep River—not the town, though her father had grown up there, but the actual river. Rapid and noisy in the mountains, wide and flowing along the south fork, summer-shallow in the north fork that bordered the town of Deep River, Luskell's beloved river welcomed her.

She still didn't like that her parents were leaving her for the whole summer, but maybe it would be all right. She missed her city friends, but she knew people in Deep River besides Klamamam. Or, she used to know people. The last time she'd visited, she'd had plenty of playmates around her age, but that seemed a lifetime ago. She'd changed a lot in three and a half years, and she assumed they had, too. Would they even remember her?

Most years, the family spent the winter either in Deep River or in the mountains with their Aklaka friends at Aku's Lap, with summers split between the city and Misty Pass, where Luskell's other grandparents lived, or an Aklaka hunting camp. This year, they had spent the whole winter and spring in rented rooms in the city. It was something to do with wizarding work of Dadad's, but Luskell didn't know the details. It wasn't the first time and likely wouldn't be the last. But this was the first time her parents had decided to leave her in Deep River for the whole summer. The previous day, the three of them had come down from Misty Pass on the afternoon coach. Because of delays, it had been late at night when they reached the coach office in Oxbow, the nearest to Deep River. Then Luskell had walked to Deep River.

She shook her head. That was wrong. Uncle Jagree was waiting for them, and they rode in his wagon. She must have fallen asleep and dreamed she was walking to Deep River. That seemed like a dull dream, yet she had regretted waking from it. What else was it about? It was right there, behind a curtain, but she couldn't remember.

She walked downstream at the water's edge and let the soothing murmur fill her mind. She could almost believe there were words in it. She was on the point of understanding when the dream came back to her.

Ketwyn. No freckles. Not a baby, a young man, but still her brother, though a spirit. He said he knew her grandfather. He said they would meet again. Could that be true? Was it real?

A human voice broke in and scattered her waking dream. "Luskell? It is you, isn't it? Do you remember me?"

She squinted up at the young man at the top of the bank. It took a moment to recognize him. "Crane? You're grown up!" She scrambled up the steps cut into the bank. He reached out a hand and helped her over the last bit.

He chuckled. "I could say the same to you."

Luskell dropped his hand and clasped her own hands behind her back. She studied the toes of her shoes. The last time she'd seen her father's namesake— they called him Young Crane to avoid confusion—he was a gangly sixteen-year-old, awkward and of little interest to eleven-year-old Luskell. Now he was a man. It had never before occurred to her to think a man handsome, but Young Crane was.

Luskell composed herself and smiled at him. He had brown eyes and dark blond hair, cut short, with a neatly-trimmed beard that made him look older than his nineteen years. He was only slightly taller than

Luskell, with a blacksmith's muscular build like his Uncle Jagree. "Why aren't you at the forge this morning?"

"Jagree went to look at a horse and gave me the morning off." He dropped onto the grass and leaned back on his elbows as he looked out over the river. "This is the best spot on a summer day. I'm lucky it's right behind my house."

Luskell sat beside him. It was a nice spot, close to the water and shaded by a big cherry tree. The branches were thick with ripening fruit. "Are these sweet cherries?"

"No, sour. I learned that the hard way." He made a face and chuckled to himself. "I saw your father this morning, so I guessed the rest of the family must be around here somewhere. Are you staying long?"

"They're not, but I'll be here all summer. I'm supposed to help at the inn." She rolled her eyes.

"We've all done that one time or another. Don't worry; Auntie Stell won't work you too hard. And you'll be here for the summer dance! You've never been, have you?"

"No, but I went to the Governor's Ball last winter in Eukard City."

He was silent a moment. "Deep River must feel like a backwater after everything you've seen. You're too sophisticated to be interested in a country dance."

"I didn't mean it like that! I'm pleased to go to the dance." She was appalled that she might have insulted him. Then she noticed the corners of his mouth twitching in a suppressed grin. "You were making fun of me?"

He flopped back on the grass and roared with laughter.

She threw a twig at him. "It's not nice to tease!" She remembered dream-Ketwyn's teasing. "I'm not your sister, you know."

He sat up again, still chuckling. "But you call my parents Aunt and Uncle, which must make you my cousin. Almost as good."

When he laughed and smiled that way, it was all she could do not to stare. He really was good looking. Maybe he would dance with her... She collected her thoughts and changed the subject. "It must be strange, being named for someone who's still living and comes to visit sometimes."

He smiled. "The way I heard it, we were both named for his father—or a name he went by."

Luskell nodded. Her grandfather had used many names in his day, but she thought of him only by the last one. "Do you remember Knot?"

"I was pretty small, but yes, some."

"I wish I did! What was he like?"

"He did magic tricks for my fourth birthday; I remember one with flowers turning into butterflies. He..." Young Crane gazed up into the branches and released an audible breath. "He wasn't like anyone else." His brow creased in a thoughtful frown. "I might be remembering wrong, but I think he died soon after that."

A pang surprised Luskell, as if she'd known Knot and the loss was still fresh. "Were—were people here sad when he died?"

"I guess the ones who knew him were. I never saw Sulika cry so much."

"I never saw her cry at all."

"So there you go. We were sad, and of course Auntie Stell still is." He gazed at her. "You've probably heard this before, but you have his eyes."

"Yes, I know." Luskell rarely thought about her dark blue eyes, or any other part of her appearance. She wasn't used to young men commenting on her looks. She liked that Young Crane had noticed, but she didn't know what to do with it and quickly changed the subject again. "Dadad had something urgent to discuss with Uncle Elic. Do you know what it was?"

"No, I was on my way out when he arrived. But he's still there. Maybe he wanted to talk over old times."

"Maybe." Luskell doubted it. Dadad had said, *It's time.* But time for what?

"Come up to the house. Mama and Sulika will want to see you." Young Crane stood and held out his hand to help her up, but she got to her feet without assistance. She liked the idea of holding his strong, warm hand more than she wanted to admit. She walked at his side but deliberately did not look at him.

They came up to the house from behind. One wing was built of wood, like Uncle Jagree's house. The older section was the more typical stone. A path led between the house and an ancient apple tree loaded with unripe fruit. A thriving vegetable garden lay just beyond the tree's shade. "Your garden is well-grown."

"Thanks to Sulika. If she touches a seed, it grows."

"You make it sound like magic."

"I think it is—a touch of Great-gram Elika's power." Crane snorted a laugh. "When we were small, I thought I'd be the wizard in the family—that it came with the name. But it seems to have skipped me."

"There's nothing wrong with that."

"I never said there was. Hey, folks, look who followed me home! Can we keep her?"

They came around to the front of the house. Dadad and Uncle Elic sat on chairs on the porch, and Jagryn perched on the porch rail. With his wavy, dark hair and freckles, the boy bore a strong resemblance to his father. The men laughed at something, but Jagryn took one look at Luskell and galloped into the house as quietly as a spooked horse. Apparently his feet had grown before the rest of him. Aunt Sunnea appeared in the doorway and smiled at Luskell, lines crinkling around her sky blue eyes. Her wheat-gold hair was sprinkled with gray. She stepped out and hugged Luskell. "Look at this beautiful girl! It's wonderful to see you, Luskell."

Young Crane and Jagryn's older sister Sulika joined them. She had her mother's light blue eyes and her father's brown curls. Luskell had always liked her; she was friendly, but with a sense of mischief and independence. It was hard to picture her *married*. She grinned at Luskell. "What did you do to Jagryn, Luskell? He looked terrified."

"What? Nothing. He ran off before I could even say hello."

Dadad rose from his seat. "It was probably me. We were just telling him about my accident, and I showed him my scar." He waggled his disfigured right hand. It was an ugly scar with a harrowing story—he had set his hand on fire with the first spell he ever worked. But even that seemed unlikely to frighten a boy Jagryn's age. Maybe he was sensitive.

"Where's Ketty?" Aunt Sunnea asked.

"Still at Auntie Brynnit's, probably," Luskell replied. "You know how they are when they start talking."

Aunt Sunnea smiled and turned back toward the open doorway. "Jagryn? Run over and remind Brynnit about the picnic we're having today. She said she'd bring the pies."

Jagryn answered from inside the house. "What about Grammy and Gramps?"

"And Grandpa Yshna, and Stell, too, if she's free."

"Yes, Mama." Jagryn slipped through the crowd without looking at anyone. Luskell watched him dash away. She couldn't imagine what might have frightened him on such a beautiful day.

Chapter 4

While Jagryn was gathering the other guests, everyone else helped prepare for the picnic. There was no way to pack the expected crowd comfortably inside the small house. Dadad and Young Crane carried the kitchen table outside. Aunt Sunnea and Sulika loaded it with bread, cheese, fresh greens, and a big platter of roasted chicken. The table wasn't large enough for everyone to sit around, but it was a picnic; as long as they had somewhere to sit, they could hold plates in their laps. Luskell helped Uncle Elic bring benches from the school to provide enough seats.

Jagryn returned with Auntie Brynnit and Mamam, each carrying a rhubarb pie. Jagryn's grandparents weren't far behind. Aunt Sudi and Uncle Ohme were Uncle Elic's parents; Dadad had always called them aunt and uncle, so Luskell did, too. Grandpa Yshna was Aunt Sunnea's father and had allowed Luskell to call him grandpa for longer than she could remember. It was too late to question it now.

Aunt Sudi greeted Luskell with a warm embrace. "What happened to the little girl I knew? Oh, it's good to have you here again!"

"It's good to see you, too." Luskell pressed her face into Aunt Sudi's glossy black hair. It was shot through with surprisingly little white, considering she was older than Klamamam, her lifelong friend. It smelled pleasantly of cooking and medicinal herbs. Everything about Aunt Sudi exuded comfort and competence. Even without magic, she was a skilled midwife who had helped Mamam train Auntie Brynnit.

Old Uncle Ohme offered Luskell his hand to shake. It trembled a little in her grasp, but his smile was welcoming all the way to his gray-blue eyes. What remained of his hair curled wildly, much like his grandson Jagryn's. He wasn't much of a talker but didn't need to be with Aunt Sudi around.

Uncle Jagree and the twins showed up just as everyone was lining up to fill plates.

"Hello, you two!" Luskell greeted the two girls. Greelit and Grynni seemed so small now. The three of them had been playmates the last time she was here, back when they were eight and she was eleven. "What's new in Deep River?"

The twins joined hands and danced around Luskell.

"We got a new horse, and she's so beautiful!" Greelit cried. She had straight brown hair like Auntie Brynnit, and she had Uncle Jagree's brown eyes.

"Pa says we get to help gentle her and choose her name!" Grynni put in. She was smaller than her sister and had black hair like her grandmother Sudi. "You're staying all summer, aren't you? You can help us!"

Greelit frowned. "She doesn't know anything about horses."

"How do you know?" Luskell asked. "Grandpa Eslo lets me help feed the horses at the Fogbank, and Mamam took me riding once."

Grynni giggled. "There's a lot more to it than just—"

Uncle Jagree silenced her with a look. "This will be a chance for her to learn more about them."

"I like to learn new things," Luskell said. "Thank you for inviting me."

Grandpa Yshna took Mamam's hand between both of his. "So, Ketty, what are the fashions in Eukard City these days? Did you bring anything I can copy?" The old tailor was so stooped that he stood no taller than Mamam, but his blue eyes twinkled when he smiled. His daughter, Aunt Sunnea, had those same eyes and had passed them on to her own daughter Sulika.

"I didn't, but Luskell has a dress you'll want to see."

Sulika laughed. "But don't let Grandpa borrow it, or he'll take it apart to make a pattern."

They all filled their plates and found places to sit and eat. The men gathered on the porch steps where they laughed loudly and all talked at once. The women pulled two benches close together so the five of them could visit more easily while they ate from plates on their laps. Luskell and Jagryn sat on the grass with Greelit and Grynni. It didn't take the younger girls long to exhaust the local news and start in again on their new horse. Jagryn didn't have anything at all to say and soon drifted over to sit near the men. Luskell feigned interest in the twins' conversation but let her attention wander to the other groups.

Aunt Sudi gently nudged Mamam. "I wish you could stay all summer, Ketty. We've got a crop of babies all due around the same time. If they all come at once, Brynnit and I will be stretched thin."

Mamam thought a moment and smiled. "Big blizzard last winter?"

Aunt Sudi nodded, chuckling. "Same old story." She turned to Aunt Sunnea. "I always wondered if that's how you got Jagryn."

Aunt Sunnea blushed. "We didn't need a blizzard. And I wouldn't have minded another one. Not that I have any complaints about these three."

"I'm glad there weren't any more. Two brothers is plenty!" Sulika said. "What about you, Auntie Brynnit? Do you wish you had more than two?"

Auntie Brynnit blushed and looked not much older than Sulika. "I imagine I could still have another, except it might be two again. But I'm glad Ketty taught me her secret so it's not up to chance."

Sulika laughed. "That sounds like a useful secret! Care to let me in on it before my wedding?"

"I'm not sure it would be any use to you," Mamam replied. "It requires certain—abilities."

"Sulika might surprise you," Auntie Brynnit's dark eyes sparkled. "She makes things grow."

Mamam studied Sulika, then nodded. "I see what you mean. All right, Sulika. Come see me this evening, and I'll tell you what to do."

Luskell didn't know the details of this secret, but she'd heard her mother speak of being *careful*. She assumed it was some piece of healer magic, and the reason she had no younger siblings. She'd wanted them once, but now it was difficult to imagine, except for the dead brother who visited her dreams.

"Twins can be a challenge," Auntie Brynnit said. "Do you remember when they had their own language? I couldn't understand them at all!"

Mamam laughed. "I had the same problem with only one. We were with the Aklaka when Luskell was learning to talk, and she picked up their language first! That forced me to learn it, but I'll never be as fluent as she is." She smiled across at Luskell, who returned the smile and looked away. It was hard not to eavesdrop, though she knew it wasn't polite. She continued to listen, but they weren't talking about her anymore.

"I wasn't even thinking," Aunt Sunnea said. "We should have invited Foli, too. I could still send someone to get him."

"No, this is fine," Sulika assured her. "It's better with just the family."

Luskell could hear the smile in Aunt Sunnea's voice. "Foli is almost family."

"But he isn't yet."

No one said anything to that. After an awkward silence, Auntie Brynnit changed the subject. "The cherry tree is loaded! Are you having a picking party?"

"I'd love the help," Aunt Sunnea replied.

That sounded more like work than a party. Luskell shifted her attention to the men.

"I have two years left, and then I'm finished," Uncle Elic said. "I won't run for mayor again."

"Who do you think will?" Dadad asked.

"I don't know. Auntie Stell would be the best—she already runs everything! But I'm not sure she needs the extra responsibility."

"Maybe I will," old Uncle Ohme said. "I have all kinds of time now that I'm retired from smithing."

"It's not often a job passes from son to father," Uncle Elic said. "But I'm sure none of this is half as exciting as what Crane's been doing. How are things in Eukard City?"

Dadad chuckled. "Not exciting. Well, we did go to a big ball last winter, and sometimes we go to concerts or the theater. Other than that, it's exactly like here—we do our work and spend time with friends."

"Your work isn't much like anyone's here, though," Uncle Elic said.

"We both put in some time with the healers at Balsam's House," Dadad allowed. "That's very rewarding work. And I still like to walk around town until I sense a need for my kind of help. It's mostly small matters, though—lost dogs and children, minor accidents, the occasional house fire ..."

"And is Luskell joining the family business?" Young Crane asked. He winked at her; she looked away, her face burning.

"She'll be helping at the Heron this summer, so—"

"Not that one! *Your* business."

"While we're in the city, she goes to school."

Luskell appreciated the way Dadad deflected the question. When she was younger, they used to talk about the things she might learn to do when her power arrived. No one had mentioned it lately. Dadad, at least, seemed to accept that magical power was not in her future. She hadn't thought about being an innkeeper, but there wasn't anyone else to inherit Klamamam's place. Maybe *that* was her future.

"It's the only chance she gets for formal schooling," Dadad continued. "I'm sure you approve, don't you, Elic?"

Uncle Elic—a teacher—grinned. "What else could I say? But I think you're being modest. You do some very important diplomatic work, too."

"Ambassador Naliskat does the important work," Dadad corrected him. "I serve as his translator. But Ketty has more *influence*."

Jagryn hung on Dadad's every word. "What about enemies? Bad wizards? Do you ever fight them?"

Everybody went silent. Mamam turned to look at Dadad with a troubled expression. Dadad smiled at her and returned his attention to Jagryn. "No. I don't think I've ever had an enemy. There aren't that many truly bad wizards—at least, not that many with the power to back up their threats."

Jagryn frowned. "But didn't you defeat Yrae?"

"I have that reputation." Dadad glanced from Uncle Elic to Mamam. "I think it's been long enough, don't you?"

Mamam nodded. "If you think your mother wouldn't mind."

Dadad took a deep breath. "Here it is, then: the truth. Yrae was not a bad wizard. And I didn't exactly defeat him."

Jagryn looked outraged. "You did, too! You must have. How else did you break the curse?"

"It wasn't a curse," Dadad began.

Mamam and another voice joined in to finish the statement. "It was an enchantment."

They all looked around as Klamamam joined the group. "I heard there was a party going on here. Am I in time for pie?" She helped herself to a slice and sat on a bench near Luskell and the twins.

Dadad grinned at her. "It's a good thing you're here. I'm about to tell about how I didn't exactly defeat Yrae. Unless you'd like to?"

"Go ahead. Maybe I'll tell my version later."

He nodded. "Yrae was not a bad wizard," he repeated, "and I didn't defeat him. I—helped him find his way home."

"That doesn't make any sense," Jagryn objected.

"It does if you know one more thing. He was my father, Jagryn. Your Uncle Knot."

Sulika sprang to her feet, her cheeks pale. Young Crane dropped his fork. Uncle Elic tried not to laugh. The young man stared at his father. "You knew? All along, you knew our Uncle Knot was Yrae?"

"Yes, I knew. I promised Stell I'd keep it secret, though I hadn't thought about it in years."

Sulika shakily resumed her seat. "But—but—but— how can it be? Uncle Knot was such a nice man. He played with us! I can't believe he was evil."

"What did Crane just say?" Uncle Elic asked. "He wasn't evil. He was lost. Did Knot ever harm anyone here?"

They shook their heads.

"No, he didn't. He gave his life for a stranger, didn't he? This news doesn't change any of that. It makes it more...interesting."

The news wasn't news to Luskell. She had always known her grandfather was the legendary wizard, but like Uncle Elic, she had kept the secret. Having it out in the open would make her life easier this summer.

Through all this, Jagryn stared at Dadad. Now he fell backward onto the grass and slapped the ground with his hands. "Your father was Yrae! And he lived here!" He seemed to be wrestling with something, and Luskell didn't know what he might do. If he was that sensitive, he might burst into tears or have a fit or something. But he didn't. He laughed long and loud. "I am the luckiest boy in the world!"

Chapter 5

Stell had spent most of the afternoon at Elic and Sunnea's, neglecting chores in order to be part of the gathering. She doted on Elic and Jagree, and their wives and children. They were like family. But nothing compared to having her own family with her. She couldn't stop smiling when she thought about Luskell spending the summer. If only Crane and Ketty could stay awhile, her happiness would be complete.

Ketty and Brynnit had not yet run out of conversation, though the men lounged on the porch in companionable quiet. Young Crane finished the last piece of pie straight from the pan. Jagryn's attention was divided between the men and the girls—Luskell and his cousins, who sat in the branches of the apple tree. Their mothers didn't seem worried, so Stell tried not to be. There was really no need. Luskell climbed like a squirrel—or like her father.

Stell got up. "I hate to be the first to leave, but it's time to start supper."

Sunnea squeezed Stell's hand. "It was good you could come for a little while. We'll probably see you later—I'm sure Elic will welcome one more meal with Crane."

Crane and Ketty both got up, too. Luskell dropped from the apple tree. "Is it time to go?"

"You don't have to—" Stell began.

"You're the one we came to see," Crane replied.

The four of them returned to the Blue Heron together. Ketty helped in the kitchen, and Crane and Luskell started on the chores Stell had left undone. At suppertime, Crane tied on an apron.

Stell shoved him playfully. "What's this? You've done enough. Sit down."

"I want to help serve, for old time's sake."

She pretended to think about it, though she knew she couldn't dissuade him. He was as stubborn as his father. She smiled. "Go on, then. You can show Luskell how it's done."

He glanced at his daughter. Luskell stared across the room at Elic's family, two mugs of ale forgotten in her hands. When Young Crane smiled at her, she twitched and ale slopped onto the floor. Crane frowned. "She'll be all right, as long as someone keeps an eye on her. She's a bit of a dreamer."

"You were no different at that age."

Stell had her own work to do, but it was hard to keep her eyes off her son. He moved through the crowded room and never bumped a table or spilled a drop of ale. She smiled and returned to the kitchen.

Luskell dashed in behind her. "I need a plate of stew for Uncle Jelf." She filled a mug, took the plate Stell handed her, and spun around. With a startled cry, she crashed into Rakkyn, the son of a local farm family. Stew splattered his shirt and ale splashed onto his shoe.

"Hey!"

"I'm sorry! I'm sorry!" she wailed.

Crane appeared at Luskell's side. "It's all right, Luskell. I'll take care of it." He waved his hand and the stew returned to the plate, the ale to the mug. "Now get a fresh plate, and slow down this time."

Rakkyn rubbed his eyes and glanced up at Crane. There was hardly anyone who didn't look up at Crane, but Rakkyn was especially small next to him. Small, but well proportioned, with the thick, dark hair and fine features girls seemed to admire. So far, he didn't return anyone's regard, but it couldn't be long before he decided to settle down.

"He got in my way," Luskell grumbled.

Rakkyn touched his now-clean shirt and chuckled. "I was just checking to see if Stell needed help, but I see she has plenty. Luskell, is it? I'm Rakkyn. No harm done, but I promise to stay out of your way."

Crane turned and smiled at Stell as if he knew she was watching. He probably did. He had his father's senses, and his smile. He was near the age Knot had been when Crane brought him home, but the years had been kinder to Crane. The joy in his life was evident in everything he did. Knot never knew such contentment until near the end.

Once everyone else had been served, Stell sent Crane, Ketty, and Luskell to sit down and eat. She took a pitcher and started to refill mugs. "Stell," Briato called. "I need to ask you something."

The weaver sat across from Jelf at one of the long tables. He had eaten at home, then come to the Heron for his after-supper ale. In their youth, he had been one of Stell's would-be suitors, but it struck her now how old he looked. He squinted all the time, and she wondered how long he would be able to continue weaving. "What is it?"

"I heard something strange that you might want to set straight." He lowered his voice to a whisper. "They say that Crane's father was actually Yrae, the one who cursed Deep River."

They say. Stell smiled to herself. That was how Yrae's legend got started in the first place. He planted false rumors about himself and let gossips do the rest.

Stell was about to reply when Jelf jumped in ahead of her. "That's ridiculous! We met Crane's father. I couldn't see him, of course, but those who did said there was no doubt about it. So what's this about Yrae?"

Stell squeezed her uncle's shoulder to silence him. "You're right, Jelf. But so is Briato."

Briato frowned. "How can that be?"

Stell drew up a chair and sat at the end of the table. "It happened like this. I was seventeen, and I knew what I wanted." She smiled at Briato. At the time, she would have been happy to marry him, or any of a list of young men who were interested. She didn't have a favorite. "Then one night a stranger walked in out of the rain. I took one look at that exhausted man, and everything I thought I wanted turned to vapor."

Jelf frowned. He wasn't there that night, but as far as Stell knew, even those who were didn't notice the visitor. But in her mind's eye, she could see again that tall young man with his dark face and compelling blue eyes—and the gruff, white-haired man he became.

"That doesn't sound much like the Mad Wizard," Briato said.

"He wasn't. Back then, he went by The Crane, though he didn't tell me that until later. What he told me were stories—true ones, things he'd seen and done. I didn't know then that he was a wizard, but I knew he wouldn't stay long in a place like Deep River. If he'd asked me to, I would have gone with him, anywhere in the world, and I didn't even know his name. He didn't ask me to do that, but I made him mine, and when he went away, he stole my heart. But he left me something." She glanced at Crane and smiled.

Silence had fallen in the room. It wasn't storytime; she had meant only to give Briato and Jelf an explanation. Now everybody was listening. But it was all locals tonight, and Elic's family already knew. From across the room, Crane gave her an encouraging nod.

"The Crane was a powerful wizard, but he didn't know how to be with people. Rather than stay and work things out, he fled. And rather than make a simple escape, out of fear and a misplaced sense of chivalry, he placed an enchantment on Deep River to keep outsiders out and insiders in, at least until my child was grown."

"How would that even work?" Jagryn asked. He seemed more curious than frightened.

"I can only tell you the effect. People on the outside forgot Deep River existed; it didn't occur to them to come here anymore. And we on the inside no longer felt inclined to go anywhere else, or even remembered the times we did. No one wondered about the identity of Crane's father, which meant no one thought to go after him until Crane himself went."

"I went along for part of the journey," Elic added. "I didn't know what the enchantment felt like until I'd escaped and returned. It didn't hurt us, but it was oppressive, a heavy hand pushing down all the time."

"He didn't consider the consequences. He changed his name to Yrae, and the enchantment became known as Yrae's Curse."

"Did she say Yrae came *here*?" someone muttered.

"She said he was Crane's father."

"I thought Knot was Crane's father."

"But—Yrae was *famous*!"

Briato stared at Stell. "So the curse was *your* fault."

She hadn't noticed Crane move, but suddenly he was there. He laid a protective hand on her shoulder. "It wasn't a curse, and it wasn't anyone's fault but Yrae's. He didn't mean any harm, but he rarely thought things through."

At the next table, Rakkyn raised his hand. "I'm confused. Who was Knot, then?"

Stell sighed. It was going to be a long night. "Knot was Crane's father."

"Formerly known as Yrae?"

"That's correct."

"The Mad Wizard."

Stell closed her eyes and counted to fifteen. Rakkyn was only being curious. She had ripped open an old secret, and they had a right to know the facts. She looked him in the eye. "That was just part of a made-up name. He never did any of those things in the stories. He started evil rumors to scare people into leaving him alone. But all he ever really did..." She closed her eyes and swallowed the lump in her throat. "... was love me."

"And you loved him back?"

Stell nodded.

Rakkyn smiled. "Happy ending. I don't know about anyone else, but that's good enough for me. No further questions."

As if it had been a trial! That comment broke the tension, and conversation resumed as Rakkyn got up and left. Stell gave Crane a grateful smile. He chuckled softly as he returned to his seat. Luskell was asleep, her head on the table. But she already knew Yrae's story from beginning to end.

How unfair to know the story but not the man when she was so much like him. Stell caressed Luskell's head. Knot lived on in the girl's hair and eyes but it wasn't the same.

"Hey, baby girl," Stell whispered.

Luskell stirred and opened her eyes partway. "Not a baby."

"I know. Come on, you'll be more comfortable in bed. You'll share with me tonight, then move up to the best room tomorrow."

"But it's not even dark yet! I want to hear your stories." Luskell sat up straight and made a show of being alert, spoiled by a huge yawn.

"This close to Long Day, it's light late. Storytime's over and you need your rest. Your folks want to make an early start tomorrow."

Luskell gave in without much fight, so she must have been as tired as she looked. Maybe she was having a growth spurt on a top of a few full days. Stell hoped the girl would reach her full height before she had to duck to get through doorways. Her height was another trait from her grandfather. Too bad the magic hadn't come down to her, though with her impulsive temperament, maybe it was just as well.

Luskell said good night to Elic's family and her parents before she disappeared into Stell's room. Crane and Ketty went to their room soon after. Stell stayed up to wash the dishes and shed a few tears in private. She was more accustomed to life without Knot than to life with him, but she would never not miss him. At least she had known him. Luskell never would.

Chapter 6

Crane woke early the next morning, but he could hear Mama already clattering around in the kitchen downstairs. He was tempted to go back to sleep. He wished more than anything that he and Ketty could stay in Deep River and take life easy for a while. But powerful as they were, they couldn't change what lay ahead. It was time to return to Eukard City.

Beside him, Ketty still slept. Her fiery hair lay in short, tousled waves on the pillow. It was a pretty picture, though he still missed the long tresses she had chopped off years ago. She found it more practical for the life they led, and it was *her* hair. Crane still wore his hair long, as most wizards did. As his father had. He wasn't expected to do anything with it—he tied it back and was done. A woman's hair had to be *fixed*. But Ketty could create at will the illusion of any amount or style of hair. It seemed a frivolous use of power, but she had plenty to spare, and it allowed her to get along in all tiers of society.

He kissed her awake. "Are you ready for this?"

She groaned. "Do I have a choice?"

"At least we get a hot breakfast first. Come on, get up. "

Mama had their breakfast ready by the time they came downstairs. She greeted them with a warm smile. "Should we wake Luskell or let her sleep?"

Before they could discuss it, Luskell stumbled into the kitchen and slumped at the table. Crane ruffled her hair as he took his own seat. "Thanks for getting up to see us off. We'll miss you."

"Mmf." She dragged her spoon through the porridge and tasted a small bite.

The rest of them didn't have much more to say. After a nearly silent meal, Crane and Ketty got up from the table. They didn't have to pack for their journey; everything they were taking could be worn or carried in a pocket. He bent to kiss Luskell goodbye. "I'll move your trunk upstairs."

She nodded but didn't reply or get up. After a moment, he left her there, disappointed that she didn't want to watch as he levitated the trunk up to the best room. Crane didn't often use magic as a performance, but he liked to show off for his daughter. He was still waiting for her to join in the act but knew better than to ask. Even without an audience, he made a good job of it. The trunk lifted and floated without touching a step or marring a doorframe. He settled it precisely at the foot of the bed. When he came back down, Luskell stood with Mama and Ketty by the front door.

Crane forced a smile onto his face. "Take good care of Deep River until we get back."

"I still don't understand why I can't go with you."

"We've been over that," Ketty said. "Things are different with the new governor. We don't know what to expect, and we can't afford to be distracted."

"Is that all I am? A distraction?" Luskell frowned and crossed her arms.

Crane stroked her hair. It was rough and tangled from a night's sleep. How much did he dare tell her? They had kept from her their acute sense of some undefined, looming danger, though he and Ketty had both felt it. A wizard's hunch was almost always more than that, but he didn't want to worry Luskell when he had no details to share. "We need to know you're safe, that's all. Then we can focus on our work."

Luskell nodded and let Crane hug her. Her Aklaka heritage showed in her height. At fourteen, she was already taller than her mother and all the women in Deep River. Most of the men, too, for that matter. She was built like an Aklaka girl, long-limbed and slender. Many of them equaled or surpassed Crane's height, though he doubted Luskell would get quite that tall. Her soft, springy curls were like Knot's hair, another Aklaka trait. It was dark brown, with red lights when the sun hit it, a color that came from Ketty's mother, Lukett. Her caramel skin tone was lighter than Crane's, darker than Ketty's. She had Mama's smile and Knot's deep blue eyes. She was a beautiful mixture of everyone Crane loved most.

His determination wavered. "Maybe we could stay a bit longer." He twirled Luskell in an impromptu dance step. "It's a shame to miss the summer dance when it's so close. We usually come too late."

"It's usually earlier," Ketty replied. "I wonder why it's so late this year."

"I think they schedule it when the musicians are available."

Ketty gave him an impatient look. "Anyway, I thought it was important that we go right back."

"It's only through tomorrow night."

"Yes, but you've already moved Luskell into our room. Besides, I have nothing to wear, and I don't care for the music."

Crane frowned. She was right about the clothing issue, though it wasn't the music she had a problem with. "What makes you think *he'll* be there?"

Luskell looked between them. "Who's *he*?"

"No one. But I don't like to take the chance."

Crane spread his hands and smiled. "You're right. We should go today." He didn't want to argue the point. When Ketty made up her mind, you didn't change it with words.

They pulled on cloaks; this early in the morning, it would still be chilly, though it was likely to be hot later. Crane counted the coins in his pocket. He had more than enough for their travel expenses. He extracted two silver duls and pressed them into Luskell's hand.

She shook off some of her sullenness. "What's this for?"

"Whatever you want. Add it to your fiddle fund or spend it at the market. Give it away, if you want." She managed most of a smile, and he wrapped an arm around her shoulders. "We have to go now."

"Is Jagree driving you back to Oxbow?" Mama asked.

"We can get ourselves there this time," Crane replied. "The luggage was all Luskell's. We're traveling light enough."

"Will that get you all the way to Eukard City?"

"No, but Oxbow is near enough not to tire us too much. We'll catch the early coach, pick up a few things in Misty Pass, and be back in Eukard City by dark."

They stepped outside and each hugged and kissed Mama and Luskell once more in front of the inn. Crane gripped his staff in his left hand and took Ketty's hand in his right. They walked west in silence.

After a moment, she squeezed his hand. "Is there time to visit Ketwyn?"

"Of course. A promise is a promise. So, magpies?"

She smiled and nodded. They were far enough off that Luskell wouldn't hear. They spoke the words of transformation and flapped into the morning sky.

Crane's first flight had been over Deep River more than twenty years before. He had been young then, and in turmoil, but the joy of flight had erased his troubles for a time. It was still exhilarating, but he knew not to overuse the ability. They'd both learned that lesson the hard way. They rarely traveled this way unless they had no other choice—never, if Luskell was along. There was no way to carry a passenger. But Oxbow was not far as the magpie flew, and flying would bring them there in plenty of time for the early coach. They could both do with the simple pleasure of it before they faced the task ahead.

In many ways, this job was nothing new. Every summer for the past fifteen years, Crane and Ketty had assisted the Aklaka ambassador in his dealings with the Eukardian government, for which they received housing, meals, and a modest stipend. Before that time, the Aklaka had kept almost entirely to themselves—so much so that many people did not know they were real. That isolation ended after the mischief of a rogue band of Aklaka caught the attention of the Governor's Guard. The Aklaka leader had decided it would be better for all of them to live in the open and take their chances.

Crane's role in all of this was not something he could have foreseen before he was in the middle of it. What did a solitary wizard and a country midwife know about diplomacy? But he had spent years with the Aku band of the Aklaka people seeking a connection to that side of his heritage. All Aklaka considered Aku the chief mountain and revered that band and its leader. Crane's youthful friendship with the future leader, the Uklak Takalanatlan, and his relative fluency in their tongue, led to his appointment as translator to her chosen ambassador. Ketty's role was harder to explain but perhaps more important. The Aklaka believed her to be the legendary peacemaking figure Aketnan, and she did seem to have a mysterious influence over both sides. She was always included in negotiations.

Those negotiations were often complicated but had so far always ended peaceably. Eukard granted the Aklaka autonomy to govern themselves and maintain their own culture within Eukard's boundaries in exchange for information about mountain plants and animals and reliable guide service through their territory. A few young Aklaka had gone to live in Eukardian towns, and a few adventurous Eukardians had joined Aklaka bands. Mostly the two societies ignored each other.

Crane feared that this peaceful co-existence might be threatened with the recent election of Governor Snowabi. He seemed benign, but there were rumors the new governor wanted the Aklaka to assimilate into Eukardian society. Crane didn't know how he meant to accomplish that. He hoped Ambassador Naliskat could change the governor's mind. But he and Ketty had both sensed trouble even before they left the city.

And there were other rumors. Crane assumed Ketty had heard them, too, but they hadn't talked about it. It was too much to accept. The rumors said Yrae had returned. Anyone else would greet this news with fear, but to Crane it had another meaning. If Yrae had returned, his father was back from the dead.

Chapter 7

As they flew over grassland and sagebrush, Ketty could almost forget Luskell's resentment. She was sorry to leave her daughter in that mood, but she didn't know what to do about it. Ketty hadn't been that way with her own mother because, by the time she was fourteen, her mother had been dead for five years.

Worry receded before the stark beauty of the morning. The rising sun turned ripening wheat fields to gold and cast long shadows from fence posts and lone trees. Red-and-white cattle grazed on a grassy slope. A solitary rider trotted toward Deep River.

Ketty tried to remember the last time she and Crane had flown together. Several years ago, somewhere in the mountains. She had never flown over the open country of the Dry Side. There had never been a need, and transformation required too much power to do it for fun.

After what seemed like only a moment in the air, Ketty glided down toward a patch of hilltop surrounded by a low stone wall, Crane right behind her. She lighted on the wall and resumed her own form. The change had been so brief she barely felt it, but she still rested a moment before hopping to the ground inside the wall. The graveyard.

Yellow climbing roses covered the wall with brambles, buds, and blooms. Among the graves, purple lupines and yellow daisies competed to provide the most cheer. In winter, the place felt desolate and grim, but in summer it was hard to believe it had anything to do with death.

"It's always so peaceful here," Ketty breathed, and even that seemed too loud. "Especially early in the morning."

They picked their way through wildflowers, past grave markers, to a particularly tiny grave, well-tended and thick with flowers. At the head stood an iron marker, worked into the shape of a flame and adorned with a single, dark red agate. Their friend Jagree had crafted the marker; the stone was a sign of Crane's promise that no matter where their lives took them, Ketty would be able to visit her first child's grave. No one could bring back Ketwyn, who hadn't lived even a full day. But many people cared enough to help her remember him.

"Mama's here, baby," Ketty murmured. "It's good to see they're still taking care of your spot."

Crane laid his arm around her shoulders. "That's Jagree for you. Keeps his promises."

"He's not the only one."

He drew in a breath and let it out, deliberate, controlled, calming the shiver of anxiety that rippled from him, over her. "Do you think, someday—a little boy...?"

"Don't, Crane. Not here."

He nodded and said no more, but he gave her a gentle squeeze and stepped away to visit his father's grave nearby.

Crane knew her story and never pushed, though he did raise the question from time to time. He didn't hold it against her that she'd borne another man's child—a man she thought at the time she loved. But Walgyn, fearing her power, had cast her out as soon as she revealed her pregnancy. She wound up on her own, staying with Crane's mother till the baby came. Crane wasn't there then; would it have made a difference if he had been? He couldn't have saved Ketwyn any more than she could. The child's death had broken her; she couldn't even drag herself out of bed for the burial. Grief stole all her power for a time. In her emptiness, she had nearly taken her own life, but the love of friends—Stell, Jagree, Knot—had helped her to a place where she could feel, live, love again. Her power returned, stronger and deeper than before. And then Crane had come back into her life after a long absence. She had borne Luskell because her love for him and her desire to have his child had been greater than her fear.

That was still true, but it seemed like tempting fate to try again.

She sighed. "We should go."

They stood by Ketwyn's grave and became magpies again.

As the main road came into view, Ketty expected Crane to turn west toward Oxbow, but he glided down to the roadside and transformed. She joined him.

"Why are we stopping here? What's wrong?"

"Maybe nothing." He pointed east along the road. Ketty squinted against the low sun. In the distance, a wagon stood by the road, not moving. "We should see if they need any help."

Ketty nodded, then sat down in the grass beside the road. This time, she felt the fatigue that resulted from even brief transformation. A short rest would restore her. Crane sat beside her and closed his eyes.

When they were both rested, they got up and walked toward the wagon. As they drew nearer, Ketty made out an animal in harness—a mule, to judge by the ears. The wagon box had the high sides and canvas cover of a travel wagon. It was possible these people were camping, though it seemed an unlikely spot. There was no obvious water source nearby, and the wagon appeared to be parked on a slant. No, the ground was level, but the rear wheel was broken. The wood had split in two places, and the iron rim was bent. A man appeared around the back as they approached.

"Good morning!" Crane called.

"Morning," the man grunted. He set down the box he was holding but stayed close to the wagon. Waves of suspicion rolled off him.

Crane glanced at the broken wheel. "It looks like you've had some trouble."

"Nothing but," the man admitted. "Five years of bad weather and bad luck." He took off his hat and wiped his forehead, pale above his sunburned face. Ketty started. By the way he moved, she had assumed he was an old man, but he was younger than Crane.

"Sorry to hear that," Crane said. "I take it you're a farmer."

"Tried to be. Failed."

"Whereabouts?"

"Up in Grouse Prairie, near the Azzar border. It's good land, if the weather cooperates, but it never did for me." He shook his head. "We're trying to get back to the city. I thought it would be easy going once we got to the main road. Then this morning, just after we started out again, the wheel broke, and I don't have a spare."

Crane nodded. "You could probably find a replacement in Oxbow."

"That's what I thought. If I left now on the mule, I should be back well before dark, but my wife is afraid to stay here alone with the children. So now we're thinking we'll load what we can on the mule and leave the wagon. Maybe I could sell the animal and get us seats on the coach."

A thin cry rose from inside the wagon. It sounded to Ketty like a small child, and not a healthy one. "Is someone ill?" she asked.

"My little girl," the man replied. "She won't be able to walk all the way to Oxbow. And she'll hate to part with that mule. I don't know how I'll tell her we have to sell Baby." He sighed. "Maybe we could sell some of our extra goods."

Ketty glanced at Crane. He smiled. He always knew when someone needed help. She turned back to the man. "I have some skill with healing. May I look at your daughter?"

He stared a moment, then nodded. "I'd be grateful."

She walked around to the back of the wagon. The man had already emptied out most of their goods. There wasn't much extra, and she had a feeling the junk dealer would pay as little as possible. Selling everything they owned wouldn't be enough, if they could even get it there. Baskets, cookware, furniture and stacks of boxes surrounded the open tailgate. The mule wouldn't be able to carry half of it, and Ketty doubted selling the mule would bring in enough to pay for four seats on the coach.

A boy of about ten crouched inside the wagon. A woman sat on a pile of blankets, holding a younger child of maybe five or six.

The man leaned in. "Here's a healer who happened by. Maybe our luck's turning."

"Good morning. I'd like to help you if I can." Ketty climbed into the wagon and knelt near the mother and child. "May I?"

The mother nodded. Ketty laid her hand on the girl's forehead. She burned with fever and shivered. "I hurt," the child complained.

"No wonder. You managed to catch winter wobbles in the summer! You must be very special." Ketty gave her an encouraging smile. "You'll feel better soon."

She spoke the fever charm and could have left it at that. It was an uncomplicated case. The right herbs would relieve most of the symptoms, and if the child could rest in bed, the disease itself would run its course in a week or two. But Ketty's herbs were all in Misty Pass, and this family was far from settled. The little girl might get worse, or the others might fall ill. Ketty called up more power and intoned a spell that would heal the infection and protect the rest of the family.

When she finished, the girl smiled at her and promptly fell asleep. Ketty felt the need of a nap herself, but it would have to wait. She climbed out of the wagon. The mother followed her.

"I don't know how to thank you. We've had nothing but bad luck for so long, and then you came along. We—" She broke off and gaped at her husband, who gaped at Crane.

Crane touched the broken wagon wheel with his staff. Only it wasn't broken anymore. "That should get you where you're going. You might want to pick up a spare in Oxbow, but you shouldn't have to sell your mule for that. The junk dealer will try to overcharge you, but don't let him. And keep your family in the wagon. He's—not respectful of women."

The mother burst into tears. The man put his arm around her and held her close. "Thank you, both of you! Will you stay and have a meal with us?"

Crane glanced at the sun. "We appreciate the offer, but—"

"We will, thank you." Ketty jerked her head toward the east. Crane looked and nodded. The early coach approached in a cloud of dust. Even flying, they wouldn't reach the coach office ahead of it. And Ketty wouldn't tell these people, but the healing had required a significant portion of her considerable power. She needed to rest and eat before she could transform again. Crane probably did, too.

They all waved at the coach as it passed. Crane assisted the farmer in repacking the wagon while Ketty helped his wife prepare a late breakfast. The little girl woke cheerful but hungry. Her mother laughed to see her well again.

"Where you headed?" the man asked when they had finished eating. "Can we give you a ride?"

Crane shook his head. "You don't need our extra weight. Good luck to you." They turned and began to walk west.

Ketty turned to wave goodbye. "We never even asked their names!"

"And they don't know ours. It's better that way. So, magpies again, or ravens?"

As magpies, Crane and Ketty flew on until they reached a stand of pines outside the town of Oxbow. A narrow, curved lake nearby gave the town its name. They alighted and resumed their own forms under the cover of the trees.

"That felt wonderful!" Ketty exclaimed. "I didn't know how much I missed it."

Crane grinned at her. She was flushed with excitement, and he couldn't resist kissing her. "Me, too. But I'm hungry again."

They walked into town and found the inn. They had plenty of time for a third breakfast (or early lunch) before the afternoon coach. They ate in silence until hunger's edge was dulled.

"I'm glad we stopped to help those people, but this changes our plans," Ketty said. "We won't make it to Eukard City tonight."

"We can sleep over in Misty Pass. Your father will be glad to see you."

She laughed. "Even if I don't have Luskell with me?" She sighed. "What are we going to do about her?"

Crane chuckled. "What can anyone do about a girl her age?"

"I'm serious! Did you hear what she said about Ketwyn? You know what that means."

"Are you sure she didn't make that up just to vex you?"

Ketty frowned. She and Luskell had been at odds recently, and there didn't seem to be anything Crane could do about it. "Maybe. But even if she did, she shines like you do! When will she start using her power?"

"I hope not before we get back. Besides, she might not be ready to use it. Or maybe she doesn't want it."

"How could she not want it? You know how rare such a gift is. She could do great things!"

"Who's to say she won't, in time? I don't think we can imagine what it's like for her. You had to hide your abilities, and mine weren't well-received. It must be completely different for her. She's been around magic all her life."

"That's what I mean—she has nothing to fear. We could teach her everything she needs to know."

"I know. I've tried. But parents aren't always the best teachers." He made a wry face. He had learned a great deal from his own father, but it hadn't been easy for either of them. "Maybe she wants to find her own way as we did. This summer apart might be exactly what she needs." Ketty made an impatient noise and continued to eat. Crane smiled at her. "Luskell is as stubborn as her mother, but she has good sense, too. After a summer without so much magic, she could have a very different attitude about her gift."

Chapter 8

The sun broke through after a drizzly morning in Eukard City and gleamed off the stones of the square. As the day turned pleasant, a young man took a seat on one of the stone benches in front of the library and watched the passing scene. Seekers of knowledge crossed the square to the library, seekers of healing, to Balsam's House. Magic users came and went from the Wizards' Hall, their social center and informal school. All but one.

With a quiet word and a subtle hand motion, the man on the bench faded from view. As long as he didn't move from his seat, he was invisible to non-magical eyes. He could observe without being observed. And take action, if he so desired.

A laughing couple paused near him, so close he could have touched their clasped hands. They didn't so much as glance his way; who notices an empty bench? Their attention was all for each other. It was easy to see why the man was so enamored. The young woman had large, dark eyes and a luxurious fall of chestnut hair that glinted red in the sunlight. She moved with alluring, quick-footed grace, and her laughter was like birdsong. The man seemed too ordinary for her, but when he pulled her close and kissed her, her eyes sparkled and the roses in her cheeks bloomed redder.

The man on the bench frowned as he watched them walk away. Someday he would have a woman like that. Someday he would have everything this city had denied him. As a boy, he had frequented the Wizards' Hall to learn to use his newfound power. Concealment was the only useful magic he'd mastered then. Someday they would regret teaching him even that. Because he didn't intend to remain invisible forever.

He flicked his finger, and the peaceful afternoon was disturbed by vague unease. People glanced over their shoulders and hurried indoors as unease turned to fear. Even the happy couple paused and looked around.

It was almost too easy.

He called himself the New Yrae, after Yrae the Mad Wizard, aspiring to occupy a similar terrifying place in legend. The New Yrae could bend the thoughts of an entire neighborhood, and they never knew they'd been enchanted. At this moment, everyone for blocks around was filled with nameless dread. He had performed this magic in other parts of the city with satisfying results. In some places, the fear was vague and unspecified; in others, he made them fear *him*, though no one knew what he looked like. It didn't matter what they feared. What did matter was that they believed, when relief came, that his employer had provided it. And if they didn't, he could make them feel that, too.

He hadn't learned this magic from his teachers at the Wizards' Hall, but on his own, from a grimy, forgotten book, lost behind a shelf in the library until he had liberated it.

The magical community should have been able to see through his concealment charm, but it was laughably simple to misdirect their attention and shield himself from their awareness. He could hide both his presence and his thoughts. Only one wizard concerned him, a man of great power and perception. The one called Crane. But he did not make a permanent home in the city, and had recently left town again. He had received his training elsewhere and rarely visited the Wizards' Hall. The New Yrae was free to instill fear, undetected.

Legend had it that Yrae the Mad Wizard had once sustained a general, pervasive enchantment over a whole town for decades. The young namesake wasn't sure where this had happened, or even if the story was true. He couldn't make the spell last more than a day or two, but that was usually enough.

Another legend told of Yrae transforming into a giant eagle to attack his enemies or carry off small children. Transformation had been denied the New

Yrae. He wasn't ready, they'd said. He lacked the power, the aptitude. He'd tried to teach himself without success, so perhaps they were right. But he wished he could have known, even once, what it felt like to change. To be something else.

No one had heard anything of Yrae in decades. There had been that one old man at the Wizards' Hall who claimed to have known and taught the Mad Wizard as a youth, under another name. But that couldn't be right; he must have been born with the knowledge and the skill. Could a legend die? The New Yrae preferred to believe he was merely in hiding, perhaps under a new name, awaiting the right moment to return.

And so the New Yrae borrowed the name and the reputation to promote his employer's career. It bothered him to use his talents for the benefit of another. Not that he wouldn't benefit, too—eventually. It felt like cheating. But this wasn't only magic. It was politics. *Someone* had to get his hands dirty.

Chapter 9

Luskell stood with Klamamam in front of the inn and watched her parents transform and fly away. When they were gone, the day seemed as empty as the sky.

"They actually left me here."

Klamamam gave her a one-armed hug. "Is here so bad? Or do you miss them already?"

"No, I miss...everything." Luskell blinked back tears.

"If you keep busy, they'll be back before you know it. Come on, let's do our chores, and then you can write to your friends in the city."

Luskell followed her back inside. How had she guessed? "Write what? There's nothing to tell."

"Then tell me about them. It'll help, I promise."

Together, they cleared the breakfast table and Luskell talked about the people she knew in Eukard City. "We lived upstairs from Keela and Wyllik, so I saw them almost every day. But you know them." Their mother was a Deep River girl who had moved to the city with her husband.

"I'm not sure I'd recognize them now, it's been so long. Keela's about your age, isn't she?"

"A year younger, but we started our bleeding the same month, so we might as well be." Luskell wouldn't have spoken so freely if any men had been about, but she was alone with Klamamam. "She looks so much like Auntie Brynnit, you wouldn't believe it. And Wyllik is a terrible tease, but so funny I can't even get angry."

Klamamam smiled and poured hot water over the dishes in the dishpan. "You should write and tell them you've seen their cousins here. And tell them to come visit us again."

"I might," Luskell allowed. "I don't think you ever met Ambug, did you? His mother used to look after me, so we know each other pretty well, though he's older."

"Is he your sweetheart?"

"No! When I was little he was my horsie. Maybe I should tell him about Grynni and Greelit's new horse." Luskell sighed. "I especially miss my school friends, Daisy and Cedar."

"Oh, I like those flower and tree names," Klamamam said. "They never caught on around here. I don't know why."

Luskell guessed it was because nothing ever changed in Deep River, but she didn't say so aloud. "Don't you like being named for your father and mother?"

"I never thought about it. Of course I can't complain when people name their child for her grandmothers." Klamamam's eyes twinkled as she squeezed Luskell's hand, then gave her a damp rag. "You can wipe off the table while you tell me about Daisy and Cedar."

"They're finished with school, so I don't know how much we'll see each other. Cedar wants to be midwife, so I guess I might see her."

"Will she train with your mother?"

"Probably at Balsam's House. She doesn't have any power that I know of, but I think she'll be good at it. She's very calm, and good with people."

"Sounds a lot like Sudi. What about the other one?"

"Daisy's mother is a dressmaker, so I suppose she'll do that, too." Luskell gave the table one last swipe with the rag. "What's my next chore?"

Klamamam sent Luskell to sweep and change the bedding in the best room while she finished washing the dishes. Being busy helped. Luskell still resented being left behind, but it was a relief not to argue about it. She wrote brief letters to all her city friends. They didn't say much more than where she was and that she missed them, but the day seemed full again.

She joined Klamamam in the kitchen. "All right, what's next?"

"Help me shape these loaves." Klamamam uncovered a ball of dough and divided it into four pieces. "I hope you have something to wear to the dance tomorrow night."

Luskell picked up a ball of dough and pulled it into a loaf shape. She liked the smooth, stretchy feel of it. "I brought all my clothes. What do people usually wear?"

"We like to put on our best."

"That would be my dress from the Governor's Ball. It should still fit—Mamam had it made a little large on purpose."

"That sounds perfect. Now, let me tell you a story..."

Klamamam told stories like no one else. Maybe it wouldn't be so bad here if she got to listen to stories all the time. But after lunch, Klamamam had to go over her figures. Not only could she not tell stories anymore but needed quiet so she could concentrate.

"Why don't you go over to the Village Hall? Myn will let you borrow my book. You can learn the stories for yourself."

"It won't be as good that way."

Klamamam kissed her. "Thank you. You can stay up and hear a few tonight."

Luskell went out. It was a sunny day, hot but with a breeze that kept the short walk pleasant. The Village Hall was dark and cool by comparison. The big meeting room stood empty, but the door to the library was open. Luskell, who had visited the library in Eukard City, smiled to herself at the use of such a grand word for the tiny room and its few shelves of books. Myn sat at the desk inside, writing in the log.

"Hello, Myn. My grandmother sent me to borrow her story book."

He looked up from his work and smiled at her. He was not yet thirty, but already his brown hair was sprinkled with gray. When he smiled, his face looked younger. "Luskell! Welcome back. Let me help you." He went to the shelf and pulled out the book. "Do you need a lamp, or is the light good enough?"

"I don't plan to sit inside! It's plenty bright out in the sun." She reached to take the book from him, but he pulled it back.

"I can't let you take it out of the Hall. You must read it here."

She scowled. "It's my grandmother's book. And I won't take it off the steps, I promise!" He didn't answer immediately. She forced herself to smile sweetly. "Please?"

"Well, all right," he said at last and let her take the book. "But not off the steps!"

"Thank you, Myn! I knew you'd be reasonable."

Luskell went back outside and sat on the top step with the book on her lap. Klamamam had told stories at the Blue Heron since she was a girl—tales she'd learned from her elders and new ones she made up on the spot. She'd always had a talent for bringing them alive for her listeners. Years later, but still long before Luskell was born, she'd started writing them down so they wouldn't be lost.

It was hotter out than Luskell was used to, but the sunshine felt good. She opened the book to the first story, an ancient tale of Old Mother Bones, set down in Klamamam's neat handwriting. Luskell heard her grandmother's voice in her mind as she read—not quite the same as hearing the tale told, but close. She shivered as she read of the skeletal old hag who could drag a living soul to the Other Side.

Soon after she began to read, a gray-striped cat rubbed against Luskell's leg. She thought she had seen it hiding under the porch at Uncle Elic and Aunt Sunnea's house the day before. It wouldn't come out with so many people around, but now it had decided to make friends. She petted it absentmindedly, and it settled down to sleep in the sun. Luskell returned to the book and was soon immersed in the stories.

"Luskell?" Jagryn stood at the bottom of the steps. The cat hopped down to his side and rested its front paws on his leg. He scratched its head.

"What?"

He looked away and dug his toe into the dust. "What—what can you do?"

She frowned. What kind of question was that? "I can read and write. I can cook a little. I'm learning to play the fiddle."

"That's not what I mean! You know...what can you *do*?"

Now she understood. He was talking about magic. Rather than answer truthfully, she pretended to miss his meaning. "I can gut a fish, dig a root, and dance if I have to." Hadn't Young Crane made her an honorary cousin? A cousin could tease.

She thought Jagryn would be angry, but he smiled and shook his head. "Fine, be that way." He sat on the step below hers. The cat immediately settled in his lap as if it had been there all day. "What book is that?" She showed him, and he nodded. "I love those stories. Auntie Stell tells them better, though."

"I know." Luskell felt bad for teasing him. He was only trying to be friends. "So, what can *you* do, Jagryn? Are you learning a trade?"

He slumped. "I should be, at my age. I started with Grandpa Yshna, tailoring. But I kept sticking myself and bleeding all over the work! I'm still amazed he kept me as long as he did. Cobbling was no better, and tanning made me sick."

"You don't have a trade, then?"

"I might. Here." He reached behind his back and held out a stem of lupine. As she reached for it, it turned into bright blue butterflies. The cat jumped and batted at them. They swirled around Luskell and brushed her face with their wings before they fluttered away and disappeared.

She stared at Jagryn. "That was well done. My father does that trick."

"Who do you think taught me? I wish he could have stayed longer. I want to learn more than one trick, but I have to wait until he comes back."

"There are books in the Hall. That's how he learned."

"I know, but Mama and Papa told Myn not to let me have them. They say it's too dangerous to have the books but no teacher."

"You heard how Dadad got his scar. He might agree with them." She pondered the boy. His big brown eyes were so eager, and he seemed to have some talent. "Did you cause some terrible accident when you discovered your power?"

Jagryn gave her a half smile and shook his head. "Never had a chance. Aunt Ketty thought she saw something in me last time you were here. I didn't know about it, but my folks kept a close eye on me. I got suspicious last year when I started to dream about flying all the time, but I didn't know for sure until Uncle Crane tested me yesterday. I guess I have enough power that he wants me to be his apprentice."

"How exciting! Too bad you have to wait, though. You should have Auntie Brynnit teach you some healing charms."

"Maybe." He didn't show much enthusiasm for that idea. "I kind of hoped you could teach me something."

"Me? I don't have any power."

His eyes widened. "You don't? Really? Everyone was sure you'd have double measure by now, with your parents as great as they are."

She slapped the book shut. The cat startled and ran for home. "Everyone was wrong." She stood and turned to go back inside.

"Don't be like that, Luskell."

She didn't reply.

She went back into the Hall and returned the book to Myn with a muttered, "Thank you." Jagryn was gone when she came back out. It was time to help Klamamam start supper, anyway. She went back to the inn, her good mood flown away like a magpie, like her parents. Why was she supposed to have power just because they did? Why couldn't she just be Luskell? Not for the first time, she wished she had a brother or sister to confide in. If only she could dream of Ketwyn again.

"Thank you for helping clean up," Klamamam said. "You should go to bed now—you look about to fall asleep where you stand."

"I am tired," Luskell agreed. She had stayed up late to hear every story. Klamamam was still in a mood to tell true tales about Knot. Tonight she had told what she knew about his years on Mount Aku, before Dadad found him. It made Luskell wish even more that she had known him. "Good night." She took off her apron and climbed the stairs to the best room.

"Tomorrow will be busier than today, so sleep well," Klamamam called after her. "Sweet dreams."

I plan on it. Luskell closed the door behind her and undressed for bed. She was more exhausted than she would have expected, but it had been a long and busy day. She climbed into the big bed and pulled up the sheet. She wouldn't need the quilt until later.

She forced herself to stay awake, a difficult task in the soft, cozy bed. She had found that if she thought about a subject clearly enough, she could sometimes dream to order. She recalled everything she knew about Ketwyn and pictured how he had appeared in that other dream, how his voice sounded, his touch, his laugh...

It wasn't working. She was wide awake. It was much too bright for sleep in this grassy field, though she couldn't find the sun in the sky. She looked around her. Where was her bed? Where was the inn? Or Deep River, for that matter?

Luskell smiled to herself. She *was* asleep, and dreaming. But she had failed to dream about Ketwyn, because she was all alone in this strange, peaceful place.

A light touch sent a tingle down her arm. "You're better at this than we thought!"

Luskell spun to face her brother. He was exactly as he had appeared before, but here, the whole scene was lit up. His hair flamed, and his eyes sparkled. They weren't Mamam's green eyes, but light blue. Luskell beamed at him. "I'm so glad to see you! I tried to dream of you on purpose."

He grinned. "So that's how you managed to come to us. Impressive. You shouldn't stay here long, though."

"Why not?"

"This is no place for the living. But I know Knot wanted to speak to you. Maybe that's him now."

Ketwyn peered into the distance, and Luskell followed his gaze. A figure approached improbably fast, but as it drew nearer Luskell could see it wasn't Knot. This was a thin woman with wild black hair and a severe expression. Luskell didn't know her, but her dark eyes seemed familiar. The woman ignored Ketwyn and marched up to Luskell. "You tell my great-granddaughter she's marrying the wrong man!" She spun on her heel and strode away without another word.

Luskell gaped after her, then turned to Ketwyn. "Who—what—?"

He chuckled. "That was Elika. She takes some getting used to, but we're all very fond of her. Especially Knot. He says he knew her when he was a child."

Elika. Luskell knew that name. She had been a healer in Deep River long ago. She was Aunt Sudi's mother; Uncle Elic was named for her.

"So I'm supposed to carry messages from the dead?" Luskell asked.

"It appears so. I'm sorry you have to go before Knot comes." Ketwyn bent and kissed her forehead.

"No, I want to stay!"

She wanted more than anything to wait for Knot. With bitter disappointment, she watched as the grassy field began to fade. The dream blurred into ordinary nonsense dreams that she couldn't remember when she woke. All she remembered was that there was something she was supposed to tell Sulika, and she probably wouldn't like it.

Chapter 10

At midmorning, while Luskell helped Klamamam with chores, the three musicians for the dance arrived at the inn, led by a tall man with a shock of pale hair.

"We'll have a bite to eat, if it's not too much trouble, and two rooms for the night."

Klamamam set her broom aside. "No trouble at all. But only two rooms? They're small to share."

"We'll manage. These two don't need much space."

The other two were shorter, but Luskell didn't see how that made a difference. They didn't argue, though. Maybe it was the thriftiness musicians everywhere were famous for. Luskell left the lamp she'd been polishing and went to the kitchen to get their meal. The tall man gave her a piercing glance as she passed, though she pretended not to notice. What had she done now? She brought out the food, then retreated to the kitchen until they'd finished and headed to the Village Hall to warm up their instruments and run through a few tunes.

Some visitors from out of town arrived in time for lunch. A few of them decided to spend the night, too. Klamamam put Luskell to work preparing all the guest rooms.

"I don't like putting anyone in the room next to yours," Klamamam fretted. "Your father trusts me to protect you."

"I'm sure he doesn't expect you to turn away paying guests," Luskell said. "It's only one night."

"True. I doubt the rest of the summer will be as busy. I'll put that nice young family with the baby next to you." Luskell didn't see how a baby in the next room was an improvement but kept it to herself. Klamamam carried on talking. "All the same, you should bolt your door tonight. The musicians can get rowdy afterward. I saw the tall one staring at you already."

"He was not!" Or if he was, Luskell didn't know what to make of it. She couldn't believe she warranted a second glance. He must have been looking at something else.

They spent the afternoon cleaning and cooking. Supper was early, and they had a crowd to feed, both locals and visitors. This one night of the year, there were no stories after the meal. Once the guests departed, Klamamam took off her apron and smiled at Luskell. "Let's get you dressed."

Up in the best room, Luskell opened her trunk and removed her good dress from the paper that protected it. Klamamam gasped as she held it up. "Is something wrong?" Luskell inspected the dress for a tear or loose button.

"No, it's beautiful," Klamamam breathed. "I've never seen anything so nice." She fingered the green silk of the skirt and inspected the many little tucks in the bodice. "How did you come to have such a fine thing?"

"Remember my friend Daisy, the dressmaker's daughter? She was dangerously ill, and Mamam healed her. Mamam wouldn't take anything in payment for herself, but the dressmaker insisted. We'd been invited to the Governor's Ball, so when she offered to make something for me..."

Klamamam smiled and helped Luskell put it on. The dress itself had no sleeves and buttoned up the back. "I don't know—bare arms in public?"

Luskell laughed as she put on the matching jacket. "See? Sleeves."

"All right," Klamamam said. "And it's lovely on you."

"Once Mamam saw mine, she agreed to have one made for herself. Hers is blue, with two different jackets. She paid for it, but I don't think the dressmaker charged full price."

"Your dress is fine. Now let's do something with your hair."

Luskell tugged at one of her braids. "There's nothing that can be done with it. I wish Mamam would let me cut it short, like hers."

"You lead a different life." She had Luskell sit on the edge of the bed and knelt behind her. "You're too young to put it up, but I remember an elegant braid we used to wear when I was a girl. Let's see if I can still do it." She undid Luskell's braids and gently brushed the springy curls before she started the new style. After a while, she sighed. Luskell felt her hands shake.

"What's wrong?"

"Nothing." Klamamam sniffed. "I hope you don't cut your hair short. It feels like Knot's."

Luskell thought for a moment that her hair was snarled, but then she understood. "And everyone says I have his eyes."

"You do. You remind me so much of him, when he was young and healthy, with a whole life ahead. Like he was when we first met."

"But he was a wizard. I can't do any of the things he did."

"I didn't know he could, either, that night. I loved him for him." Klamamam gave Luskell a hand mirror she'd brought from downstairs. "There, you're ready to turn some heads."

"I don't care about that, but thank you for fixing my hair." Luskell studied herself in the mirror. Her hair was pulled back into one long braid, with a few curls arranged to frame her face. She liked it—she looked dressed-up, but not as if she were trying to appear older.

Klamamam changed clothes and brushed her hair. She liked to wear it loose in the evening. Then they left for the dance, along with everyone else who hadn't already gone to the Hall. The sun was not down yet, so

Luskell had a clear view of all the variations on "best dress." In some cases, this seemed to be a less-faded version of a woman's everyday dress, but others wore a more fitted style in a finer fabric. Nothing came close to Luskell's green silk.

The music had already begun, and Klamamam had a dance partner as soon as they were through the door. Luskell peered around the dimly lit hall for someone she knew. Before she could discern a familiar face, Grandpa Yshna darted up with surprising quickness for a hunched old man.

"Is this the dress Ketty told me about? The city dress?" he shouted over the din of music and voices.

"Um—yes, it is."

"Lovely! Silk, isn't it? Years since I saw any, but I recognized it from across the room—nothing takes color like it."

Grandpa Yshna exclaimed over each detail as he examined the stitching, the cut, the fit. Luskell glanced around anxiously, certain everyone was staring at her, the city girl showing off her city clothes. Aunt Sunnea came to her rescue as he knelt to examine the skirt's pleated flounce.

"Papa, you're embarrassing Luskell. Come, dance with me."

"I only wanted a closer look," he grumbled, but he allowed himself to be led away.

Aunt Sunnea looked over her shoulder. "Sorry about that. Jagryn's over there if you're looking for someone more your own age." She nodded toward the refreshment table.

Luskell went over and sat next to him. He gave her a nod, then devoted himself to eating a small cake. At least he didn't stare.

The next number was a circle dance that didn't require a partner. Jagryn remained seated, but Luskell joined in. Although she didn't know the steps, it was simple to learn. She forgot to feel overdressed and began to enjoy herself. As she came around to face the door, Sulika entered on the arm of a young man Luskell recognized as Foli. She didn't know him well, but he was old enough not to have changed much in three years. He had a round, boyish face, but his black hair was already receding. He held Sulika's arm like he owned her, though he didn't look at her. Luskell couldn't understand why not. With her dark hair in ringlets and a blue dress that matched her eyes, Sulika was the prettiest girl in the room.

When the song ended, Luskell turned back to her seat, but someone touched her shoulder. "You look like the princess in one of Auntie Stell's stories."

She blushed and smiled at Uncle Elic. "Thank you." She held the full skirt out. "I thought this might be too much."

"Don't worry about it. You have the mayor's approval. Come on, this is an easy one." He helped her learn a partner dance. She stumbled at first but soon got the pattern of it. "You've done this before!"

"No, but I learned the Guards' Reel last winter. It isn't that different."

She danced the next number with Uncle Jagree. He wasn't as good a dancer as his brother Uncle Elic but worked hard to get the steps right. Luskell did her best to follow, and they laughed at themselves when they got it wrong. When the song ended, she returned to her seat to rest. The air had grown stifling. She slipped off her jacket and hung it on the back of the chair. She hadn't sat long before Young Crane stood in front of her with his hand out. "Dance with me, Cousin!"

She tried to pretend she wasn't flattered. This dance was more complex, but Young Crane was an excellent dancer and easy to follow. He made small talk as they danced, and her heart fluttered until she realized his attention wasn't on her. She glanced over her shoulder. He gazed at, and guided them nearer to, a girl with straight black hair tied with a red ribbon. She stood with a compact young man who looked familiar.

Luskell indulged in a moment of jealousy and disappointment but no more than that. Young Crane was handsome, and she liked his attention, but could she really believe he would wait for her to grow up? She didn't plan to stay in Deep River, anyway. This black-haired girl was probably a better match for him. "Who is she?" He missed a step for the first time. They took a moment to sort themselves out. "Well?"

He sighed, then smiled. "Bramynna."

The way he said the name told Luskell everything. She remembered Bramynna now, too, though she'd grown up a lot in three years. Then, she'd been an older girl too dignified to play with Luskell and the twins, though she probably hadn't been much more than twelve or thirteen.

Crane nodded toward Bramynna's companion. "That's her brother, Rakkyn."

"Rakkyn. Yes, we've met." If dumping stew on someone counted as an introduction. "Do you want to dance with her?"

"Oh, do I!"

"Then let's switch. Maybe Rakkyn will dance with me."

Young Crane didn't answer. She glanced at him. His face was so red under his tan that it was all she could do not to laugh out loud. "Go on, ask her."

"I'm—no, I don't think I can."

Luskell couldn't bring herself to tell him he was the best looking man in the room, but it was easy to see Bramynna thought so. "Go on, she's waiting for you to ask."

"No, she isn't. She doesn't even have the courtship ring yet. I heard her mother tell my mother she's getting it on her seventeenth birthday."

Luskell was familiar with this old-fashioned ritual that had somehow hung on in Deep River, if nowhere else. A single earring marked a girl as available for courtship, while two proclaimed her betrothed.

"I thought you were smart. You're not asking the girl to marry you. You're only asking her to dance. You didn't have any trouble asking me."

"That was different."

Luskell shook her head and glanced around at the other dancers. Foli and Sulika stumbled past. As they struggled with the steps, he still didn't look at her. "That's odd."

"What is?" Young Crane asked.

"Foli is watching Bramynna, too. Isn't she a little young for him?"

Young Crane turned his head to follow Foli. "And she's some kind of cousin to him. Distant enough, I guess; most of Deep River is related one way or another. But I don't suppose Sulika is pleased."

"I don't think she noticed, but you're right. It seems rude."

"He's probably just out to irk Myn."

"How so?"

"Bramynna is Myn's sister's child. Anything connected to Myn, Foli has to try for. Those two have always competed."

Luskell laughed. "Maybe Foli should marry Myn and be done with it."

Young Crane snorted. "You really are from out of town!"

The music stopped again. They were close to Bramynna and her brother, but Foli looked like he was moving in. Luskell gave Young Crane a gentle shove. "Ask her now, before he gets there."

He nodded, and as she turned away, Luskell heard him make his invitation. She smiled to herself as Foli was left to converse with Rakkyn. Luskell returned to her seat and sat back to watch the dancing. Jagryn had gone to food table again, and someone else had taken his seat. Luskell was glad to have a jacket she could use to save hers. Sulika twirled past, in Myn's arms this time. She was laughing, and neither of them stumbled. As she watched, Luskell had a flash of memory. She was supposed to tell Sulika—something. Someone had given her a message...But that made no sense. She had been in Deep River only three days and had barely

spoken to anyone except Klamamam. It must have
been a dream.

Chapter II

Luskell enjoyed dancing, but she was nearly as happy to watch and rest. Toward the end of the tune, Jagryn sidled up and stood near her. All the seats were taken. When she smiled at him, he looked away. She wasn't sure what to think. He had been friendly when he thought she could do magic. He hadn't even spoken to her since, though he'd had plenty of opportunities tonight.

A new, faster tune began, one she knew, called "The Blacksmith's Courtship." She stood and turned to Jagryn. "Well? Shall we?" He stared at her but didn't reply. She grabbed his hand. "Come on, let's dance." Still mute, he nodded and followed her onto the floor.

He wasn't quite as good a dancer as his brother, but he wasn't bad. She wondered if he would grow up to be as good looking, then forgot everything in her enjoyment. It was an active dance with a lot of stomping and clapping, so they didn't have to be graceful, or even touch each other much. They weren't the only ones who ended the dance red-faced and puffing for breath.

"We're going to take a short break," the fiddler announced. "After that last tune, you could probably use one, too! But we'll be back for another set, so don't go far!"

Jagryn grinned at Luskell. "That was fun! I'm parched, though. Do you want a—?" He waved his hand toward the drinks table.

"Yes, please." He got two mugs of cold tea and handed one to Luskell. She took a grateful swig. "Ah! That's good. Let's go outside and cool off."

Most of the dancers headed out in pairs and groups. It was still warm out and not yet dark. The full moon shone out of a clear sky still tinted with sunset colors. Klamamam went out ahead of Luskell and Jagryn, guiding blind Uncle Jelf as she chatted with Aunt Sudi and Uncle Ohme. Some of the out-of-town visitors were leaving, and Uncle Jagree helped them hitch up their teams in the lot next to the Hall. Luskell nudged Jagryn and pointed out his brother, walking and talking with Bramynna. Not far away, Foli and Rakkyn continued in animated conversation.

"Do you go to a lot of dances in the city?" Jagryn asked.

"No. Why do you ask?"

"It seemed like you'd done it before, and you have the fancy dress."

She chuckled. "I've been to one dance before. We went to the Governor's Ball last winter, on my birthday."

His eyes widened. "I can't even imagine that! What was it like?"

"Elegant. Refined. Stiff." She scrunched up her nose, and he laughed. "I danced one reel, with my father. The rest of the night, I just sat there. It was dull."

He nodded, looking thoughtful. "At least you had a good partner. He's supposed to be the most graceful person ever to come out of Deep River."

She laughed at that. It was a nice break from the usual hero-wizard talk. And she was glad Jagryn had decided to be friendly again.

"What's he like?" he asked.

"Who?"

"The governor."

"Oh, Governor Snotwabi? I don't like him."

Jagryn stopped walking and stared at her. "Is that what you call him? He's important!"

"Well, not to his face." She tried to be serious but had to let the laughter out. "I'm kidding—I've never even met the governor. He showed up at the ball long enough to wave at everybody, but I was all the way at the other end of the room. I could barely see him. I still don't like him."

"Why not?"

"I don't know, I just don't." Luskell looked around the groups gathered outside the Hall. "Who's that with

Grynni and Greelit?" The twins were chattering away with a pink-cheeked girl in a rose-colored dress. She'd wrapped her golden braids around her head like a crown.

"That's Ruvhonn. I thought you knew her."

"I wouldn't have recognized her! She looks so grown-up."

"She's almost sixteen. Ruvhonn's only a few days older than me."

Just then, Ruvhonn looked around and smiled.

Luskell poked Jagryn's shoulder. "You should ask her to dance."

The color drained from his face so his freckles stood out in contrast. "No, I shouldn't."

They headed toward the group, Jagryn suddenly silent again. They passed the musicians where they stood smoking. Luskell overheard the fiddler's name. It was familiar, but she didn't know why at first. Then she remembered and forgot everything else. "Excuse me, Jagryn, I need to talk to someone." Before he could respond, she turned away and approached the fiddler.

He was tall and thin, though not as tall as Dadad, with bright blue eyes and unruly pale hair that could have been blond or white. He looked down at her with an amused smirk. "Well?"

"Is your name Walgyn?"

"Yes, it is. What can I do for you, pretty girl?"

She blushed at the compliment, acutely aware of her bare arms. "I—what I mean is—you play very well."

He laughed. "I admire your taste, but what are you comparing to?"

She frowned. "I've heard other fiddlers! I even play a little myself."

"Oh, well then—any good?"

She shook her head. "I'm still a beginner. That isn't what I meant to tell you, anyway. You knew my mother."

He drew on his pipe. "Did I?"

"Yes. I'm Ketty's daughter."

Walgyn lost his smile and stared at her. He glanced at his companions. "Give us a moment, will you?" They moved off a few steps. "It's been a long time. Is she here?" He gazed around the crowd.

"No, they're in Eukard City by now. I'm staying with my grandmother, Stell."

He nodded. "Yes, I saw you at the inn this morning. Now I know why you seemed familiar. You look something like your mother. What's your name?"

"Luskell."

"Nice to know you. How old are you, Luskell?"

"Fourteen. I'll be fifteen on Short Day."

"Tall for your age." He gazed upward a moment as he puzzled over something. "But fourteen? Then you've got nothing coming to you, if that's what you're after. You're some other man's brat."

She glared at him and stood taller. "Did I *say* you were my father? No, thank you. I know my father very well. He's a great man."

Walgyn gave her an unperturbed smile. "Then you're a lucky girl, though I think you exaggerate. Great men don't come from Deep River."

"One did."

He nodded. "What do you want from me?"

"Nothing. Only you're Ketwyn's father, and he's my brother."

He drew a shaky breath but didn't say anything right away. He squatted down and cocked his head up at her. "Ketwyn? A boy?"

"That's right. It's an interesting coincidence to meet you here."

"Not really; I come here every summer, though I had no idea Ketty had settled here." He looked around again, though she had already told him her mother wasn't there.

"She didn't. She came to Deep River to have her baby."

"A son. My son." Walgyn smiled a little. "Is he here, too?"

Luskell shook her head. "No. Well, sort of." She swallowed. "He's—buried here."

Walgyn sagged. "You sure know how to make a man feel bad, you know that? It wasn't enough that I never saw my child. Now you have to tell me I never will."

"Whose fault is that? You're the one who threw my mother out of the house."

He sighed. "True. I regret that, though it probably wouldn't have worked out between us. She's better off with the great man. Well, what was Ketwyn like? Tall and funny-looking like me, or small and beautiful like his witch of a mother?"

Too late, Luskell realized she had spoken of Ketwyn as if she had known him in life. But no one in this world had heard his laugh or seen the grin on his grown-up face. She still wasn't sure her dreams were anything more than that. "He had red hair," she said at last.

"He was your brother, and you can't tell me any more than that?"

"No. He died at birth. I never knew him, either."

Walgyn stared at her. "If I play sad songs the rest of the night, it's your fault." He stood up and started to go back inside, then turned again. "Maybe tomorrow you can show me Ketwyn's grave?"

She nodded and watched him go in. It was hard to imagine Mamam with Walgyn. He wasn't as bad as she made him out to be, but he seemed too ordinary for her. He was a talented fiddler but not half the man Dadad was. Even Ketwyn preferred Dadad. Hadn't he said, "Walgyn has no power?" No one could say that of Dadad, or Mamam, either. Luskell imagined her parents in Eukard City on their important diplomatic mission. They were both great, probably greater than any of those powerful government people they had to deal with. For the first time in weeks, she was proud to be their daughter.

Chapter 12

Arriving in Eukard City at last, Crane stepped down from the coach and stretched till all his joints cracked. The coaches were reasonably comfortable but built for someone with shorter legs. The step, on the other hand, was more to his scale. He helped Ketty down so she wouldn't have to hop.

The coach office in Eukard City was located in Old Town, a central neighborhood of solid stone buildings and old brick mansions. Although only a short walk from the Government District, Old Town was no longer a fashionable address. But the library was here, and two former mansions housed the Wizards' Hall and Balsam's House, a hospital for the very sick or very poor. Others had been converted to rooming houses for workers and students. So if it wasn't a fashionable neighborhood, it was almost always lively.

Crane and Ketty had rented rooms nearby over the winter, but now they would have quarters at Embassy House. They had sent their belongings ahead before the trip to Deep River.

Ketty squeezed Crane's arm and smiled up at him. "At least this part of the journey was uneventful. Maybe the rest of the summer will be dull, too."

"We can only hope. Do you want to walk, or should I hire a cab?"

"It's a fine evening—let's walk."

"Good." After half a day confined to the coach, Crane was happy to walk to the Government District. It was near suppertime, but traveling stole his appetite. Walking would restore it—and meals were part of his pay for working with the Aklaka ambassador.

The warm, bright evening was a welcome surprise. It had been raining when they left the city a few days before and probably would be again before long; the weeks around Long Day were often cloudy and cool. They joined the crowd of people headed home or out for the night.

"It feels strange, not having Luskell with us," Ketty said.

Crane squeezed her hand. "I love that girl, and I love being a father. But it was nice having you to myself last night."

She glanced up at him. A lovely flush crept up her face. "Like we were young again."

"You still are. I—" In one quick motion, Crane dropped Ketty's hand, tossed his staff from his left hand to his right, and reached behind him to catch the hand that was almost in his pocket. He turned. The hand belonged to a skinny, sharp-featured boy. His hair was tangled, and nothing about him was clean.

"Lemme go!"

"I could do that. Look, there's a Guard over there. Shall we go talk to him?" The boy shook his head and lowered his gaze. "Ketty, what do you see?"

"I see a little boy terrified of the scary man looming over him."

"What? Oh." Crane crouched to bring himself closer to the child's eye level.

The boy straightened himself and glared at Ketty. "I'm not little! I'm almost eleven."

Crane studied him more closely. Although a lot smaller, he wasn't much younger than Luskell. "Sorry. It's hard to see properly in this light. So, Ketty, nothing else?"

"Not what you're looking for."

Crane sighed and nodded. If the boy had any power, they could take him to the Wizard's Hall, which might keep him out of trouble. As it was ... "How about we take you home, then? Do you live around here?"

"You could say that."

"All right, where?"

"Wherever."

Crane took a quick look at the boy's thoughts and saw the truth in the answer. He slept wherever he could—alleys, back rooms, vacant houses. "Sorry to hear that. What does your father do?"

"Dunno. Never met him."

Crane knew how that felt. He tried to cover his growing sympathy with a stern look. "What about your mother?"

"Died last winter."

"Rough. So you're supporting yourself, are you?"

"Trying to. Stealing's better than begging."

"Except it's not a good idea to pick a wizard's pocket. I'm surprised you haven't learned that already if you're working this neighborhood."

"I'm ... new to it."

Crane glanced hopefully at Ketty. She shook her head. "No, Crane." Then she spoke to his mind. *We're not in a position to take in a child—especially not one who needs as much watching as this boy. Think about it. We sent our own child away from the city.*

Crane gave her a nod to show she was right, then turned his attention back to the boy. "I wonder if we could find you more honest work." Crane dug in a pocket and found a slip of paper and a charcoal pencil. "What's your name, young man?"

"Druner."

"May I use your back as a desk, Druner?" Crane half expected Druner to run as soon as his hand was free, but the boy turned around and held still while Crane wrote a short note. He pulled out the moneybag the boy had meant to steal and extracted a silver dul. Druner stared at the coin while Crane folded the note around it. He gave the little package to the boy. "Take this to Berdona, the landlady at the Otter. I know some people in this neighborhood, but she knows everyone. If she doesn't have work for you, she'll know who does. And if there's no work, the coin should buy you a room or a couple of meals."

The boy immediately tried to unwrap the coin, but the note wouldn't come off. He frowned at Crane.

"You think you might buy the meals and skip the work? You won't be able to unwrap it. Only Berdona can."

"Is she a witch?"

Crane laughed. "I don't think so. But she has a good heart, and I think you'll learn to appreciate steady work. Much better than picking a wizard's pocket. You never know what they might do." He winked and stood up. The boy looked at him, then at the wrapped coin, and ran off in the direction of the tavern.

Crane watched him go and hoped he'd done the right thing. Ketty was right—they weren't in a position this summer to adopt a child, especially a half-grown, scruffy orphan who needed a lot of watching. But he couldn't help wondering what it would be like to have a son. Not instead of Luskell, who was irreplaceable in her father's heart. But in addition. Was that so wrong? When she was born, he'd assumed other children would follow, but Ketty was always *careful*. He had to respect her choice to use her power in that way. He couldn't know what it must have been like to lose Ketwyn; he only knew he was lucky to have even one child. But that one was challenging enough for three.

As a small child, Luskell had been energetic and curious, always running, climbing, asking, "Why?" and "How?" Crane and Ketty had tried to keep a close watch on her but failed often enough for the child to sustain an impressive roster of minor injuries. She was lucky to have a skilled healer for a mother; there wasn't a single scar on her. By the time she was seven, she was persuading other children into explorations. Crane still remembered the time she'd led five Aklaka children deep into an abandoned coyote den. The entrance tunnel was too narrow for an adult. All the parents had been forced to wait until Luskell and her faithful followers emerged at the end of their expedition, filthy from head to toe, with their hair full of bugs and debris, but proud of their fortitude.

Now that Luskell was older, Crane had to admit she was less challenging for him than for Ketty. She had inherited her mother's intelligence, stubbornness, and temper. She took Ketty's suggestions as criticism and advice as demands; they'd endured a lot of stamped feet and slammed doors in the past year or two.

And then there was the girl's power. Ketty had first detected it when Luskell was thirteen or so. The conversation got no further than, "When you get your power—" before Luskell shouted, "I won't!", burst into tears, and stomped out of the room. Ketty had to shield herself from the outburst; she was sensitive to any emotion, but especially that of her child. She took it personally.

So they were back to watching. Crane didn't know whether Luskell was actively rejecting her power, though it was possible. Expectations had always been high for her; it was a lot to live up to. She hadn't tried using magic and didn't seem interested, so he hadn't pushed her to talk about it. He hoped she would open the conversation when she was ready. Maybe with her grandmother, who had the benefit of distance and no power of her own. A summer apart might be the best thing for all of them.

Chapter 13

Even after more than a decade, Ketty doubted she would ever get used to the luxurious surroundings at Embassy House. Thick rugs and heavy drapes muted noise from the street or from other apartments. Servants cooked and served meals, washed clothes, and cleaned the rooms. Ketty and Crane's elegant bedroom, the smallest of their three furnished rooms, was more comfortable than the best room at the Blue Heron and larger than their whole house in Misty Pass. It was a long way from the two bare rooms Crane had rented in Eukard City years ago.

They had taken their time getting up that morning and ate a late breakfast prepared by others. For Ketty, who had done all the cooking since girlhood, this was a special luxury. She waved her hand over the unmade bed. The silk coverlet rustled into place and smoothed out while the pillows plumped themselves.

She felt Crane's approach before he spoke. Love and affection streamed off him, mixed with worry. "You don't have to do that."

She turned to him with a smile. "I'll never get used to having chambermaids."

"Enjoy it while you can. Maybe we could rumple up these covers again."

He took her in his arms and kissed her. It was tempting. In their itinerant life, the family often shared one room, and moments of intimacy were limited. Much as she missed Luskell, Ketty had enjoyed the freedom of the past two nights away from her.

She broke away. "We shouldn't. We have appointments today."

Crane sat on the side of the bed so she wouldn't have to look up at him. "Do you think I'll fall asleep?"

"I *know* you will." She stroked his jaw. He had shaved his beard, as he always did for the diplomatic season. Beards were not in fashion among politicians and diplomats, and he had no wish to stand out. Ketty missed the beard, but it would grow back quickly enough. "That's not the problem. We'll both need all our power if we're to learn anything useful when we meet the governor. I can't afford to divert any purely for pleasure."

Ketty was so attuned to her body's rhythms that she could avoid conception more or less at will. At some times, it required little effort, but this was not one of them. The effort would leave her physically and magically depleted, two things she couldn't afford today. Crane nodded with understanding and drew her onto his lap. "Maybe—you could stop using your power that way. See what happens."

She shivered, though the room was warm. That was how Ketwyn was conceived.

"I don't know," she said. "Do we really want to travel with a baby again?"

He smiled and kissed the top of her head. "It wasn't so bad before. And we're not getting any younger. Besides, why waste all this luxury and privacy? If something gets started, we can go back to Deep River at the end of the summer and stay there until it's born."

Ketty laughed in spite of herself. "*It*? Did you think of Luskell as *it*?"

"If I remember correctly, I thought of her as *he* until you set me straight. So, what do you think?"

They both started at a loud knock. "I think we should talk about this later. That's probably Naliskat. Aren't you glad he didn't interrupt something?"

She ducked out of Crane's arms, left the bedroom, and crossed the sitting room to the foyer. It still made her giddy just to *have* a foyer. The people in Misty Pass and Deep River had probably never heard of such a thing. She opened the door to reveal two men taller and darker than Crane, both dressed in dappled deerskin clothing.

The elder of the two stepped inside. "We have come," he said in accented Eukardian.

"Naliskat! I guessed it was you. And Pataknan, welcome!" Ketty spoke in equally labored Aklaka. She held her hands out palm up in their formal greeting. Naliskat returned the greeting by placing his hands palm down on top of hers.

"You may call me Liski," he reminded her and gave her the more casual, family greeting—a bear hug that lifted her off the floor.

Crane offered a welcome and received his own affectionate hug, though Naliskat couldn't quite lift him. An embrace between the two men was a relatively new thing. They had once been rivals. Crane turned to Pataknan. "It's good to see you, Takni. This is your first visit, isn't it? What do you think of Eukard City?"

"I'm glad to have the experience, but it makes me nervous. It's so—built." He gave them a weak smile. "I thought you would be disappointed Chamokat didn't come."

"I did expect him," Crane allowed. "What happened?"

Naliskat grinned. "Kala thought our son needed a father figure while I'm away. Nalaklak is a talented Listener; he'll learn a lot from Chamokat. And it was time for Takni to spread his wings."

Ketty hid a smile. She wasn't sure whether Naliskat knew his brother-in-law Chamokat could literally spread his wings when he wished to. Maybe Pataknan could, too.

An Aklaka Listener understood the language of plants, water, the earth itself. A good Listener could pick up warnings, interpret signs, and help his or her leader discern the best path for the people. Ketty had grasped, years before, that the Listeners' ability came from the same place as her magic. She and Crane had taught his friend Chamokat a few of their spells, including transformation. He kept it quiet because some members of his band did not approve of that kind of magic. But his sister Takalanatlan, their leader, did not mind at all. She even had some ability herself. An injury when Laki was born made it dangerous for her to bear more children, but she was capable of the same technique Ketty used and did not have to turn her husband away.

"Do we meet with the governor today?" Pataknan asked.

Crane shook his head. "There's a reception this afternoon where we can see him in person and shake his hand, but the real business begins tomorrow."

"Have supper with us tonight, and we can plan," Ketty offered.

Naliskat smiled. "Thank you. We will come."

Naliskat had an even grander apartment than theirs, across the hall, where he never felt at home. He usually slept in the garden. If it rained, he moved under a tree or onto the porch. And, though he didn't mind Eukardian food, he felt self-conscious about the utensils. Ketty had noticed that he ate more and seemed happier if there was business to discuss or plans to make during the meal.

Over their everyday forest clothes, the two Aklaka put on ceremonial capes made of cedar bark, adorned with feathers. Crane wore his best tunic, and Ketty changed into a well-made but understated summer dress in light gray. She preferred brighter colors, but this was not the time. She created the illusion of a simple hair bun at the back of her head. The less attention she drew, the better.

The four of them went together to the Governor's Mansion, an imposing yet graceful edifice of white stone. A curving drive swept up to a gated courtyard with a fountain in the center. Broad steps led up to the main entrance. Another staircase, partly visible off to the side, was rumored to lead to a rooftop terrace, but Ketty had never seen it herself.

The reception was held in a long, high-ceilinged room with many windows, open to the breeze. The space and light seemed to put Naliskat at ease, but Pataknan still looked nervous. Ketty gave his arm a squeeze as they joined the line to greet Governor Snowabi. She smiled to herself as she remembered Luskell's mocking name for him. She would have to use great self-control not to say "Snotwabi" aloud.

The delegations from the neighboring countries of Azzar and Foryin had already arrived, as well as a number of local trade groups. Those who had been through the line already were drinking wine and beginning to talk business. Music played in the background.

They reached the head of the line, and a functionary introduced them. "Governor, may I present the Aklaka delegation."

Governor Snowabi remained seated in a large, ornate chair as he greeted his guests. Ketty frowned. Governor Dillet had always made a point of standing for these receptions. But he had been an energetic man. Snowabi looked round and soft in his fine clothes. He smiled warmly as he gave each member of the group a quick glance. "Some of you are not Aklaka." His blue eyes twinkled as if he had told a clever joke. He peered at Crane. "Although you might be."

Crane smiled and made a respectful bow. "Greetings, Your Honor. You have a keen eye. I have some Aklaka heritage on my father's side. This is Ambassador Naliskat, and Pataknan, his—advisor. My name is Crane, and I serve as their translator. And—"

Snowabi interrupted before Crane could present Ketty. "Can you make a living as an Aklaka translator? I can't imagine there's much call for it."

"I have other work."

One of the governor's attendants cleared his throat. "Your Honor, Crane is too modest. You see before you one of the greatest wizards in all Eukard."

Snowabi raised his eyebrows. "Indeed? And they have you working as a translator?"

Crane smiled. "I volunteered. We have been friends since my youth."

"Friends? How interesting. I have heard much about them, but it is a pleasure to see their barbaric regalia up close. Perhaps they will dance for us later?" Crane opened his mouth to reply, but the governor's attention had moved on. "And who is this lovely lady?"

Ketty started and forced a smile. Her attention had been on the page, who had recognized Crane. The young man had the same blue eyes as the governor. There was something else about him, but she couldn't say exactly what.

Snowabi smiled so much his eyes disappeared into the crinkles. He beckoned Ketty closer and held out his hand. She reached for it, but instead of shaking, he grasped her fingers and kissed them. She used the opportunity to learn what she could from his emotional state, but he didn't give her much.

"Ketty is my wife," Crane said, "and a full member of the delegation."

"And what do you do, my dear? Make the breakfast?"

The blood rose in Ketty's face. He seemed to think his joke was charming, but his charm was wearing thin. Before she could answer, Naliskat said, in Eukardian, "She is Aketnan, the Peacebringer. She sees the truth."

Snowabi stared at Naliskat, then looked to Crane. "I can't understand his jibber-jabber. What did he say?"

Ketty hastened to explain. "I settled a dispute for them once, so they include me in all negotiations." Given the governor's attitudes, it might be an advantage if he didn't know Naliskat understood him. Her own role was difficult enough to explain, even to herself. She hosted a spirit from another culture's legend, a being she'd never even heard of until just before it began speaking with her voice. She'd come to accept it, though she didn't control it. Aketnan was an influential force for justice and peace, their delegation's secret weapon.

Crane stepped forward and grasped the governor's hand. "It is very good to meet you, Your Honor. We shouldn't hold up the line."

The Aklaka shook hands with the governor, and the four of them moved off to join the other delegations. Ketty took a glass of wine as soon as it was offered. Crane also took a glass, but Naliskat waved the server away. Instead, he and Pataknan sought unfermented drinks. Aklaka sometimes drank a fermented beverage of their own, but nothing as strong as this wine and never during the day. Ketty knew from experience that if Liski had too much to drink, the governor might see him dance, but not the way he expected. It would not involve ceremonial robes, or much else in the way of clothing.

Ketty exchanged greetings with those she knew from past years. There weren't many other women, so the Lieutenant Governor, Klanya, stood out. She was a tall, dignified woman with stylish silver hair. She had received enough votes in the election—including Ketty's—to finish second and be awarded this mostly-ceremonial position. Ketty doubted Snowabi would use his "make the breakfast" line on her.

Crane bent to whisper in her ear. "What do you think of the governor?"

"He has charm. I can see why *some* people voted for him."

Crane nodded. "He's made some good proposals, but Luskell distrusted him from the first."

"Young people know everything." Ketty sipped her wine.

"And you? Did you learn anything?"

"Not much," she murmured back. "I think his page is related to him, but what else is new? And Snowabi is a true politician. He had his feelings closely guarded."

"But he's not a wizard?"

She frowned. "Not so much as a sparkle. Why?"

"He's hiding something, but I couldn't bring it to light. Maybe he has someone shielding him."

She smiled. "After all, he doesn't want to give up state secrets to every wizard who comes along. Is that Dokral?" At the far end of the room, someone played a harp. As she drew closer, she recognized the musician as their old friend and Crane's former landlord. She hurried to him.

"Dokral! How did you get this job?"

"I was recommended by someone on the governor's staff who heard me play at his niece's wedding." He continued playing as they spoke and never missed a beat. "It's wonderful to see you, Ketty. Hello, Crane. And where is the charming Luskell?"

"She's in Deep River this summer," Crane said.

"What a shame! I had hoped to continue our fiddle lessons."

"Perhaps some other time. It's good to see you, Dokral. The music business has been kind to you."

"I pick up the occasional important party," Dokral agreed. "I'm glad to see you both looking well. I think we'll all feel safer now that you're back."

Crane chuckled. "Safer? Why?"

"Haven't you heard? There's a new wizard in town who has people mighty scared. But you could probably stop him."

"I'm sure I could. What's his name?"

Dokral continued to play, but his fingers shook on the strings. He gestured with his head for them to lean in so he could whisper. "Yrae."

Crane flinched as if the harpist had struck him. Ketty's heart pounded. She'd heard the rumors but not from any reliable source—until now. She swallowed. "That isn't possible. Yrae is—"

"What has he done?" Crane interrupted. He stared at Dokral with an intensity that made even Ketty uneasy.

"Nothing that I know of—yet. But it's only a matter of time. Everyone knows he's a killer."

Chapter 14

"I miss Governor Dillet," Naliskat said. "He was a reasonable man. I could trust him. I'm not so sure about this Snowabi. Why did you change leaders?"

Naliskat and Pataknan had come to supper at Ketty and Crane's apartment so the four of them could discuss plans for the following day. They sat around a table still cluttered with the remains of the meal, the windows thrown open to catch any hint of a breeze.

Ketty glanced at Crane, but he seemed not to have heard Naliskat's question. "I liked Dillet, too, but he served his two terms," she said. "Snowabi is new, but that doesn't mean he won't be as good."

"What do you know of him?" Pataknan asked.

Crane shook himself. Ketty read surprise on his face and caught a whiff of it in his feelings. He'd forgotten they were there; his mind was somewhere else. "He has made some popular proposals," he said. "A few have already been put in place. He increased Guard patrols around the markets and docks to deter petty crime, and he opened food stations for the destitute."

"This hasn't happened yet, but he expressed an interest in taking over the Free School," Ketty added. "It sounded like he wanted to set up government schools on that model."

"I'm not sure how he plans to pay for any of this," Crane said. "So far, he hasn't raised taxes, but how long can that last?"

Naliskat waved this off. Aklaka did not pay taxes. "What does he intend for us?"

Crane shook his head. "I don't know. I heard something about assimilation, but no details. And it was only a rumor, not anything reliable." His brow furrowed, and his attention drifted away again.

Ketty absorbed his wash of worry and longing. She knew what distracted him and felt it herself; they remembered a different rumor. Although Dokral had been genuinely frightened, when Ketty heard the name Yrae applied to a living person, she could barely hide the spontaneous rush of joy.

She didn't want to talk about this news until after the Aklaka had left. Crane didn't seem to want to talk about it at all. Later that night, he lay quietly in bed beside her, but she knew he was awake and troubled. She found his hand under the covers and held it.

"You don't suppose—"

"No!"

Ketty flinched; Crane rarely snapped at anyone, least of all her.

His tone softened. "I'm sorry. It's just so—I'd heard the rumors, but—Yrae, alive?"

"If anyone could come back, he could."

He drew her into his arms. "But why as Yrae? He was a better man as Knot."

She thought about that. Why, indeed? "Maybe he doesn't remember."

Crane stiffened. "Then we have to remind him, before anyone gets hurt."

Just when the New Yrae thought everything was going according to his employer's plan, the astute wizard was back in town with his Aklaka comrades. He had shaved his beard, but anyone that tall was hard to miss. And he seemed to suspect something.

Though large and strong in body, the Aklaka posed no real threat. They kept to themselves. They spoke no more than a few words of Eukardian, and no one but their translator could understand their gabble. Still, the little group made an impression. While technically not *foreign*, the Aklaka were *exotic*.

The New Yrae had heard the name Crane and seen the man before, but he hadn't put the two together. Crane didn't waste more than a glance on the New Yrae, but he had felt Crane probing for thoughts. The woman in their party seemed a formidable adversary as well. It took all the New Yrae's power to shield his employer's mind from those two at such close range.

Under different circumstances, the New Yrae would have liked to talk with Crane. Where had he studied? Was there anything he couldn't do? He behaved generously—humbly, even—but he carried himself with more confidence and authority than the New Yrae had seen in any other wizard. If only he could have studied with such a teacher. But it was too late now.

Crane's business in town would bring him close to the New Yrae's employer on occasion, and he was not as easy to fool as the local wizards. If they weren't careful, he was powerful enough to extract the whole plan from their thoughts.

He always shielded their minds when there might be wizards about. That effort alone took a toll, but he would have to do more. Any meeting must be delayed as long as possible while the New Yrae arranged a distraction to keep this Crane's mind occupied. A distraction that would seem to have nothing to do with them, or magic of any kind. Something that might occur naturally. The weather would do. The New Yrae was not a skilled weatherworker, but this didn't call for finesse. A local heat wave should cause enough discomfort and fatigue to unfocus even the most perceptive mind.

But *would* it? Perhaps more direct action was called for—a dramatic piece of misdirection? An act of violence would no doubt have the desired effect, but it could draw attention as easily as deflect it. They couldn't afford too much attention this early in the plan. To succeed at all, it had to remain secret until all the pieces were in place.

But he had promised to do whatever it took to advance his employer's interests. The reward in the end would be worth it. And perhaps a heat wave would be enough; violence might not be required at all. Although he had borrowed a name that still evoked terror, the New Yrae had not yet drawn blood.

Chapter 15

The baby in the room next to Lukell's woke early the morning after Deep River's summer dance, so Luskell did, too. Yawning, she went downstairs to the kitchen.

"Good morning! I was about to come get you." Klamamam always rose early, baby or no. "We'll have a full house this morning."

As Luskell finished a hasty breakfast, guests began to appear in the common room. She wondered if the baby had roused them, too. It was happy now, playing with its fingers and giggling when Luskell served the parents' breakfast. Walgyn beckoned Luskell over to the other long table, where he sat with his bandmates.

"Luskell, isn't it? Remember your promise?"

"I remember." She almost regretted that promise now. It was difficult to imagine her mother with this man who was not her father. Mamam rarely spoke of him and never kindly. But she must have seen something in him once. And he was Ketwyn's father. "We can go after breakfast."

"What's this about?" one of the other musicians asked. "I thought we were heading back to Sweetwater after breakfast. We don't have time for you to dally with a local girl."

Luskell's face grew hot, and she glared at him, but Walgyn smiled. "You don't understand, Skyne. I need to visit a grave here, and this girl knows where it is. Luskell, this is Skyne, and that's Poplar."

"Like the tree," Poplar added, though she didn't need the clarification. Tree and flower names were common enough in Eukard City, if less so in Deep River.

Skyne drummed his fingers on the table. "How much time will that waste?"

"That depends on how much time Walgyn wants to spend." Luskell's own doubts had vanished. She would bring Walgyn to his son, no matter the obstacles. "But it's not like you need to make a special trip—the graveyard is on your way if you're going to Sweetwater."

Klamamam joined them. "Good morning, everyone. I trust you slept well?"

"Very well," Walgyn replied. "I think we're ready to settle our bill."

"Good. Luskell, come with me, please." She smiled but took Luskell's arm in a firm grip and propelled her to the kitchen. For a small woman past fifty, she was surprisingly strong. "You're awfully friendly with that crowd," she said, her voice barely above a whisper. "You might want to steer clear of that tall fellow. If you knew who he was..."

"I do know who he is," Luskell replied in normal speaking tones. At Klamamam's gesture, she spoke more softly. "Have you ever told Mamam he comes here every summer?"

Klamamam's mouth dropped open, and she let go of Luskell's arm. "No. Why stir up old troubles? But I think she suspects—she's never here the day of the dance. And I'm sure she'd rather you stayed away from him."

Luskell crossed her arms. "I'm going to show him Ketwyn's grave."

Klamamam shook her head. "I'm sure you mean well, but I can't let you do that. I'm responsible for you."

"But I promised! Where's the harm in showing him the graveyard?"

"Are you even listening to yourself? You want to go to a remote spot with a man you don't even know. Where is the sense in that?"

Luskell frowned. "You're one to talk about strange men."

"Yes, I am. Maybe I learned a lesson you should heed." She began to figure Walgyn's bill.

"Anyway, we won't be alone. It's on their way, so Skyne and Poplar will be with him."

Klamamam glanced up. "Musicians? That doesn't make me feel any better. You should at least take along someone you know."

"Like who?"

Before she could answer, the front door opened, and Jagryn popped his head in. "Is there any work for me this morning?"

Klamamam smiled at him. "Yes, there is. Would you go with Luskell to show the musicians the graveyard?"

He grinned. "That's a funny job, but I'd be happy to. As long as she doesn't mind."

Luskell sighed. There seemed to be no point in further argument. "No, it's fine. I'll tell Walgyn." She left the kitchen, forced a smile onto her face, and crossed to Walgyn's table. "We can leave as soon as you're ready. I hope you have room for one more. My grandmother insists that Jagryn come along."

Walgyn smiled. "You're lucky you have people looking out for you." He paid his bill and joined his friends outside.

It was a sunny day and growing warm. Luskell and Jagryn rode in the back of the musicians' open cart with Skyne and his drums. He did his best to ignore the two young people. Poplar drove, with his flutes tucked under the seat. Walgyn carried his fiddle case with him like a baby. They didn't talk much, either to Luskell or among themselves, and Jagryn's mind seemed to be on something he didn't choose to share. Luskell didn't mind. After the noisy inn, she enjoyed the quiet.

The graveyard sat on a rise outside town, not far from the road. When it came into view, Luskell pointed it out. "Stop here." She and Jagryn hopped out of the cart. Walgyn climbed down from the seat and walked up the path with them. The other two stood by the cart and smoked while they waited.

A low stone wall surrounded the graveyard. The yellow roses that covered the wall had recently begun to bloom, and lupines filled the warm, still air with their sweet scent. It was the cheeriest graveyard Luskell had ever seen.

Luskell led Walgyn to the tiny grave with its iron marker in the shape of a flame, decorated with a dark red agate. "Ketwyn? Here's your father, come to visit you."

Walgyn admired the marker. "This is beautiful work."

"My Uncle Jagree made that," Jagryn said. "And he looks after the grave. He says he promised Ketty."

Walgyn gave him a sharp glance, then returned his attention to the grave marker. "How did he fix the stone to it? I don't see a weld."

"Jagree didn't do that; my father did," Luskell said. "That was a promise, too." Walgyn and Jagryn exchanged a baffled look. "After Knot's funeral, he asked Mamam to marry him. Well, he'd been asking her, but this time she accepted. They wouldn't be settled anywhere, but he promised they could come back here anytime she wanted."

Walgyn nodded slowly. "You said he was a great man. What does your father do, Luskell?"

She shrugged. "He's a wizard. He can do anything."

"A wizard?" Walgyn shook his head and gave her a half-smile. "That would suit Ketty better than a fiddler. Are you a witch, too?"

"Me? No!"

"Fair enough. There'd be no shame in it if you were."

"Of course not!" Jagryn cried. "Why would there be?"

Luskell glanced at him. Why should he leap to her defense over something she was not? But he probably knew Walgyn had cast Mamam out because of her power. Maybe he was defending himself.

Walgyn glanced back toward town. "I didn't know Deep River produced any wizards."

Luskell and Jagryn grinned at each other. "He wasn't the only one," she said. "His father was born near here, too. Do you remember—Yrae?" She could as easily have said Knot; he had some renown under that name. But she had a feeling the old name would make a bigger impression.

Walgyn's eyes widened. "I'll say I do. He was from here? Then I take back what I said about no one great coming from Deep River." He frowned. "Yrae. I heard an odd rumor recently that Yrae had returned. Do you know about that?"

"I hadn't heard that, but I know he's buried here, too."

Walgyn knelt and opened his fiddle case. He tuned up and began to play a soft, mournful melody completely unlike the dance tunes he'd played the night before. Luskell and Jagryn withdrew to give him some privacy, but the quiet notes followed through the warm, scented air.

Luskell glanced at gravestones and recognized a few names—Elika, Stoli, Soorhi. Jagryn interrupted as she tried to work out how she might be related to these people. "I thought your mother was already expecting you when Knot died."

"She was."

"But you just said your father asked her to marry him that day."

"He did. He'd been asking, but she couldn't bring herself to say yes before that."

Jagryn looked puzzled, then shocked as the light dawned. "So they *had* to get married?"

"No, they *wanted* to. As I said, he'd been asking her for months." She grew pensive as they reached Knot's grave. His birth date was uncertain, so the stone had only his name and date of death. "Dadad didn't know his own father until he was grown. That was the other part of the promise—that he'd be there for me."

Jagryn nodded as he gazed at Knot's grave. "I still can't believe Yrae was your grandfather! How old would he be, if he were still alive?"

"I don't know. In his sixties, I guess, like your grandparents. He was older than Klamamam."

"I wish he were here, so he could teach me. Then I wouldn't have to wait for Uncle Crane to come back."

Luskell nodded. She wished the same. Of all her grandparents, Knot had led the most colorful life by far and had even gained a measure of fame. More than that, she felt close to him in a way she couldn't explain. Maybe because she had begun as he was ending.

Walgyn stood up from Ketwyn's grave and joined them. "All right, then. I'm ready to go. Thank you for bringing me here and for telling me what happened."

"I thought you should know."

He nodded. "I often wondered, but I didn't know where Ketty went or how to find her." He sighed. "I wish I could see her again. Is she coming back here?"

"Yes. I don't know exactly when—sometime later in the summer. I think they plan to stay awhile."

"Could you maybe send word to me in Sweetwater?"

"I don't know if I should. Would she want to see you?"

"Probably not, the way I treated her. But I'm not that scared young fool anymore. Now that I know what happened, I'd like to be man enough to at least tell her I'm sorry."

"Maybe I can get her to write to you."

"I'd appreciate that." He smiled and shook her hand.

Feeling very grown-up, Luskell returned the smile and looked up into Walgyn's bright blue eyes. Ketwyn had those same eyes. She couldn't tell Walgyn, because how did she know that? All she could do was show him this grave and try to persuade Mamam to write to him. He had thrown away his chance at a family, but he deserved a chance at forgiveness.

Chapter 16

Luskell and Jagryn walked back to the cart with Walgyn. Skyne and Poplar were impatient to be on their way, so he didn't linger. They drove away, and Luskell and Jagryn headed back toward Deep River on foot. As they walked, Jagryn performed the lupine-to-butterflies illusion over and over.

"Why are you doing that?" Luskell asked after what must have been the eighth time.

"I can only do this one thing, so I'm going to get really good at it." He produced a ninth stem of lupine. The butterflies appeared at once but clung to the stem a moment before puffing away in a big cloud. He did it again, but this time, each floweret became a butterfly in succession, peeling away in a long streamer.

"You already do it perfectly."

"Thank you. But you see why I want to learn more?" He gazed after the butterflies as they vanished in the air.

"Yes." She watched as he performed the trick for the eleventh time. "Maybe I can help you."

Jagryn spared her a glance. "How? You said you didn't have any magic."

"I don't, but I could tell you some spells. I've heard enough of them."

He looked troubled. "I don't know. I think I'd rather learn from someone who knows what he's doing. No offense, but what if you remember a word wrong?" He shuddered.

That was a danger she hadn't considered. She had overheard many common spells throughout her life. She knew what was supposed to happen, but not what the words actually meant. "There must be *something* I can do."

"It's nice that you even want to help. Don't worry about it; I can wait."

She nodded but didn't answer. He wanted to learn more, and he had an obvious talent. Besides, she didn't think she could stand to watch the same trick over and over for the rest of the summer. It was unfair that he had to wait for Dadad when there was a shelf of spell books at the Village Hall. Maybe Jagryn wasn't allowed to borrow the books, but no one had said anything about her. If she had to be stuck here, she might as well be useful. Not that the books would do anyone any good if Myn wouldn't let her take them out of the building.

They passed the vacant house at the edge of town. Since Luskell's last visit to Deep River, the roof had been patched and a new door fitted. "That was Elika's house, wasn't it?" There was something about Elika that Luskell was supposed to remember. The only thing that came to mind was a spooky old rumor. "Do people still think it's haunted?"

Jagryn chuckled. "I'm not sure anyone ever really did. But no, I haven't heard the story much since Jagree started fixing it up. I helped, so maybe I'll get to live in it someday."

Luskell smiled at him. "Yes! Make it a magic house again!"

He did his illusion one more time and sent a cloud of butterflies in one window and out the other. Luskell had watched a lot of student wizards during her stays in Eukard City. She had never seen such precise control so early. She decided not to promise Jagryn anything yet, but she set her mind on getting those books.

They continued toward the Blue Heron. As they passed Uncle Jagree and Auntie Brynnit's house, Grynni and Greelit called to them from where they sat on the pasture fence. "Hey, you two! Come and see our new horse!"

They climbed onto the fence next to the two girls. A moment later, Uncle Jagree led a horse out of the stable, and Luskell had to catch her breath. It was compact and muscular, a beautiful chestnut color with a creamy mane and tail. "What do you call that combination of colors?" she whispered to Grynni.

"Pa said she's a sorrel."

Greelit frowned. "*Everyone* knows that."

"Well, I didn't." Luskell knew better than to be offended. Greelit had been a know-it-all almost from the day she started to talk. "Does she have a name yet?"

"No, we're still thinking about it," Greelit said. "Stay and help us work with her."

Jagryn climbed down from the fence. "I can't, but I'll let Auntie Stell know where you are."

"Thanks. I think she'd let me stay awhile."

The filly seemed alert in every fiber of her body, quivering with energy. Luskell thought she would be both agile and strong. She had no tack on, not even a halter, only a loose loop of rope around her neck. Uncle Jagree held the end of it and walked beside the horse, not leading or controlling her in any way. He spoke quietly to her. His ability to talk to animals was well known, so perhaps he did have some control. The horse shied when one of the twins couldn't resist an admiring cry, but Uncle Jagree led her away from the fence and soon calmed her.

He looked back at the girls on the fence. "She's getting used to me. Let's see how she does with two people. Luskell, you're our guest. Why don't you go first?"

She gripped the fence rail. "I don't know how to ride."

He smiled at her. "Don't worry, no one's riding her today. After she's used to new people, she'll be able to take some weight—not too much until her bones and joints are fully grown. Any of you girls will be light enough, but we'll work up to it gradually—a blanket at first, then a saddle, then a rider, bareback. But for now, I only want her to get to know you."

Luskell longed to get closer to the horse but still held back. She had no fear when climbing trees, but this was a creature with a mind of its own. "I don't know ..."

"Go on!" Greelit said. "This part is easy."

Grynni gave her a little push, and Luskell climbed down on the pasture side.

"Walk over here by me," Uncle Jagree said. "Stand where she can see and smell you, and don't make any sudden moves."

Luskell had guessed that much on her own. She walked slowly to Uncle Jagree. She kept her eyes on the horse, and the horse kept her eyes on Luskell. Her tail swished, and she pawed the ground. Her ears went back.

"She's a little nervous," Uncle Jagree said.

Luskell gave him a shaky smile. "So am I."

"Maybe talk to her."

"I—I wouldn't know what to say."

"*What* doesn't matter so much as *how*. You're trying to soothe a frightened child."

She nodded and began to murmur, nonsense at first and then real words. The sharp tang of horse sweat filled her nostrils, so strong she could taste it. Luskell had never liked horse smell, but it didn't bother her now. It was one part of the animalness of the creature before her, and it dredged up a long-forgotten memory—sitting incredibly high up on the back of an elderly chestnut mare. When and where was that? It didn't matter. She continued to murmur. After a moment, the horse flicked her ears forward, then stretched her head toward Luskell and sniffed at her. At an encouraging nod from Uncle Jagree, Luskell stroked the horse's soft nose.

"That's the idea," he said. "What was that?"

Luskell continued to gaze at the horse as she answered. "What was what?"

"You were singing something, but I'd never heard it before."

"It just came to me. It's an Aklaka lullaby, the most soothing thing I know." She glanced at him. "They say it can calm a volcano."

His eyebrows shot up. "That's a powerful lullaby. What other secrets are you hiding?"

"It's no secret—Dadad and Knot both knew it!" At this outburst, the horse snorted. "I'm sorry, shh." She sang another verse of the lullaby, and the horse nosed her skirt pocket.

Uncle Jagree laughed and pulled a carrot from his pocket. "I'll take your word for it. But you may have a future as a horse trainer. Girls, should we let Luskell name our new horse?"

"Yes!" Grynni cried.

Greelit frowned. "I wanted to!"

Grynni squeezed her twin's arm. "Oh, we should let Luskell do it. We'll have other horses, right, Pa? But how often does Luskell come for the whole summer?"

Greelit continued to scowl, then gave up the fight and smiled. "Oh, all right. I guess that's fair. What will you call her?"

"I don't know anything about her!" Luskell protested.

"I can fill in some," Uncle Jagree said. "She's descended on her sire's side from my old horse, Aunt Rosy. Do you remember her?"

That hazy memory returned. And for a moment, she also saw herself as Uncle Jagree must have seen her, a tiny child dwarfed by the big, gentle horse. "I think so. You sat me up on her once, didn't you?"

"That's right. I'm impressed. You couldn't have been more than two then. And one of her grand-dams is a horse Brynnit and I helped deliver." He smiled dreamily. "I *saw* Brynnit for the first time that day, though I'd known her all her life. I think that's when I fell in love."

Luskell nodded. "That might help. May I think about it? Klamamam is calling me."

Uncle Jagree glanced toward the inn and chuckled. "No, she's not, but I like the way you take your assignments so seriously. Take all the time you need."

At that moment, Klamamam stepped out of the Heron. She smiled and waved. "Luskell! Time to come home now."

Luskell went in for lunch, then helped with afternoon chores and supper preparations. She didn't have a chance to think about the horse's name again that afternoon. It had been a long day, and by the time Klamamam sat down to tell stories after supper, Luskell longed for bed.

"Tell us more about Yrae," Rakkyn begged. "The *real* Yrae."

Luskell paused with her foot on the first stair. She wasn't *that* tired. She sat on the step to listen.

"Yes, he lived here such a short time," Aunt Sudi said. "We never really knew him, whatever he called himself."

Klamamam smiled mysteriously. "He spent more time in Deep River than you know. He used to visit me in secret."

Some listeners seemed shocked, but Aunt Sudi nodded. "I wondered. How did you manage that?"

"You remember Crane's journey," Klamamam said. "When he was only seventeen, he went looking for Yrae to learn how to lift the enchantment. He found him, and he found his answer, but he also realized soon after meeting him that Yrae was his father. Crane could have come home and lifted the enchantment on his own, but he persuaded his father to come back with him. He wanted to bring us together again. He wanted his family. It took some doing, but Yrae finally agreed.

"It turned out to be a more difficult journey than either of them expected. They were both in bad shape by the time they got here, and Yrae only made things worse when he tried to get back to the mountain. He had good reason—the mountain was about to erupt, and he was the only one who could stop it. But instead of explaining, he fought Crane—weakened him and nearly killed himself. They both had a long recovery. I let everyone know that Crane was back, but I kept his father a secret. He didn't want to be Yrae anymore, but he doubted any of you would see the difference."

"So that's when he took a new name?" Rakkyn asked.

Klamamam nodded. "I *gave* him a new name. He'd used many names in his life, but none of them fit anymore. He couldn't remember what his mother called him. I was just getting to know him myself, but I had to call him something! So I chose a new name for him that spoke of our bond ... and of his stubbornness." She sighed. "He couldn't stay then, but he came back in secret many times, and he never used another name. Knot took that one to his grave."

She told other tales after that. Luskell listened, with less interest, but stayed awake to help clean up after the guests had left. "Klamamam, why are you telling so many stories about Knot? I've never heard you speak of him so openly outside the family."

Klamamam gazed at her a moment. "I'm not sure why. I guess I was finally ready."

Luskell frowned. "What do you mean, ready?"

"The night he died, Knot asked me to tell his story. I promised I would, and I tried, but it never came out right. It was always, 'Once there lived a mighty wizard,' not 'Once there lived a man, and I loved him.' Maybe I couldn't believe his story was finished. Sometimes I'm sure I'll turn around and see him there, or wake and find it was only a dream, and he didn't die." She blinked and wiped her eyes with her apron. "Neither of those things will happen. He's gone. But I can keep my promise."

Luskell went to bed thinking of Knot and of names. Her own name was a blend of Lukett and Stell, her two grandmothers. Dadad's name was one his father had used. It was an honor and a challenge to be asked to name someone or something, and she didn't want to rush, even if she was naming a horse. She didn't have much information, but maybe it was enough.

She drifted into a doze, thinking about what Klamamam had said about Knot. She named him when she barely knew him at all. He was much more complex than a horse. Knot. If you pronounced all the letters, it sounded kind of like an Aklaka word, *k'nala*, especially if you did a click instead of the "k" sound. She smiled to herself. Yes, that would work. She would have to modify the pronunciation for Eukardian tongues, and the spelling. But based on what Uncle Jagree had told her, it was perfect.

Luskell woke early, even with no baby to disturb her. She dressed and ran downstairs. "I'll be right back!" she called to Klamamam as she passed the kitchen. Breakfast could wait. She ran to Brynnit and Jagree's house and pounded on the door. Auntie Brynnit answered her knock.

"Luskell! You're here early."

"I know. I need to talk to Grynni and Greelit."

Brynnit smiled. "You're lucky they're early risers. They're in the stable helping their pa with the horses. They haven't even brushed their hair yet!"

Luskell hurried to the stable. As she neared it, Grynni came out. Her black hair floated loose and uncombed around her head.

"Grynni, you look like Elika!" Luskell cried.

Grynni stared at her. "How do you know? Even Pa never saw her."

Luskell halted, baffled. How *did* she know? "You know, just from—what I've heard. Dadad remembers her, and—"

Grynni laughed. "Well, you're right. Everyone who knew her says so. Did you want something?"

"I thought of a name for your horse."

Greelit ran out to join her sister. "What is it? What is it?"

"You should call her Kanala."

The twins exchanged a puzzled glance. "I've never heard that name before," Greelit said.

Luskell grinned. "I know. It's an Aklaka word. It means 'love.'"

Chapter 17

The New Yrae was exhausted. Even before the heat
wave began to bake Eukard City, most of his power
went into shielding his employer's thoughts from the
wizard, Crane, and his woman. The heat was supposed
to focus their attention elsewhere, but meanwhile
everyone suffered. The New Yrae himself had not slept
well since it started.

But Crane would not be deterred in his search for
the truth. Although the rumors about the New Yrae
must have reached him, he didn't respond with fear so
much as curiosity. The man seemed immune to the
general unease in the city. He continued to ask
questions about everything from the governor's plans

for the Aklaka to funding plans for free schools; questions that came perilously close to the mark.

This called for a more direct distraction than mere uncomfortable weather. If Crane believed a violent and unpredictable wizard was loose in the city, he would have no thought to spare for secret plots. The New Yrae was prepared to play that wizard. His talents for stealth and shielding meant he could plan his attacks for locations where they would have the most impact. He could attack and disappear, attack and disappear, as often as necessary. Let Crane try to stop him!

The weapon was prepared. His hands shook as he hid the knife in his belt, but that was only fatigue. There was no room in this plan for squeamishness or fear. He stilled the tremors and went out. It was time to earn his name.

Crane paced the sitting room in the predawn darkness. It was too hot to sleep, and he didn't want his tossing to wake Ketty. He opened all the windows to catch any breeze but did not light a lamp. Darkness felt cooler.

The weather in Eukard City had been pleasant when they first arrived a week ago but turned hot soon after. Days had passed, and the heat wave showed no sign of breaking. Crane was tempted to do something about it, if only to get a decent night's sleep. But he didn't play with weather lightly. Drawing cooler air to the city might bring drought or storm elsewhere, perhaps destroying crops or taking lives. It was also possible some other wizard's meddling had caused this anomaly, in which case he didn't want to make things worse. It was relatively simple to change the weather in crude ways, such as bringing rain or clear skies. It required great skill and power to actually control the weather's subtle patterns.

It wasn't only the heat that kept Crane from his bed. When he managed to sleep, his dreams were full of threat or warning. Once, he sat straight up, certain he would find his father in the room. But that could never happen.

Or could it? Was Yrae really back?

The day after the Governor's reception, when it was still cool enough to think, Crane and Ketty had tried to find out. When his father was alive, Crane and Knot each had a sense of the other's presence. If he was in the city, Crane should have been able to locate him merely by seeking. But when he reached out with that long-unused sense, he found nothing. Ketty used her skill for mindtalking and called out to Knot. She received no answer. But that didn't necessarily mean he wasn't in the city. He could have hidden himself—

A floorboard creaked, and Crane whipped around. "Who's there?"

"Just me," Ketty yawned. "Who did you think?"

"No one. Did I wake you?"

"No, something else; I don't know what. Is something wrong?" She lit the lamp on top of the little writing desk. She had never been as at home in the dark as he.

"I'm not sure. Every time I fell asleep, my dreams woke me, so I thought I'd get up and Listen. I can't hear anything, though. Maybe I'll write to Luskell while it's quiet." He sat at the desk.

She rested her arm across his shoulders. "And tell her what? There's nothing happening here."

"That's not true. The Aklaka arrived, and we saw Dokral." Whether or not there was anything to tell, he had promised Luskell he would write every week. The first letter had reported little more than their safe arrival. He kissed Ketty. "Do you still want to go to Balsam's House after breakfast?"

"At least that will be useful. I hate this waiting around."

"I do, too, and it's a good way to find out what's happening in town. Get some sleep now. One of us should be rested."

After she returned to bed, he laid a sheet of paper on the desk and began to write.

Dear Luskell,

I write this before sunup. It has been too hot to sleep for three nights in a row. I suppose it is even hotter there, so I shouldn't complain, but I'm sure it is also dryer. Here it is sticky, something I will never get used to. I'm tempted to join Naliskat and sleep outside! He arrived in time for the governor's reception. He brought

Pataknan this year. An excellent
Listener, but I miss Chamokat.
Kala needed him to stay and
train Laki, which is more
important, I guess.

Dokral was playing at the
reception and asked about you.
Now I wish we had gotten you a
fiddle of your own before you left
the city so you could keep playing
over the summer. Maybe we will
bring one when we come, as we
might be staying in Deep River
awhile. I hope you're not bored by
it, because I am ready for a long
visit if we ever finish up here. I am
frustrated because we have been
here a week and have not had a
real meeting with the governor
yet, only with advisers who
couldn't tell us anything. I don't
think Snowabi will be difficult to
influence, but in the meanwhile
we're just waiting. To fill the time,
we're going over to Balsam's House
to offer our services as healers.

He considered writing about the rumors of Yrae. There was little else newsworthy to report, and she might find the story interesting. But he didn't want to worry her. She had friends in the city; it would be distressing to imagine them in danger, though he doubted the danger was real.

> I was pleased to learn of Jagryn's abilities. He shows real promise, and I think he will learn quickly once I can spend some time training him—one reason I want to stay in Deep River. Encourage him, but don't let him do anything foolish! He's seen my scar, so I don't think he will, but you know how boys are.

Crane smiled to himself. What with Laki, Ambug, and Elic's sons, she had enough surrogate brothers that she *should* know how boys were by now.

> Write and let us know how you enjoyed the dance. I was sorry to miss it yet again, but maybe next time. Give our love to your grandmother and everyone.
> -Love, Dadad

He sealed the letter. They could drop it at the coach office when they went out later. As the sun rose, he blew out the lamp and crawled back into bed for a few winks of sleep. But it seemed he had barely closed his eyes before the serving girl brought breakfast, and another day began.

They went out right after the meal into a morning already growing hot. Crane was thankful for the large trees that shaded most of the streets in this part of town, but even the shade was hot. People who had to be out moved slowly, and most looked like they'd slept no better than Crane.

As they passed the tavern near Balsam's House, a youthful voice called out, "Hey! Wizard!" Crane paused and looked in the direction of the shout. A boy darted out of the dim interior of the tavern and ran up to him.

"Druner?" Although it had been only a short time, Crane almost didn't recognize the young pickpocket. The boy's face and clothes were cleaner, for one thing. He'd had a haircut and already looked better fed. Crane crouched down to get a better look at the boy. "You're the first person I've seen today with any energy."

Druner frowned. "Who wouldn't, with a good bed and regular meals?"

"You make a good point. Perhaps the rest of us are spoiled. So I take it Berdona found something for you to do?"

"Did she ever! Did you know her daughter got married and moved away the day before? So she needed to hire someone, and here I came."

Crane smiled. "I didn't know that; I had a feeling she'd know who needed help. So she needed a hand herself."

"And she says I can go to school when things settle down."

"That sounds better than stealing. I'm glad to hear it."

"Yeah, probably." Druner looked doubtful, then grinned and hurried back to the tavern.

Crane watched him a moment, then rejoined Ketty and continued toward Balsam's House. She glanced up at him and shook her head. "No, Crane."

"No, what?"

"I can read you without even trying. No, we're not having another baby just so you can find out what it's like to have a son." She wasn't angry, but that sounded final.

"I wouldn't ask that. But I can't help how I feel."

Ketty took his arm and gave it an affectionate squeeze. "I know. It's not that I don't think you'd be—"

A man stumbled out of an alley into their path. He clutched at Crane's tunic. "Help me!" Blood soaked the man's shirt. He slid to the ground.

Crane caught him and lowered him gently. He glanced at Ketty. "What was that you said about nothing happening here?"

Blood welled from the man's neck, but at least it didn't spurt. Ketty knelt beside him and pressed her fingers to the wound while she spoke a healing charm. Crane reached out with all his senses. He didn't detect the assailant nearby, and of the small crowd that gathered, no one had witnessed the attack. Patrols had been increased in this area, but Crane couldn't see a single Guard.

He crouched beside the man. "You're safe now," he said. "Who did this?"

The victim's mouth opened and closed, but no intelligible sound came out. His thoughts were too chaotic to read. The flow of blood had slowed but continued to ooze around Ketty's fingers. "It's taking all my power to control the bleeding," she said. "We have to take him to Balsam's House *now*."

"Good thing we're almost there." Crane lifted the injured man.

Ketty walked close by his side with her hand on the wound as they covered the remaining distance. Crane could feel her trembling as they climbed the steps and crossed the porch of the big brick house. This really was taking all her power, and he knew how much she had. They stumbled inside where it was dim and much cooler. A young woman came to meet them.

"Get Balsam," Ketty whispered.

The healer hurried away and returned with the gray-haired mistress of the house. "Ketty? Crane? What is this?"

"I'm not sure," Ketty gasped. "All my power, and I can't stop the bleeding."

"Bring him in here and let me see." They followed her into a nearby room, one of three partitioned out of the mansion's front parlor. Crane laid the man on a pallet there. Ketty removed her fingers from the wound. It bled freely while Balsam examined it. She pressed a dressing against the cut. "Enchanted blade," she said. "Or a cutting spell. We have to perform the counterspell, or the wound will never close."

Ketty stared at her. "Of course," she murmured. "Why didn't I see it? I'm so muddled!" She sank down on another pallet. She was pale and still trembling.

"We haven't slept well," Crane explained. "Our house is not as cool as yours."

There were only a few spells that could have caused such an injury, and between Balsam and Crane they soon hit on the correct counterspell. Now it was a normal wound, and Balsam could clean and dress it effectively.

"He was lucky to bump into you two," Balsam said. "He probably wouldn't have made it this far on his own. He might have died in the street."

The man stared at Crane. His lips moved, but Crane couldn't hear him. He bent closer until he could make out the faint whisper. "Yrae. The New—Yrae."

Chapter 18

Ketty rested on the pallet until she had recovered her strength. It wasn't often that a healing drained her that way, but this one was unusual. Balsam gave her a restorative. She drank it and almost immediately felt better.

"Do you want to go home and change?" Crane asked. "There's a lot of blood on your dress."

"And go back out into that heat? No, thanks." Clean aprons hung on the back of the door. She took one and put it on to cover the stain. "I might as well be useful as long as I'm here."

"I'm sorry I already sealed Luskell's letter," Crane said. "This would be something to tell."

Ketty shuddered. "I'm more convinced than ever that we were right to leave her in Deep River. We know she's safe there."

For the rest of the morning, they helped treat the usual illnesses and injuries, plus several heat-related disorders. Ketty was especially alert for more cursed wounds but didn't see any.

"I feel stupid that I didn't recognize the first one," she said to Crane as they sat down for lunch with the healers.

"Why? Have you seen one before?" he asked. "I hadn't."

"No, but with my training and intuition, I should have known. I just can't think."

"It's the heat and lack of sleep. You'll feel better when it cools off."

"I know. I wish it would rain." She gave him a little smile. "Could you ...?"

He kissed her. "I wasn't going to, but for you, I might."

"No, never mind. These things don't usually last, and I know you don't like to play with the weather."

"Not like my father, no." He looked thoughtful. "This heat could be the result of someone else playing, though. We should stop by the Wizards' Hall. They might know something about it, or about this—New Yrae." His face worked as he struggled with emotion. "He isn't—he would never—"

Ketty felt his distress. It pained her, but she preferred that to the alternative, where he walled off his feelings from her. She laid her finger to his lips. "No. He isn't your father." It hurt to admit that after the hope, but it was a relief to say it. The dead stayed dead and did not come back wrong. But that left the question: Who was this New Yrae?

The Wizards' Hall stood across the square from Balsam's House. It was a place where wizards could meet and share knowledge or socialize. Neither Ketty nor Crane had spent much time there, but they were on speaking terms with a few of the regulars, and Crane knew many of the apprentice wizards who met their teachers there. In many cases, he had been the first to detect their power and refer them for instruction. It was as good a place as any to seek information on this mysterious wizard. She wished they didn't have to. They were guests in town, and this seemed like a matter for the local magic community—except the apparent villain had chosen *that* name.

Before she knew Knot, before she even met Crane, Ketty had held a grudge against the old Yrae. He was a powerful wizard who had let her mother die when he had a chance to save her. Maybe it was already too late, but he hadn't even tried. For Ketty and her father, this added to Yrae's already wicked reputation. Years later, she came to understand the real reason for his inaction—he'd failed someone he cared for and didn't dare risk another human bond. She forgave him, learned from him, loved him. If someone was committing evil under that name, Ketty took it personally.

It was difficult to leave the cool hospital for the blazing afternoon. The square was unshaded and hot. Crane rapped on the door of the Wizards' Hall. A slender, dark-eyed boy opened it. He looked to be about Luskell's age.

"We're not changing the weather," he said wearily before they could ask anything. Ketty suspected he'd been giving that answer for days.

Crane grinned. "That's all right, Dalmer. If I wanted to change it, I would have by now. Is Bardin here?"

The boy stared. "Master Crane? I didn't know you without the beard. Yes, Bardin's here." He stood aside. "Come in out of the heat, and I'll call him."

He left them in the large common room just off the front entry and went out by another door. Small groups sat talking or eating in the dining room, visible through an arched doorway. A few people slept on mats on the carpeted floor of the common room.

"It must be cooler here than in their houses," Crane whispered, and Ketty nodded agreement. It wasn't as pleasant as Balsam's House but cooler than her bedroom.

A straight-backed old man crossed to them, his arms out in welcome. Bardin was taller than Ketty but nowhere near as tall as Crane, with a sparse fringe of white hair and a grizzled beard. "Crane! Welcome! It's been a long time. Hello, Ketty."

They shook hands. "I have a mystery," Crane said. "If anyone knows the answer, you will. What do you know about someone calling himself 'The New Yrae?'"

Bardin sucked air through his teeth. "Not as much as I'd like to. I've heard the rumors, but I haven't seen anything yet."

"We have today," Ketty said. "A man with a cursed wound."

"Someone you knew?"

"No, a stranger," Crane said. "He literally stumbled across our path, and we took him to Balsam's House. We couldn't get much sense out of him—he'd lost a lot of blood—but he managed to say who did it. The New Yrae."

Bardin nodded. "It's a start, though if this New Yrae has any kind of power, why don't I know who he is? I can't believe he's one of ours."

"The old Yrae wasn't," Crane muttered.

Bardin gave Crane a puzzled smile. "I wouldn't know. But taking a name like that, I would guess this new fellow is young, with something to prove."

Crane and Ketty exchanged a glance. That description fit Crane's father as a young man. "We'll let you know if we meet anyone like that," Crane said.

Bardin smiled. "I appreciate that. I don't like seeing people afraid of our kind. I'll be happier when he's out in the open."

They left the square, posted the letter, and returned to their sweltering apartment. Ketty's mind was on the New Yrae. It wasn't difficult to enchant a blade or curse a wound. But he had hidden the curse from her, and she could usually read blood and bodies like a book. Was it only the heat, or was it something more?

Chapter 19

Luskell hoped her trip to the graveyard would lead to more dreams of Ketwyn, but she didn't dream of anything memorable for the next week. At least she wasn't homesick anymore. She had written to all her city friends and was getting reacquainted with those in Deep River. Her days were filled with work at the inn and helping train Kanala. Perhaps those earlier dreams had grown out of her own loneliness.

"Finish the breakfast dishes, and then you'll get a treat, " Klamamam said. It was two days past Long Day and already hot. "We get to help Sunnea pick cherries. They're all ripening at once, so she needs help to pick and preserve them before they spoil."

Luskell looked at her in disbelief. "That sounds like work, not a treat."

Klamamam winked. "A change is as good as a break."

Apparently anything different was so rare in Deep River that another kind of work was viewed as fun. Pathetic. But Luskell kept this opinion to herself.

Klamamam gathered several pails and bowls, and they headed for the small house behind the school. When they got there, they found Sulika already up a ladder against the big old cherry tree. Auntie Brynnit held the ladder, while Aunt Sunnea stood ready to receive the filled pail and pass up an empty one. Old Aunt Sudi supervised Grynni and Greelit as they picked from two smaller trees nearby.

"This is getting to be a regular orchard back here!" Klamamam exclaimed. "I didn't know the little trees were bearing yet."

Sulika smiled down at her. "I'm very proud of them. They grew from pits I stuck in the ground when I was a child. We don't have enough water for a real orchard, though. Imagine how it was in Greelin's day, when the river ran full! It was all orchards back here."

Aunt Sudi—Greelin's daughter—looked around with a smile. "It was still like that in our day, wasn't it, Stell?"

Klamamam's smile looked forced. Luskell could guess the reason; Knot had changed the river's course soon after they met, one of many acts with unforeseen consequences. The river had water again but it would never flow as deep as it once had.

Sulika handed off her filled pail and descended the ladder. "That's as high as I can reach. Luskell, you're taller. How do you feel about ladders?"

In answer, Luskell grabbed an empty pail and scampered to the top. She had grown up climbing Aku's slopes, perching on high cliffs with the whole world laid out below. A ladder up a cherry tree was nothing.

Klamamam chuckled. "She's a mountain goat, like her father."

Luskell was pleased to have cheered her up. She began to pick, well above the limit of Sulika's reach. "I can't quite get the ones at the top."

Aunt Sunnea laughed. "That's all right. We'll leave a few for the birds. As if they haven't stolen enough already!"

They picked for the rest of the morning. After a break for lunch, they gathered in the shade of the house to pit the cherries so they could be made into pies and jam. Grynni and Greelit went home to see their horse when they got bored with pitting. Luskell could have joined them but found she enjoyed the steady, almost mindless rhythm of the task that left her free to listen and converse.

"Sulika, tell me about your wedding dress," Klamamam said.

Sulika held up her hand. "Just a moment." She pitted a cherry and dropped the fruit into a bowl, but did not discard the pit. She put it in her mouth and held it there for a moment, then spat it out and poked it into a clay pot full of soil. She had eight of these pots at her side and had planted cherry pits in two of them so far, though she had tested and discarded far more than that.

"How do you know when a seed is a good one?" Luskell asked.

She smiled. "It tells me. I want to sell these seedlings at market, so I don't want to waste time on weak seeds. These should be strong sprouts by the time it turns cold, and I have a south-facing window in my room where I can set them for the winter."

Aunt Sunnea gave her a puzzled look. "You won't be in that room this winter."

Sulika stared at her mother, then shook her head and smiled. "You're right. I—can't believe it's real."

"But your dress," Klamamam insisted. "What color is it?"

Aunt Sunnea answered for her. "It's a lovely dark blue, with the finest cream-colored stripes and lace at the neck and cuffs. It's nearly done—or it *was*." She rolled her eyes at Sulika in mock exasperation. "At the last moment, she decided it shouldn't have sleeves!"

"It's summer," Sulika defended herself. "When I saw Luskell's beautiful dress, with no sleeves, and the little coat—"

"Mother would have been shocked, but Papa seemed to welcome the challenge," Aunt Sunnea said. "He took the bodice apart and started over without a complaint."

"I saw the material when it was still on Pa's loom," Auntie Brynnit said. Her father was old Briato, the weaver. "I can hardly wait to see it on you, Sulika. I suppose you'll have a bigger wedding than I did. Have you set the date yet?"

"Whenever Crane and Ketty come back," Sulika said.

"How does Foli feel about the delay?" Aunt Sudi asked.

"He hasn't complained."

Luskell thought back to the dance. She hadn't known many betrothed couples, but these two seemed an odd match. "Why are you marrying Foli?" she blurted.

Conversation died for a moment as the other women stared at her. They all looked shocked. All but Sulika, who answered calmly, "Because he asked me."

Aunt Sudi chuckled. "So anyone could have asked, and you would have said yes?"

"*Anyone* didn't ask. Foli did."

"That's no reason!" Luskell exclaimed. "Why do you need to get married at all?"

Aunt Sudi nudged Klamamam. "Listen to the girl!" she whispered, but in the silence, everyone heard her.

Luskell thought Sulika would be upset, but she remained calm. "I'll be twenty-two this winter. I want my own home and a family before I'm too much older, and Foli can give me that."

Luskell wanted to ask why she had delayed the wedding if that was the case. She thought better of it and merely nodded, though she didn't understand.

Klamamam smiled. "You can have a family without being married, though I'm not sure I'd recommend it."

Luskell turned to her, pleased to bend the subject, if not completely change it. "If you'd been Aklaka, that's what would have made the marriage official."

Klamamam frowned. "What do you mean?"

"Having a family. As long as they're of age, any two Aklaka can form a social marriage simply by moving in together." Luskell liked knowing something the adults didn't and warmed to her lesson. "There's no ceremony or formality. They just do it. But once they have a child, there are promises and contracts. If there's a ceremony with special clothes and everything, that's when they have it."

Sulika laughed. "*Any* two? You mean a man and a woman, of course."

Luskell shook her head. "No, any two adults who want to be together. The community accepts the couple as a unit, but there's no legal significance unless they have a child. That usually means a man and a woman, but not always. There have been adoptions when both parents had died. But the point is they don't have to sign a book in order to sleep together."

Aunt Sunnea flinched. "Luskell!"

Aunt Sudi blew a ladybug off her arm and glanced at Aunt Sunnea. "My parents never signed the book."

"They didn't need to," Klamamam said. "Elika loved Greelin as much as I loved Knot."

Elika? Luskell nearly choked as the dream returned. *You tell my great-granddaughter...* She looked at Sulika. "Elika says you're marrying the wrong man."

Stunned silence descended again. Everyone stared at Luskell. Even Sulika looked troubled. "'Elika says?' What—what do you mean?"

"Nothing. Never mind. I had a dream that seemed real, but it was only a dream." Cheeks burning, Luskell concentrated on the bowl of unpitted cherries she held in her lap.

"Did she happen to mention who the right man might be?" Sulika asked. Luskell shook her head.

They continued pitting, the silence filled with the ping of pits, the plop of fruit. Aunt Sunnea's soft voice broke the quiet. "Really, dear, did you give anyone else a chance? How many suitors did you have?"

"Four, Mama. How many did you have?"

Aunt Sunnea blushed and smiled. Everyone knew she and Uncle Elic had been a fixed couple since childhood. "All right, it's not a contest. But did you see any of the others more than once?"

"No, but that was their doing. Rakkyn took me out once, and we had a good time, but he's almost like a third brother. We couldn't quite picture being anything more than old friends and playmates. And Tibreff smelled like horse sweat." She wrinkled her nose. Everyone but Auntie Brynnit laughed.

"What's wrong with a little horsey smell on a man?" Auntie Brynnit asked.

Sulika wrapped an arm around her aunt. "Jagree's different. He smells like Jagree. He's special."

As they all nodded agreement, Luskell wondered if Uncle Jagree had any idea how many women adored him. He seemed to have the same effect on them as he had on horses.

"So that was it for those two," Sulika went on. "My only other suitor besides Foli was Myn."

"Myn?" Aunt Sunnea asked. "I don't remember that at all."

"I don't know why not. He was the first."

Luskell wasn't at all surprised about this, but maybe Aunt Sunnea hadn't seen Myn and Sulika dancing.

"He's a poet," Klamamam said. "Or so Jelf says."

Luskell had heard this before, though she didn't know whether it was true, or whether he was any good. She tucked the information away; perhaps she could use it to flatter him into lending her the spell books. She'd been trying to think of ways to get the books, but this was the first good idea she'd had.

"He might be," Sulika said. "All I know is that when I was twelve and dressed up for the dance for the first time, Myn danced with me. I didn't expect to dance with anyone that night besides Papa, Uncle Jagree, and my grandfathers. It meant a lot to have someone from outside the family ask me, even if he was just being charitable." She smiled at Luskell. "You know what I mean."

Luskell started. "I do? Oh, of course." Her face grew hot again. "Yes, it was sweet of Young Crane to ask me."

Aunt Sunnea and Sulika exchanged a glance that Luskell couldn't quite interpret. "Crane is an excellent dancer," Aunt Sunnea said. "He makes a point of dancing with every woman there before he dances with anyone twice." She smiled. "I can't say what Jagryn was thinking. I didn't see him dance with anyone else."

Luskell laughed. "Jagryn didn't ask *me*. *I* asked *him*, or he wouldn't have danced at all."

"That sounds more like my Jagryn," Aunt Sunnea said. "But Myn asking Sulika when he was twenty, and she was only twelve? I'm not sure I like that."

"Mama, it was in public, in front of everyone. It's not like he tried to take me off by myself." Sulika smiled and looked sidelong at her mother. "But when I asked if he was courting anyone, he let on that he was waiting for me."

Aunt Sunnea gasped. "That doesn't seem proper at all!"

Sulika laughed. "You sound like Grandma Ati! He was only being nice, but it meant a lot to me at the time. And the next couple of summers, he always saved a dance for me. It was our little joke. Then he seemed to forget about it, but when I got my courtship ring, he was the first to invite me to go walking."

"So he *was* waiting for you?" Auntie Brynnit asked.

"I think he just likes to keep his promises," Sulika said.

A tiny smile flickered over Auntie Brynnit's lips. "I thought that about Jagree once, too."

"Myn barely had two words to say to me all evening," Sulika continued. "Then Foli came calling, and Myn didn't ask me again. He'd—fulfilled his duty, I guess." Luskell couldn't be sure, but Sulika seemed wistful.

Aunt Sudi sighed. "Those two always competed for everything. They both wanted to be Jelf's apprentice, and he couldn't choose between them. If Foli hadn't gone back to the mill, I suppose they'd still be doing the job together. It figures they'd both be interested in the same girl."

"Except that Myn didn't try to compete," Sulika said.

They pitted in silence again for a time, and once again, quiet Aunt Sunnea broke it. "I haven't seen as much of Foli lately."

Sulika made an exasperated noise. "Oh, Mama, we went walking two nights ago. No, three. And we're having supper at the inn tomorrow night."

Aunt Sunnea smiled. "I guess it is more important that *you* see him."

"Yes, it is, as I'm going to marry him," Sulika replied. "I don't want to talk about it anymore."

Luskell and Klamamam returned to the inn when it was time to start supper. Aunt Sunnea had given them a big bowl of pitted cherries to take with them, and Klamamam had an idea for a cherry cake that could be eaten as a dessert or for breakfast.

"Thank you for coming along, Luskell. Our quiet pastimes probably seem dull to you, but you were a great help."

"No, I had fun. I liked being part of a group of adults for a change."

Klamamam chuckled. "I thought you must be bored to tears if you were taking an interest in small-town gossip."

Luskell laughed, too. They went inside and started cooking supper. She didn't mind that there was no break in the work, except there wouldn't be time to ask Myn for a spell book.

"So," Klamamam said after they had been working awhile. "You had a dream about Elika?"

Luskell looked up from sprinkling sugar over the cherries. "Yes, a week or so ago."

"And you recognized her?"

"No, Ketwyn told me who she was."

"Ketwyn told you ..." Klamamam swayed and dropped into a chair. "Have you—seen anyone else from our graveyard?" Her voice failed, but Luskell knew who she was thinking of.

"They're just dreams, Klamamam. They're not real."

Klamamam managed a wan smile. "Your father used to dream of flying."

"Doesn't everyone?"

Her grandmother didn't answer, and when she spoke again, it was of other, inconsequential things. The supper crowd was gathering, so Luskell went to serve them. Rakkyn sat by himself at one of the small tables. She'd seen him at supper often, but she hadn't served him since that first disastrous evening. He usually joined Uncle Elic's family if they were present, but tonight he was on his own.

"You're Rakkyn, right?" Luskell carefully set down his mug of ale.

"Yes. And you're Luskell."

She smiled. "You remembered my name!"

"It's hard to forget a girl who flung supper at me." Her face grew hot, but he smiled. "You probably don't remember, but I helped Sulika look after you once, years ago. You were probably three or four. Even then, you were always in a hurry. Kept us on our toes."

"Sorry, I don't remember. But Sulika looked after me lots of times."

"I saw you at the dance, too. I almost didn't recognize you in your ball gown. Such a color, and that fabric!" He sighed.

"I don't wear silk every day." They laughed together as Luskell did a twirl in her plain work dress. "I saw you there, too, when I was dancing with Crane. I think he was—interested in your sister."

Rakkyn raised an eyebrow. "Bramynna seemed just as interested, but who wouldn't be? What girl wouldn't be?"

"He's a handsome fellow," Luskell allowed.

"It's a fine family. Sulika is my oldest friend, and Jagryn seems a good sort. You'd know better than I would, though." He winked at her. "The two of you seemed quite friendly."

The blood rose in her face again. "It's not like that! Our families are close, and we're near in age—"

"Rakkyn! Good to see you!" Foli joined them. "May I sit here?"

"Please," Rakkyn said.

Luskell went to get ale for Foli and supper for both of them. They were immediately deep in conversation, laughing and talking as if there were no one else in the room. Foli seemed more attentive to Bramynna's brother than to his own intended bride. Did he think he could somehow have two girls? Or maybe he thought there was still time to change his choice.

Luskell laughed at herself. Klamamam was right— she must be bored if she cared about small-town gossip. But the truth was, she did care. These people and their stories had become her people and her stories. Deep River was starting to feel like home.

Chapter 20

The next day was busy again, but Luskell finally got away in the middle of the afternoon. She went straight to the Village Hall, a relief from the bright day. Her eyes were still adjusting to the dim interior when Myn called to her from the library. "Hello, Luskell. I wondered when you might come back."

"You did?" How could he know her plan when she hadn't even told Jagryn?

He smiled. "Do you want to read your grandmother's stories again?"

She relaxed. "Not this time." She wasn't sure how best to work into her request. It might sound suspicious to ask for a spell book straight out. She had thought of using flattery to get around him, but if she opened that way, it would be obvious she wanted something. But there was something else she was curious about. "May I see the register?"

"What do you want the register for?" Myn asked but got up and walked over to the shelf. He took it down and laid it on the desk.

"I think I'm listed."

Myn nodded. "Yes, you were born here, weren't you?" He found the page and pointed out the line: the date, her name, her parents' names, with Uncle Jelf's spidery signature. A few lines earlier was the marriage of Crane and Ketty—Dadad and Mamam—immediately preceded by the death of Knot, and a few lines above that, the marriage of her grandparents, Knot and Stell. It was nothing but writing on a page, but there was something powerful about seeing all that family history noted down. And she learned something new.

"*You* performed my parents' wedding?"

Myn laughed. "The first one I ever did. I was all of fourteen and still in training, but Jelf thought it was time."

"And now you do all of them. But who would do yours?"

He closed the register and resumed his seat, no longer smiling. "That isn't likely to happen. Is there anything else?"

"Somebody said you're a poet."

His head jerked up. "Depends who you ask. Foli had another name for it."

Luskell smiled at him. "I'm not Foli."

He relaxed some. "Fair enough. At least I learned not to put my poems in the logs. Do you like poetry?"

"I don't know," she replied truthfully. "But I'm fascinated when people make something out of nothing."

He grinned. "That sounds more like magic than poetry."

She shook her head. "Wizards might change one thing into another, or give the illusion that something is there when it isn't, but they hardly ever *make* anything. And nothing against potters and weavers, but they make something out of *something*. Music and stories are different, made out of thought, out of breath, out of—I don't know what. We have a friend in the city, a musician, who makes his own tunes. Where do they come from? And Klamamam, inventing stories—"

"Why do you call her that?" Myn interrupted. "I've always wondered."

"It's what Aklaka children call their grandmother. We were with them my second winter, and I learned to talk from my friend Nalaklak." She smiled to herself as she thought of Laki. He was like a brother to her, even born the same year as Ketwyn. She wondered where he was camped this summer. Whatever he was doing, it had to be more interesting than a summer in Deep River.

Myn interrupted her musings. "What's grandfather?"

"Kladadad. I—never got to use that one."

"I suppose not. I'm sorry," Myn said. He furrowed his brow. "But your other grandfather is living, isn't he?"

"Yes, but I have to be careful and call him Grandpa. He's not as comfortable with the Aklaka as Mamam and Dadad."

Myn nodded. "My father had strong opinions about such things, too. Do they—the Aklaka—have poetry?"

Luskell frowned as she thought about it. "I don't know. They sing their stories, so that's kind of like poetry." She grinned at him. "May I please hear one of yours?"

"You really want to? All right, I have a recent one here." He dug around in a drawer and pulled out a sheet of paper. "It's called 'Morning Glory.'" He stood up and began to read.

He had a pleasant voice, not ringing or dramatic, but simple and warm. The language wasn't quite like natural speech, nor like Klamamam's stories, but neither were the words unfamiliar. They were put together in a prettier fashion, something like a song but not exactly. She could see the flared blue flowers on their climbing stems, but the poem also seemed like it could be about a person. Someone specific.

He finished reading and laid the paper down. His cheeks were red. "That's the idea, anyway. I don't read very well." He cleared his throat.

"No, it was very nice," Luskell assured him. "Thank you. Has anyone else heard it? Or read it?"

"Sometimes I read them to Jelf, but you're the first person I've shared this one with." He put the poem back in the drawer and closed it. "Is there anything else I can help you with?"

She hesitated. They were getting along well, so she took her chance. She cast a casual glance at the bottom shelf. "I'd like to borrow one of those books. The red one."

Myn shook his head. "I don't think I can do that."

"Who do they belong to?" It was Luskell's one hope.

He sighed. "Crane, when he wants them, but—"

"That's what I thought. He might want to have them rebound." So far, everything she'd said was true, though her father hadn't actually voiced any such plan. She launched into deceit. "I need to go through them page by page to see how badly they're damaged."

"In the wrong hands, they could be dangerous," Myn protested.

"I can't do anything with them but look at the pages. I won't even be able to read them, so where's the danger? I'll take them one at a time and bring them back as soon as I'm finished. I promise."

By his hesitation, she knew he was thinking about it. At last, he nodded. "I'll tell you what. I'll let you take a book out if you'll do me a favor."

"What favor?"

"Tell Sulika I want to see her."

"Why can't you tell her yourself?"

"I—seem to have lost the ability to talk to her."

"You didn't have any trouble asking her to dance."

He turned redder than the binding of the book Luskell wanted. "She asked me. Foli had left her to go make a fool of himself, as usual, and I happened to be standing there."

Luskell knew her guess about the poem was correct. If she helped him, she could have all the books she wanted. And, though she didn't know all the details, she had taken sides. "Fine, I'll carry your message. I was going over there, anyway. But if you can't talk to her, what's the point?"

He ruffled his hair. "I don't know, but I have to try. Maybe I'll read her something." He smiled. "That's not your problem. I'll write a note for you to take. You may pick up a spell book tomorrow."

"Tomorrow? Why can't I take one now?"

"Because I need to know you've delivered the message. Besides, I'm going home as soon as you leave." He wrote something on a slip of paper, folded it up, and handed it to her. "Thank you, Luskell."

She took the note and left the Hall. She was tempted to read it, but Myn came out right after her. She went straight to the house behind the school. Sulika and Jagryn were in the garden, thinning carrots. Luskell thought it was sad to yank up such eager new growth, but the remaining plants would grow better with the extra space. The ones they pulled were more greens than carrot at this point, but the skinny little roots were bright with their telltale color.

"Sulika, this is for you."

Sulika placed a bunch of tiny carrots in a basket; nothing went to waste. She brushed the dirt from her hands and accepted the note. "Who's it from?"

"Read it."

Frowning, Sulika unfolded the note. Her eyes widened. She stood and turned her back as she read. Without a word, she folded the note and put it in her skirt pocket, then went to the wash bowl on the porch to rinse her hands. She hung up her apron and smoothed her dress. "Myn wants—one of my seedlings." Her voice seemed louder than necessary. She went to the line of pots along the house wall.

Jagryn laughed. "They haven't even sprouted yet!"

"They will. Here, this is the strongest one." She selected a pot that looked no different from the others. Sulika walked away toward the Hall without another word.

Jagryn stared after her, then turned to Luskell. "What's happening?"

"I don't know," she replied as innocently as she could manage. Then she gave him a conspiratorial grin. "But I mean to find out." She started to follow Sulika.

"No, you don't!" Jagryn grabbed her arm and held her back. "I know better than to pry into Sulika's business. If she thought we spied on her—"

Luskell shook him off. "She won't know. Besides, I agreed to carry the note. I want to see how this turns out." She started across the road.

Jagryn made an impatient noise and followed. "Why do you care? She's my sister, and I don't care." But he couldn't hide his curiosity as he glanced toward Myn's house. Sulika was at the door, knocking. They hid at the corner of the Village Hall until she had gone inside.

"Come on!" Luskell whispered.

"Only to keep you out of trouble."

They hurried across the dry grass to the side of the house. It was built into a slope; the foundation was knee-high on the downhill side, where they were. The windows were set just above Luskell's head.

"The windows are closed!" Jagryn hissed. "We won't be able to hear anything, and we sure can't see. Come on, let's get out of here."

The curtains had been drawn against the afternoon sun, but one of them had caught, leaving a gap big enough to see through. Luskell gripped the sill and used foundation stones as toe-holds to climb high enough to look in. Myn and Sulika stood just inside the door, talking. She smiled and gave him the pot. He accepted it and set it on the table. He picked up some papers.

"He's reading something," Luskell whispered to Jagryn. "I think it's poetry!"

"Poetry? Sulika will crush the poor fellow!"

"She's listening . . . She's turning away. Is she leaving? No, she's—oh, my. She's crying."

"Sulika, crying? I didn't think she remembered how."

"Now she's saying something. She looks angry, but I can't tell for sure. I wish we could hear!" Luskell watched as Myn gently wiped a tear from Sulika's face. She was about to report this to Jagryn when things got a lot more interesting. "He kissed her! On the mouth!"

"I'll bet you anything she slaps him."

She smiled down at him. "Are you sure you want to bet? Because you'd lose money."

"What? What do you mean?"

"She's kissing him back, like she means it."

Jagryn's eyes widened. "Can she do that? What about Foli?"

"She's not thinking about him right now." Luskell had seen her parents kiss when they didn't know she was around. It was mortifying, but kind of reassuring, too. They still loved each other after so many years. The kiss between Sulika and Myn was as ardent as that, but—hungrier. It was scary and fascinating, and she couldn't look away. Then the kiss ended, but they continued to hold each other, to lean on each other, as if they'd fall down otherwise. They seemed to speak a little, but Luskell couldn't hear or guess what they were saying.

They broke apart and turned toward the window. Luskell ducked out of sight. When she pulled herself back up, they were gone, but she caught a glimpse of a skirt hem as it disappeared into another room before the door closed.

She dropped down from the window and grabbed Jagryn's wrist. "Come on. We were never here and we didn't see anything." She ran with him back down the path and didn't slow until they reached the road.

"I know I didn't," he puffed. "What's the hurry?"

"No one can know about this."

"I won't tell, but why the big secret? So Myn read Sulika some poetry, and she kissed him. So what?"

They walked back to his house and dropped into the grass by the garden. Luskell stared across at Myn's house. "How many rooms are in there?"

"Three. Two, if you don't count the storeroom—the front room and the bedroom. Why?"

"They're not in the front room anymore, and I don't think they're in the storeroom."

Jagryn stared at Luskell. He looked even more shocked than she felt, and no wonder. Luskell wasn't from here, but she was familiar enough with the small town to know this was a scandal if anyone found out. The mayor's unmarried but betrothed daughter was in the bedroom—most likely the bed—of a man other than her intended. And Luskell felt responsible. She had carried the note. She had taken sides. But she hadn't expected this.

When they followed Sulika, she had thought maybe Sulika would show Myn how to care for his potted cherry pit, and then leave—a neighborly kindness, nothing more. Or perhaps he would read her some poetry, and she would laugh in his face. Or perhaps she would even decide to break her engagement. That would have been scandal enough for Deep River, but nothing compared to what was actually happening. On the other hand, Luskell suspected her favor for Myn had worked out better than he could have dreamed.

Jagryn shivered in spite of the heat. Then he started to laugh. Soon they were both giggling hysterically at the situation. "Who's going to tell Foli?" he gasped.

"Not us." Luskell took one of the immature carrots from the basket, wiped it on her skirt, and ate it in one bite. She glanced at the low sun and leaped to her feet. "I'm late! I have to get back. Remember, don't tell."

She hurried back to the inn. A few guests were already at supper. Klamamam looked up but didn't comment on her lateness. Luskell tied on her apron, washed her hands, and got to work.

Foli and Rakkyn were sharing a table again. Was Foli still trying to get into Bramynna's good graces? Luskell smiled to herself. Two could play at that game. As she went to serve them, Sulika came in. Her face was flushed and her dark hair frizzy, strands escaping from the once-neat braid. She hadn't even changed her dress. Her skirt had a smudge of garden soil and a grass stain near the hem. It looked like she'd remembered her supper date with Foli at the last moment—not surprising, all things considered.

"Sorry I'm late." Sulika kissed Foli's cheek.

He glanced at the grass stain. "That's all right. I know how you get with your garden."

"You guessed it! That's where I was! Hello, Rakkyn."

Rakkyn stood. "Here, take my seat. I can move." He waved toward the communal tables.

"Nonsense, stay and eat with us," she said. "We're all old friends."

"Yes, do," Foli agreed. Rakkyn smiled and resumed his seat.

Luskell did her best to serve them without staring, but she didn't trust her voice. She was silent as she set down the mugs of ale and plates of stew. As she set a plate in front of Sulika, the young woman turned to Foli. "Maybe we should get married right away."

He patted her hand but only half looked at her. "No, we can wait for Crane and Ketty. It won't be long, and I think it's the right choice. They're like family to you. Right, Luskell?"

She jerked. "Right," she squeaked.

Sulika gave her a strange look, then whispered something to Foli that got his full attention.

"What makes you ask such a thing? No. I appreciate the offer, but we'll wait like everyone else does. There's plenty of time for *that* after we're married." He winked at Rakkyn and took a gulp of ale.

Uncle Elic rushed in. The rest of the family followed. "*There* she is. You had us worried, Sulika. What do you think you're doing?"

"Having supper with Foli. I thought you knew."

"We did," Aunt Sunnea said. She gave Uncle Elic a look and took his arm. "We just forgot. I'm sorry, dear." Uncle Elic seemed about to say something more. "She's of age," Aunt Sunnea reminded him.

They went to sit at one of the communal tables. As Jagryn passed, Luskell caught his sleeve. "I didn't tell," he whispered.

"Good." She smiled at him. From the look of things, Myn owed her at least one spell book. "Meet me at Elika's house tomorrow after lunch. I'll have a surprise for you."

Chapter 21

Embassy House sweltered with the rest of Eukard City. Rather than wait in their apartment, Crane and Ketty returned to Balsam's House. They could be useful, and it was cooler behind the heavy brick walls. Crane almost wished they could sleep there, in spite of the lack of privacy. But their second day brought three new patients with cursed wounds. The only thing that connected these people was their presence in Old Town at the time Crane and Ketty were helping at the hospital. It felt personal.

So when a messenger brought word the next morning that the governor would meet with the Aklaka delegation that afternoon, Crane received the message with relief in spite of the short notice.

"Thank you, we'll be there." Crane closed the door and returned to Ketty in the dining room. "About time."

"Did he say why it took so long?" She nibbled a piece of cheese from the breakfast tray.

He shrugged. "The Azzar delegation had to shorten their stay, so all their meetings were pushed up. I'm just glad to have something official to do. I hope you slept well."

"Well enough. I must be adjusting to the heat. I'm fine as long as nobody touches me."

Crane chuckled in agreement. The heat had rendered moot any thought of a second child. "I'll tell the others. We have some time to plan."

He crossed the hall and knocked on Naliskat's door. Pataknan opened it and waved him inside. "Liski, the governor summons us to a meeting this afternoon."

Naliskat nodded. "Good. I'm tired of waiting. I want to know what Snowabi means by assimilation."

"I do, too—if that's even his plan. We've never been given so little information." Crane turned to the Listener. "Takni, what do you hear?"

He shook his head. "Nothing. It is very peculiar. Perhaps it requires different skills to Listen in the city."

Crane squeezed his shoulder. "I hoped it was only my lack of skill. Keep trying."

The four of them had a meal together before the meeting. Without detailed information on the governor's plans, they couldn't develop a specific plan of their own. They wrote out a list of questions based on the vague rumors they'd heard, as well as potential compromises. A general plan was better than nothing.

The delegation walked to the Governor's Mansion together. The afternoon sun beat down, but it was pleasantly cool within the mansion's stone walls. A red-uniformed guard met them inside the entrance. Crane stiffened out of habit, then deliberately relaxed. Years ago, members of the Governor's Guard had greeted him and his Aklaka friends with hostility and threats. But in recent years, Crane had sometimes worked with them; he'd spent the previous winter and spring helping them track down an arsonist. The firebug wasn't using magic, so Crane shouldn't have been better equipped to find him than any other observant person. But he'd always had an affinity for fire and a sense for hidden things. Catching the perpetrator went a long way toward warming Crane's relationship with the Guards.

"This way." With great courtesy, the guard showed them to a closed door where two more guards stood. They were equally cordial and waved the party inside.

This was not the grand reception hall but a smaller meeting room, plain and businesslike. A large fireplace stood at the far end, unused on this hot day. Four smaller chambers opened to the sides. Heavy curtains at the entrances had been looped back, but they could be closed for privacy. Food and drinks had been laid out in one chamber. The governor and a huddle of advisors conferred at a long table that ran down the center of the main room.

Crane recognized Ganyk, a member of the Legislative Council who specialized in diplomatic matters. Klanya, the lieutenant governor, was also present as an observer. Her duties were mostly ceremonial, but she was allowed to offer insights and opinions in such meetings. Crane welcomed her presence; her thoughtful intelligence had impressed him enough to win his vote.

Snowabi looked up as they entered. He rose and crossed the room to them, trailed by two attendants. He wasn't much taller standing than seated, but it was good to see that he could actually move under his own power. He smiled warmly and shook hands with each member of the delegation.

"Welcome, friends." Snowabi addressed Crane as spokesman. "Thank you for your patience with the delay. I trust you have found worthwhile pursuits while you waited."

"We have, sir," Crane said. "Although in this heat, it is difficult to be active at all."

Snowabi nodded sympathetically, and Ganyk chuckled in agreement. One of Snowabi's attendants smiled, but the other maintained a stony face. He was the page at the reception who had known Crane's reputation, the one Ketty had guessed was related to the governor. Although taller and of a more angular build, the young man resembled Snowabi in some of his facial features.

"We seem to have adapted to this weather, so it is getting easier. Ketty and I have kept busy dealing with the work of a rogue wizard. I could almost believe he was trying to distract us."

Snowabi looked concerned. "What wizard is this?"

"I'm sure you've heard of him. He calls himself the New Yrae."

"I've heard the name, yes. And you believe this villain is deliberately hampering your efforts?"

Crane laughed at the ridiculous notion. "No, I spoke facetiously. Why would the New Yrae would bother with a couple of healers? Probably just coincidence."

Snowabi smiled. "I see. Very good." He turned and whispered something to the serious page, who nodded and left the room.

"Forgive me a presumptuous question," Crane said. "Is that young man related to you? There is a resemblance."

"You are very perceptive. He is my sister's boy, Trenn. I promised him a job if I was elected, though I'm not sure he expected to start at the bottom." Snowabi gestured toward the long table. "Shall we proceed?"

He resumed his seat with his advisors. The remaining attendant took up a position behind his chair. Naliskat sat across from the governor with Pataknan on his left and Crane on his right. Ketty took her place beside Pataknan. Ganyk and Klanya completed the group.

"We are all busy men—and women—" Snowabi smiled at Ketty, then at his lieutenant governor, "—so I will get straight to business. Ganyk?"

The councilmember stood and read a summary of the previous year's meeting, pausing frequently so Crane could translate for Naliskat and Pataknan. There had been a few minor conflicts over hunting and fishing rights and an episode of a lost Aklaka youth who wandered into Stony Creek, a remote village on the Dry Side, where he was assaulted by superstitious villagers. The main item was a road to be built south of Mt. Aku.

The Aklaka had approved the route. Naliskat himself knew that area well and had agreed to provide detailed advice on placement in order to avoid landslides and other hazards. There had once been a winter camp on that slope, but it was long abandoned.

"Is this report correct, as you recall it?" Ganyk asked.

Crane conferred with Naliskat. "It is."

"Where do these matters stand?" Snowabi asked.

"The hunting and fishing issue was resolved amicably," Crane replied. "The people of Stony Creek have been educated about Aklaka ways, especially their traditional foraging grounds in that area. And the road project is underway, with completion expected in another year."

The governor smiled. "Very good. Let us move to the business at hand." He took a moment to look directly at each person gathered around the table. "Fifteen years ago, Eukard welcomed the Mountain Folk—these *Aklaka*—into our great nation."

He paused, and Crane translated. It wasn't strictly accurate, but he translated literally to give Naliskat a fair idea of what they were up against. There would be time to give the true version of things later.

"My predecessor made few demands of them," Snowabi continued. "They were not taxed nor asked to contribute to society in any other way." This was true as far as it went, but Crane didn't like the trend of the presentation. He translated for Naliskat and allowed the governor to continue. "We have seen no progress. They continue to live on our land like squatters. They do not build. They do not make anything useful."

Naliskat had remained calm until now, but when Crane translated this, the Aklaka's eyes burned with indignation. "Wait," Crane advised.

"A few of the Mountain Folk have settled in our towns and been welcomed as true members of society. It is time they all do so. I propose that by Short Day all Mountain Folk resettle, either in existing towns, or in a new town that will be constructed for them on the Dry Side. They will be taxed in order to pay for said construction."

Naliskat leaped to his feet as soon as Crane finished translating. "No! We will not!" He spoke in Eukardian, but Snowabi looked to Crane for translation.

"The ambassador objects strongly to your proposal, as I am sure his Uklak would, as well. Allow us time to—clarify our counter-proposal."

Snowabi granted their request. The others stood up to stretch and converse over refreshments while the Aklaka delegation moved to one of the side chambers. Crane pulled the curtain across. They sat around a small table. Pataknan appeared too bewildered to speak. Ketty frowned, deep in thought. Naliskat slapped the table and leaned forward.

"This Snowabi lies. Why do we even listen to him?"

"Because if we ignore him, he will put his plan into action by force," Crane said. "We need to persuade him to abandon it, or at least explain his reasoning. What does Eukard gain by moving the Aklaka into towns?"

"What is he thinking, with his demand that they move by Short Day? He can't be serious." Ketty's face wore a fiery aspect that had nothing to do with her red hair or the heat.

Crane smiled. "This is a welcome development. It appears Aketnan the Peacebringer has joined us."

Naliskat gave her a triumphant grin. "Aketnan will persuade him. She should be the one to speak."

"I'm willing," she agreed. "So, the demand is startling, and the schedule...?"

Pataknan spoke up at last. "It's ridiculous, of course. But maybe that's the point."

Naliskat gave his Listener an approving smile. "Explain."

"When I was young, sometimes my mamam would ask me to do something right away. If I complained, she might relent and let me do it later. I felt like I'd won something, but I still had to do the chore. So maybe Snowabi thinks we'll get so involved negotiating the schedule that we'll be happy when he gives in on the date, even though the demand is unchanged."

Naliskat nodded. "Yes, you may be right. We must stand up for ourselves and avoid getting bogged down in petty bargaining."

Ketty understood Naliskat's Eukardian well enough to take down a list of all the reasons they disagreed with Snowabi's plan. Crane allowed his mind to return to the main chamber. He had been unable previously to get any sense of the governor's thoughts or motives, but during this break, Snowabi seemed relaxed. Crane reached out carefully, and this time he detected something. Something about power or wealth, but veiled and hazy. Then even that was gone. But it was better than nothing.

When the Aklaka delegation returned to the meeting table, the others resumed their seats. Both Snowabi's attendants were present now and took up their places behind his chair as the meeting continued. Ketty stood to speak. As Aketnan, she felt taller.

"The Ambassador objects to the Governor's proposal. It appears to be based on mistaken assumptions, which I have been appointed to correct. By your permission—?" Ketty inclined her head toward the governor.

Snowabi smiled in the tolerant fashion of a father listening to a small child's recitation. "Please, enlighten me." He folded his hands over his belly and sat back.

Ketty felt the fiery glow increase, though she kept her face and voice calm.

"First, the Aklaka were not invited to join Eukard. They were always among us but in hiding for their own safety. They were successful enough to be regarded as mythical by many in Eukard—myself included. But then the Governor's Guard began to regard them as not only real, but as a threat. In reality, the threat arose from a small rebel band, but the consequences would have fallen on the Aklaka as a whole, no matter how peaceful."

She glanced at Naliskat. He bowed his head. He had led that rebel band, and there had been consequences. Naliskat nearly lost his wife and son, and his actions indirectly caused Knot's death. The governor did not need to know the details now, but those affected would never forget.

Ketty continued. "At this time of misunderstanding, when the danger to the Aklaka was perhaps as great as it had ever been, their leader had the courage to step into the open. Takalanatlan offered to live openly, in peace, with the people of Eukard. Governor Dillet accepted that offer and granted the Aklaka autonomy within Eukard's borders. Since then, these annual meetings have seemed an effective way to air grievances and solve conflicts."

Snowabi leaned forward to listen more attentively as he fell under Aketnan's influence. Ketty glanced at Crane. She could feel his pride and admiration for her, though he kept them from showing on his face. As Aketnan, she had single-handedly reconciled the two rival Aklaka bands, then announced that an Aklaka ambassador would meet with the governor. She was proud of her role in the peace deal, too, but this was not the time to bring it up.

"It is true that the Aklaka pay no taxes," she continued. "They also don't use government services, such as roads and Guards. They do not use currency, but perhaps they would be willing to pay something— dried fish, maybe—if the tax gatherer would come to them."

Naliskat barked a loud laugh at that. Although they now lived openly, the Aklaka were still difficult to find. The winter camps were remote and well hidden. The rest of the year, the bands moved around to where the gathering, fishing, and hunting were best. You were more likely to find them by accident than by looking.

Ketty made several more points involving the small population of Aklaka, their traditional way of life, and the bands located outside Eukard's borders. Before she finished, Snowabi was whispering with his advisors. Her voice faltered; she regained control and concluded. "We do not see how there is anything to be gained from moving the Aklaka people into towns. Unless you can explain the benefits, we will continue to object to your request." She resumed her seat. Aketnan's fire faded.

Snowabi stood. "Thank you, my dear. That was most interesting. We will consider this information as we make our final recommendation. Let's plan to meet again in a week's time."

Before anyone could object to this additional delay, the governor and his entourage rose and left the room. Klanya glanced back once, a look of sympathy on her elegant face.

"Ketty, you presented that very well," Crane said. "If I were governor, I'd be persuaded."

"If you were governor, we wouldn't have this problem." She frowned. "Maybe I'm still not rested. Aketnan filled me, but I didn't feel very influential. It was like talking to a wall."

Naliskat nodded. "Snowabi *is* a wall," he said gruffly in Eukardian.

"I did pick up something," Crane said. "It was fuzzy, but Snowabi seems to have a hunger for power."

Ketty rolled her eyes. "The man ran for governor. Of course he likes power."

Crane shook his head. "It's something more than that. I wish I'd gotten a clearer picture."

They left the building to find that the weather had changed. The air was much cooler. A strong breeze blew off the water, and thick clouds were gathering.

Ketty smiled and hugged Crane. "Did you do this?"

"No, but I'm glad to see the change." He grasped her hand. "Let's walk to Braffin's Garden."

"That's a long way from here."

"I know, but we haven't been there in so long, and it would be a pleasant walk now that it isn't as hot."

She didn't have to think about it long. The garden was one of her favorite places in Eukard City. She squeezed his hand. "You're right. Let's go."

Chapter 22

Crane turned to Naliskat and Pataknan. "We're taking a walk. You're welcome to come, too."

Naliskat glanced at their clasped hands and grinned. "Go. You don't need chaperones. I plan to sit under my tree and wait for the rain."

"I will try again to Listen," Pataknan added. "Perhaps it will be easier with this change in the weather."

"Good. We'll see you tomorrow, then." Crane walked away with Ketty down the tree-lined street toward the heart of the city. He relished the feel of her hand in his. It was no longer too hot to touch.

As they walked, they tried to make sense of the day's business but still had more questions than answers.

"I feel like we don't know anything," Ketty said. "No matter how much we talk about it, it doesn't make sense. Why move the Aklaka into towns?"

"We won't solve that problem today," Crane agreed. "I wonder how Luskell is getting along? Do you think she'll still be angry with us when we get back?"

"Surely she's over it by now. She probably thinks she's bored. Deep River is a quiet place after Eukard City. But I envy anyone who doesn't have to deal with this governor."

Crane laughed. "He's not that bad. Ambitious, perhaps, but I think he'll see reason. I—" He broke off abruptly as something hidden pricked his wizard's senses. He looked over his shoulder in both directions. They had left the district of fine houses and government buildings for a more tightly-packed neighborhood of small shops and rented rooms.

"What's wrong?" Ketty asked.

"I thought I sensed something."

"What kind of something? Another pickpocket?"

He shook his head. "I don't know. Maybe. Or someone following us, but the feeling's gone now, and there's nobody there. I'm still jumpy after those attacks."

They entered a large market. Everything seemed calm and orderly as people bought and sold goods. The increased Guard patrols were visible here, and no one appeared worried about the New Yrae. Crane shook off his own uneasiness. There was no danger here.

A short time later, they reached the garden, an island of beauty in the heart of town. The grass was turning brown, and some of the flowers had wilted, but the roses bloomed riotously. The humid air was heavy with their scent. Crane and Ketty walked together to the center of the garden where there were benches. They sat and looked up at the monument to King Braffin, the last king of Eukard.

"Do you remember the first time I brought you here?" Crane asked.

"How could I forget? That was the day I found you again." She squeezed his hand and shook her head. "I was scared, but I trusted you."

"After all these years, that's still hard to believe."

"That I trusted you?"

"No, that you could be afraid of anything."

Ketty smiled. "Usually I get angry first." She gazed into his eyes. "But that day, I was afraid—of you. I had to trust the one who could hurt me."

"I'll never understand that when you have at least as much power as I do."

"It's not about that kind of power."

Crane nodded. They had both tried to hide love they believed unrequited. "We should have just stayed together. It would have been easier."

Ketty laughed. "Oh, I should have married you when I'd known you just a few months? I was only sixteen."

"So? You were already a good cook."

She slapped his shoulder, then nestled against him. "Maybe it would have been easier. But those years apart made us who we are."

"Probably." He gazed up at the stern face of the bronze king. "Do you still think I look like him?"

"More so when you have a beard. I'm hungry—let's go to the Osprey for supper. We haven't seen Ellys and Ambug since we got back."

Crane nodded and stood. "We should go to Dokral's first while we're in the neighborhood. I told Luskell we'd buy her a fiddle."

Dokral was getting ready to close his shop for the day when they walked in. "Good to see you're not too fine for the old neighborhood," he greeted them. "Your old room is available if you want it."

Crane laughed as he shook Dokral's hand. "Thank you, but I think we can do better than that these days. We want to buy a fiddle for Luskell."

"I was hoping you'd say that." The shop was filled with instruments in various stages of completion or repair. Dokral selected a finished one from a rack. "I thought of her when I was making this one." He plucked a string, and then bowed a few warm, sweet notes.

Ketty laughed, a single startled "Ha!" Dokral stopped playing and looked at her with raised eyebrows. "It sounds like her," Ketty explained. "Youthful, and a little mischievous."

Crane paid for the fiddle. Dokral locked up and walked with them to the nearby Osprey for supper. It was a pleasant evening with old friends; Crane could almost forget his questions about the governor.

While they were in the tavern, it started to rain. Crane stepped out at the end of the meal and let the rain pour over his face. It washed away the lethargy of recent days, and if he Listened, he was sure he would hear the rain's voice. But that was Pataknan's job; Crane would leave it to him.

Under ordinary circumstances, Crane would have walked home in the rain. Out of deference to the fiddle, he paid for a horse-drawn cab. They still lived simply most of the time, but there were times when some comfort was welcome.

As they rode back to their rooms, he pondered again what Snowabi might be up to. He closed his eyes and saw again the bronze face of Braffin. The last king…In that moment, an answer came to him—an unlikely, laughable answer, but an answer all the same. He opened his eyes and turned to Ketty.

"I think I know what Snowabi wants."

"And what would that be?" she asked.

"He wants to be a king."

Ketty gave him a skeptical look. "He may *want* to be, but it won't happen. Not here. Eukard got over kings a long time ago. No one could live up to Braffin."

Crane was inclined to agree. Hundreds of years ago, Braffin's successor had failed to meet expectations. The people overthrew him, abolished the monarchy, and seemed content with elected leadership. Crane smiled. "You're right. It would be ridiculous to even try." He wrapped an arm around her shoulders and pulled her close. "Let's not talk about the governor anymore."

Lying next to Ketty, Crane fell asleep easily, but he woke with a start in the middle of the night. It was quiet and cool. A dream must have roused him. He couldn't remember it beyond a hint of a feeling he used to have when he was with his father on Mt. Aku. But as he lay awake, listening to the rain fall, his certainty about the governor's ambition returned. It *was* a ridiculous notion, but...He couldn't shake the feeling that he was missing something important.

What if Snowabi really did want to rule as king? It wouldn't be easy to achieve, but there was a chance. The governor served at the will of the people. The people had abolished the monarchy, and they could reinstate it—unlikely, but possible. Crane considered Snowabi's first proposals: public safety, feeding programs, free schools. Were these all efforts to endear himself to the masses, to win their approval, perhaps make them regard him as a father? A king?

But these programs would eventually cost more than the treasury could sustain. So far, Snowabi hadn't raised taxes, but how popular would he be when he had to take that step? Unless he could acquire treasure some other way.

Crane rolled over. It was late; as much as it vexed him, this was not his problem to solve. He had power, but not that kind. When it came to politics, he was a citizen like any other. His work with the Aklaka brought him closer to the governor than most, but his job was to make sure the Aklaka understood what was said and were treated fairly. That was all. If Snowabi wanted to be king, he was welcome to try.

Crane closed his eyes and drifted toward sleep. *Nothing will come of it*, he thought. *Nothing but a good story for my grandchildren about how I guessed it first.*

Chapter 23

Luskell went upstairs to bed, her mind filled with Klamamam's stories and Deep River's secrets. After the long, hot day, her room was stifling. She opened both windows all the way. The night air was still warm but cooling now that the sun had set. She had plenty besides the heat to keep her awake, but a breeze and the day's work combined to send her to sleep almost as soon as she lay down. It seemed only moments later that her eyes opened again. Moonlight gleamed off the wild silver hair of the man seated across from her bed.

Luskell wasn't afraid. "What do you want?"

"Only to speak with you, Luskell. Do you know who I am?"

She couldn't see him clearly, but her whole being swelled with joy to be in his presence. "You're my kladadad." She wished she could run to him, climb into his lap, and throw her arms around him. For some reason, she couldn't move her limbs. "I'm so happy to see you."

Knot smiled, a beautiful smile like her father's, but different. "I'm happy to be here." He gazed around the room. "I'm glad she gave you the best room."

"It's my favorite."

"Mine, too. You've seen your brother, haven't you?"

Luskell grinned. It had been so long she'd almost forgotten her visits from Ketwyn. "Yes, more than once. He—oh. It's a dream, isn't it?" The joy shrank down again.

"It is the only way we can come to you."

"Why do you come to me at all?"

"You have my eyes. You see as I did."

"I have your hair, too," Luskell grumbled. "I don't understand what you mean."

Knot sighed. "Your parents—don't hear me. They're using their power for other things. But you are open."

"Open to what? If you think *I* have any power—"

"This isn't something I *think*. You—hoo hoo." Knot's mouth continued to move, but after the strange hooting, she could no longer hear his voice. He faded from view. She opened her eyes and sat up, really awake now. Moonlight shone on an empty chair.

Luskell listened to the night sounds: the river, insects, the yowl of a distant cat. Nothing loud enough to wake her. An owl hooted. She listened harder. She had heard that owl call before, but not here. That was a forest owl.

Luskell leaped from her bed and leaned out the open window. The owl hooted again, and she gave the answering call. A shadow separated itself from the darkness under the cottonwood tree.

"Luskell?"

"Shh!" She knew that voice and was glad to hear it, but they didn't want to wake the town. "What are you doing here?" she whispered. "No, wait, I'll come down." She slipped out of her room, down the steps, and out the back door. "Laki?"

"Here." A tall figure appeared out of the shadows.

Luskell ran to him and threw her arms around him. "You don't know how glad I am to see someone taller than me! Come in, but be quiet." She spoke Aklaka, as he had; she was more fluent in Aklaka than he was in Eukardian. They tiptoed past Klamamam's room. "Are you hungry?"

"Yes."

"Wait at the top of the stairs." She went to the kitchen and collected the thick heel of a loaf of bread and a wedge of cheese. She joined him upstairs and opened the door to her room. "We can talk in here if we keep our voices down."

Luskell perched on the end of the bed, and Laki sat in the chair where—no, nobody had been sitting in that chair. She shook her head to clear it. Laki eyed the bread and cheese hungrily. She handed them over and let him eat, though she could hardly wait to question him.

"So, what are you doing here?"

"I ran away." He smiled. "No, I flew away. That's why I'm so hungry."

"Transformation? I didn't know you could!"

"It turns out there's little difference between Listener and wizard. Your dadad taught Chamokat, and Chamokat taught me. He told me to keep it secret, but I don't think he expected me to use the skill to escape."

"But why would you want to come *here*? You don't know how much I've wished I was camped out with the Aklaka, instead of stuck in Deep River."

"I had to get away from the expectations."

Luskell nodded in recognition. Everyone expected her to have great magical power because of who her parents were. That nudged a memory of...something. Then it was gone.

"Someday, I'll be Uklak," Laki continued. "I'm always learning duties and being attended wherever I go. Why can't I just be a Listener?"

"Can't you be both?"

"I don't want to be in charge."

"You'll be good at it when the time comes. Will you be called Nalaklaknatlan?" She giggled, then pressed her fist to her mouth to stifle the sound. "I don't think I can say all that!" she whispered.

"I'll always be Laki to you, Luskell." He seemed about to say more but only gazed at her in silence. His eyes shone with reflected moonlight.

"That's a relief. But we won't have to worry about it for a long time. Kala is young and healthy."

"So was my kladadad, but things happen." Laki frowned, then perked up and gave her a smile. "We were camped along the south fork of the river, not too far away, and I knew you were here. I sneaked out of camp, changed to an owl, and came to find you on my own. A little adventure."

She squeezed his hands. "I'm so glad you did! But don't expect much excitement. Nothing ever happens here."

"I'm sure it's not that bad. Have your parents already gone to Eukard City?"

"Yes, about two weeks ago. Dadad wrote as soon as they arrived, but there wasn't anything much to tell. I don't know why I couldn't go with them this year. It's not like anything ever happens there, either."

"Maybe this time, something will. A new governor, and everything—" He looked thoughtful. "Why did you change? Did the other one die?"

"No, Dillet served as long as he was allowed, fourteen years. It was time to elect a new one."

"So they're not born to it? How do they know what to do?"

Luskell laughed. "I don't know." She could see how it might work better if leaders trained all their lives for the job, as the Uklak did. But Eukard had abolished its monarchy hundreds of years ago. Nobody wanted to go back to that. "I suppose they observe and have advisors. The new governor was on the Legislative Council, so it's not all new to him."

Laki nodded. "Is he *my* governor, too?"

Luskell frowned. "I don't know. You rule yourselves, and you don't vote...but from what I hear, old Snotwabi wants to tell you what to do."

Laki grinned. "I should meet the governor."

"If you do, don't tell him I called him Snotwabi."

"Maybe you should learn some respect. But I meant when I'm Uklak. Mamam hasn't met one yet, but I'll make sure I do."

He yawned. Transformation took a lot of energy; he had to be exhausted. Luskell hopped off the bed. "Come on, the room next to mine is empty. You can sleep there."

"Will your klamamam mind?"

"I don't know. We'll talk to her in the morning. Right now, we both need to sleep."

She tiptoed to the door. He stood but didn't follow her from the room. When she looked back, he stared at her. "Luskell, you—shine."

"It's the moon."

He shook his head. "You *are* the moon. And I will teach you to fly."

Chapter 24

Stell rose early to make breakfast and prepare for the day. No guests stirred yet, but it was time to wake Luskell so she could eat and start her chores. Stell sometimes detected resentment in her granddaughter's attitude, but she could ignore that. It was the age.

She paused at Luskell's door when she heard a snore from the next room. That room should have been empty. Out of consideration for Luskell, she had refrained from putting guests there except for the night of the dance when all the rooms were full. It wasn't much, but it gave the illusion of privacy.

She knocked softly and got another snore in answer. She pushed the door open and gasped. "Crane?" She knew she was wrong as soon as the name was out. The shirtless young man sprawled on the pallet did resemble her son, at least as he had looked twenty years ago: tall and thin, but darker and more muscular. Stell knew an Aklaka when she saw one. She poked his shoulder. "Hey! Who are you?"

The young man sprang awake, wide-eyed, and fumbled around to pull his deer-skin shirt over his head. Awake, he looked less like Crane. His eyes were darker and had a different shape, and his nose was much longer. He looked more like Crane's friend Chamokat, whom Stell had met once, years ago. The young man stood and stared at her, his hands out in a placating gesture. She almost laughed—how intimidating could one tiny, gray-haired grandmother be? But she had a right to know what this stranger was doing in her place.

"How did you get in here?"

"Please forgive my trespass," he said. "I am called Nalaklak. You are Luskell's klamamam?"

"Yes." Stell was relieved he spoke her language, if with an accent. She knew almost no Aklaka words. She recognized 'grandmother' only because Luskell had never called her anything else. "I'm pleased to meet you—Nalaklak. But what are you doing here?"

"I—" He frowned. "I come to see my friend. Luskell. Hard to explain."

"Maybe she can help you." Stell went to the next room and knocked. "Luskell?" The girl answered with a groan. "Get up, dear, and introduce me to your friend."

She heard a muffled shriek, followed by rustling and thumping. The door opened. "I'm sorry! I swear I didn't know he was coming until he was here! Please let him stay!" Luskell was dressed, but she hadn't done anything with her hair yet. With those wild curls and deep blue eyes, she looked more like Knot than ever. A lump rose in Stell's throat. "Please don't be angry."

"I'm not angry, Luskell. I hoped you might help him explain what he's doing here."

Luskell threw her arms around Stell. "Thank you! I knew you wouldn't send him away!"

"I haven't promised anything. Let's all go to the kitchen and talk this over."

Stell returned to the kitchen. The two young people clicked and chattered unintelligibly for a moment, then followed. She could tell Nalaklak was trying not to look at the fresh loaves. She dished up three bowls of porridge and sliced the warm bread. "Let's start with breakfast and introductions. Luskell?"

The girl gave her a nervous smile. "Klamamam, this my friend Nalaklak. He goes by Laki. Laki, this is my Klamamam Stell. She doesn't speak Aklaka, so you'll have to speak Eukardian."

He nodded. "I will try."

"Thank you. You seem to speak it well," Stell said. "Now, why are you here?"

Between them, they filled in the story. Stell was glad to learn that Laki knew and respected Crane and Ketty. She didn't let on, but she was impressed by his parentage. His father was the Aklaka ambassador to Eukard, and his mother was Uklak, the leader of their band. Laki would someday inherit that role. An important person—but he didn't want to be important. Stell decided to treat him like any other guest.

"I'm concerned your parents don't know where you are."

"Dadad is in Eukard City with Crane and Aketnan," he said. Stell had to think a moment to remember this was what the Aklaka called Ketty. "He doesn't know I am gone."

"But your mother will be worried."

He nodded. "Mothers worry. Uklaks worry. But I am not a child."

Stell couldn't argue with that. He was around the same age Crane had been when he left home for the first time. Among his own people, Laki was an adult.

"Please don't send him back!" Luskell begged. "You won't, will you?"

Stell shook her head and smiled. "No, I won't. Laki, is it possible to send word to your people to let them know you're safe?"

He smiled. "I can send a message to Chamokat."

"Thank you. In that case, you're welcome to stay." Luskell and Laki grinned at each other. Something in the boy's smile reminded Stell of Knot when he was young. That could be a problem. "There will be rules, though. Luskell, I promised your father I'd watch over you, so if you two are in a room alone, you must leave the door open."

Luskell looked mortified. "Klamamam! We wouldn't—"

"I promised. And Laki, if you stay here, you'll have to work. What can you do?"

He opened his mouth, then closed it, frowning. Then he brightened. "I learn fast."

Stell smiled. "I won't overwork you. Luskell, this afternoon after the chores are done, you should take Laki out and introduce him to your other friends."

Luskell looked startled but recovered quickly. "Yes! Grynni and Greelit would love to show him their horse. And I think Myn would like to meet him. Oh, and Jagryn..." Her smile was almost crafty. Before Stell had a chance to interpret it, the expression was gone.

Chapter 25

"It's not fair!" Luskell complained. Klamamam had assigned Laki and Luskell enough chores to keep them busy—and separated—all morning. "Don't you trust us?"

Luskell helped with cooking and cleaning indoors while Laki worked in the garden and cleaned the chicken coop. She had no desire to clean the chicken coop, but she did want to be with her friend. They hadn't seen each other in months, and he had made a great effort to visit her.

"Is there some reason I shouldn't?" Klamamam's eyes twinkled. "I thought he'd be happier with outdoor work. They don't live in houses, do they?"

"No, not exactly," Luskell admitted. "And Listening is easier outside."

"I've heard your father talk about that. What *is* Listening?"

Luskell scrubbed the porridge pot and frowned as she puzzled over how to explain it. "It's a special kind of—awareness. A Listener can hear messages in the wind, in snow, in trees and rocks. I don't know how it works but it's important."

Klamamam smiled. "A sense for hidden things. Can all Aklaka do this?"

Luskell shook her head. "No, a Listener is like a wizard. Mamam says there's no difference."

Klamamam kneaded a ball of dough. "So it's a learned skill?"

"If you have the ability. Chamokat taught Dadad how to Listen, and Dadad taught him some spells. But many Aklaka still don't trust that kind of magic."

"We used to have that problem here." Klamamam sighed, then shook herself. "I expect your grandfather learned to Listen, up there on his mountain. He had to know when she needed him."

"And sometimes Listeners have ..." Luskell swallowed. She'd been about to say "dreams" when her voice failed. There was *something* about Knot and dreams.

"Sometimes they have what?" Klamamam prompted.

"Visions. Chamokat does, anyway. And Laki started having them when he was little, before he was trained at all."

"No wonder you get along so well."

"What do you mean?" Luskell asked uneasily.

"You've been surrounded by magic all your life. You feel at home with it."

Luskell didn't answer. She supposed it was true, but the thought made her uncomfortable for reasons she couldn't quite grasp. She didn't care about magic. She didn't want to care about it. When it was time to clean the upstairs rooms, she was happy to get out of the kitchen and away from Klamamam's knowing gaze.

She paused a moment to watch Laki from the upstairs window. Klamamam had given him some of Dadad's old clothes to wear so he wouldn't ruin his own. From a distance, he didn't look that different from anyone else in Deep River. He had finished in the garden and was starting on the chicken coop. Instead of fluttering around in a panic, the hens dutifully went where he directed them. Luskell chuckled to herself. He seemed to have a power like Uncle Jagree's. Now *that* kind of magic could be useful.

When Laki finished with the chickens, he cleaned up and put his own clothes back on. They had lunch with Uncle Jelf and Klamamam in the kitchen before any guests arrived for the meal.

"You two have been very helpful this morning," Klamamam said. "You've earned a break. Luskell, why don't you show Laki around town?"

"Yes, take him over to the Hall," Jelf said. "Myn will want to put something in the log."

"I thought so, too." Luskell hurried out the door with Laki and started for the Village Hall. She wanted to go straight there, but Laki was too big to hide. Auntie Brynnit was visiting with Aunt Sudi on the older woman's front step across from the Heron. They looked around as the door closed behind Luskell.

"Luskell, who's your friend?"

"Hello, Aunt Sudi, Auntie Brynnit. This is my friend Nalaklak. He plans to stay here awhile. Laki, Sudi and Brynnit are midwives here in Deep River."

He smiled at them. "Brynnit has some power. Yes?"

Auntie Brynnit's mouth dropped open, but then she smiled, too. "Yes, I'm a healer. How did you know?"

"I can see your light."

"Oh! Like Ketty!"

"We call her Aketnan. She saved my life once."

Auntie Brynnit seemed about to say something more, but Luskell nudged Laki. "We have to go. We're meeting Myn at the Village Hall."

"It was nice to meet you, Nalaklak," Aunt Sudi said. "Enjoy your stay in Deep River. I'm sure we'll see you soon."

They got a little farther up the road before they met Kolma, a near neighbor. Luskell was better acquainted with her grown son, Liko, and his wife Alill; they were brewers, and Klamamam was their best customer. Kolma stared up at Laki and pointed. "What—?"

Luskell didn't know whether to laugh or be indignant. "Kolma, this is my friend Nalaklak."

"But he's a—a—"

"Aklaka," Laki supplied. "It is very nice to meet you."

They left her staring and reached the Village Hall at last. As Luskell put her foot on the bottom step, the door flew open. "No, not here," someone inside said. "Find another place. I have to go!" Sulika ran down the steps without looking and collided with Laki. "Oh! I'm sorry. I—" She stared up at him. Her face was flushed. "I'm sorry," she repeated and dodged around him.

Laki watched her go, but Luskell pulled him inside and across to Myn's library.

"Myn? This is my friend Nalaklak."

Myn looked up from his work. He didn't seem surprised that a towering Aklaka youth had just ducked through his doorway. He smiled, a dazed expression that had nothing to do with the dusty books and antique bric-a-brac that surrounded him. "Hm?"

"Laki surprised us by coming to visit," Luskell explained. "Uncle Jelf thought you might put something in the log. Laki, this our Keeper, Myn."

Myn stood. "Hello, Nalaklak. Welcome to Deep River." He held out his hand.

Laki, unfamiliar with Eukardian handshakes, extended his hands, palm up. Myn looked uncertainly at Luskell. She held her own hands out, palm down, and Myn copied her to complete the Aklaka greeting. Laki beamed. "I am happy to meet you."

Myn started. "You speak the language very well."

"I started late, but Luskell is a good teacher. I am happy for the practice."

"You said I could have a book," Luskell reminded Myn.

"Yes, help yourself." Myn returned to his work, still smiling and now humming to himself.

Luskell stifled a laugh, grabbed the red book, and hurried from the Hall before Myn could change his mind.

Laki glanced over his shoulder. "Is something wrong with that man?" Now that it was only the two of them, he slipped back into Aklaka.

"With Myn? No." She smiled. "I think he's in love."

Laki nodded. "With that girl we saw?"

"Don't tell anyone. They think it's a secret."

He tapped the book in her hand. "What is that?"

"It's one of the magic books my father learned from when he was a boy. I'm borrowing it for a friend who has some talent." She slid it into the large pocket on the front of her skirt. It pulled her dress and slapped against her leg, but at least it was hidden.

"Why can't he borrow it himself?"

"His parents think it would be dangerous." Luskell rolled her eyes. "He knows one spell. One! And they want him to wait until Dadad comes back before he learns any more. Oh!" She halted and turned to face Laki as a new idea presented itself. "*You* could help him! You know some spells, right?"

Laki frowned. "Yes, a few, but I'm not sure that's such a—"

She grabbed his hand and started to run. "It's a great idea. Come on!"

Luskell hoped they could reach Elika's house without meeting anyone, but Grynni and Greelit were in the pasture with Kanala when they passed. They waved and called until Luskell went to meet them at the fence.

"Can you train with us today?" Greelit asked.

Grynni stared at Laki. "Who's that? A giant?"

"Grynni, Greelit, this is my friend Laki. I'm showing him around today, but maybe we can both help you tomorrow."

"You have a beautiful horse," Laki said.

"He talks funny," Grynni said. Greelit whispered something to her, and her eyes widened. "Oh! So he really *is* a giant? Laki, you'll like this—we named our horse Kanala."

He raised his eyebrows and grinned. "I do like it. I think you had some help." He glanced at Luskell.

"Yes, I suggested it. We need to go now. See you later!" She tugged him away. They reached Elika's house without any further delays. Luskell looked around to make sure no one was watching, then pushed the door open.

The last time she had looked inside this house, a few years ago, the front door was off its hinges, weeds were growing up through the floorboards, and there were big holes in the roof. Not only had the door and roof been repaired, the whole floor had been replaced with new boards that filled the single room with a fresh, resiny scent. A wood box full of scraps stood next to the hearth. Across from the door, Jagryn troweled patches of fresh mortar between some of the wall stones.

He turned, smiling when he saw Luskell. He laid his trowel next to the hod of mortar. "I decided to do something useful while I waited. I thought you might have forgotten, but—" He broke off as Laki entered.

"Jagryn, this is my friend Nalaklak—Laki. He arrived last night, and yes, he is Aklaka. Laki, this is Jagryn, the friend I was telling you about."

"I can see that." The two boys did not exchange greetings but looked each other over, assessing. Laki walked around the room, touching the walls here and there. He had an intent look. "This place has known magic," he murmured as if to himself.

Jagryn stared. "Is this the surprise you promised me?" He had lost his smile.

"No, this is." She pulled the book from her pocket and held it out to him.

He released a little gust of breath. "But I'm not supposed to— How did you—?"

She grinned. "Remember the favor I did for Myn? He's letting me borrow all the magic books, one at a time. Happy as he looked, I think he would have let me take them all at once, but I didn't want to press my luck." Jagryn blushed, and she remembered she was implying things about his sister they weren't supposed to know. "Myn thinks I'm only checking the books for damage, so we can't keep any one of them too long. But there should be time for you to learn something."

Jagryn nodded. He sank onto the floor and opened the book. "Oh!"

"What?" Luskell sat beside him. Laki leaned against a wall and crossed his arms.

"I couldn't read it, but then the letters arranged themselves so I could." Jagryn read in silence for a bit, then frowned. "It starts in the middle of something. There must be pages missing."

"It's probably an introduction," Luskell guessed. "Skip to something that's all there."

Jagryn flipped ahead and continued to read. "I've come to a spell, but I'm not sure how to pronounce it."

"I know what they sound like," Luskell said. "Maybe I can help."

"Would you? I'm afraid something terrible will happen if I get it wrong." He passed the book to her.

Luskell took it from him and looked where he pointed. It was an unintelligible jumble of letters. She chuckled. "But I won't be able to..." She trailed off as the letters reorganized themselves under her gaze. She recognized the spell as one she had heard often throughout her life—the fire spell. This was the first spell her father learned, the one responsible for his scar. But she shouldn't have been able to read it at all; you had to have—you had to be—

The hair on the back of her neck stood up. She shook off the chill. "This is an easy one. You pronounce it like this." As she spoke the words, her voice gained a strange, crackling overlay, and a sense that she couldn't stop speaking if she tried. Heat in her belly spread up her chest and down her arms. Her fingers tingled with intense warmth, and a bright flame burst from the page. She shrieked and threw the book onto the floor.

"Stop that!" Jagryn cried. The flame went out, leaving charred marks in the middle of the page and on the floor.

Luskell stared at Jagryn. His eyes were round in a face drained of color. "Hah!" she shouted. She threw her arms around him and kissed him exuberantly on the mouth. Then they broke apart. Cheeks burning, Luskell turned away from Jagryn and found herself facing Laki. He scowled, an expression that made him look like her father.

"What?" she asked.

"Maybe you and your friend wish to be alone." He spoke Aklaka.

She slipped into the same language. "No, it wasn't—that's not why—" She glanced at Jagryn, who was studiously not looking at her. His ears were red, and she could tell he was smiling in a dazed fashion similar to Myn's. *Now* what had she done? She thought back over her encounters with Jagryn since she'd arrived in Deep River. He'd been acting odd from the start. Did he—*like* her? If she wanted to discourage him, kissing him wouldn't help. *If* she wanted to discourage him...She shook herself. "It didn't mean anything. But did you see what we did?"

Laki nodded. "You performed a spell poorly and nearly burned up your precious book. Jagryn instinctively corrected your mistake. Perhaps he deserved his reward." He looked away.

Luskell frowned. "His—Laki, are you jealous? Do I have to kiss you, too?"

He didn't answer, but he lost his scowl. She'd meant it as a joke but saw too late that he was serious. Now everybody in the room was embarrassed together. After a long moment, he spoke. "Someday I'll be Uklak. If I have a daughter, she'll follow me. I have always hoped that my daughter would—be like you."

"What are you saying?"

He glanced at her and quickly looked away. "Nothing. Never mind."

"I think I should leave." Jagryn started to get up. "You two want to be alone."

Luskell jumped to her feet and blocked the door. Boys! Idiots, every one of them. She stamped her foot, and they both came to attention. "You're not going anywhere. Pick up that book and sit. Laki, please speak Eukardian around Jagryn. You are both my friends, nobody wants to be alone, and we have work to do."

Laki blinked, then nodded and sat on the floor a short distance from Jagryn. Luskell sat between them.

Jagryn cleared his throat. "You did a spell. You said you couldn't."

Luskell shrugged. "I didn't know I could."

Laki chuckled. "I did."

She gave him a puzzled frown. "But the last time I tried, nothing happened."

"The last time?" Jagryn asked. "When was that?"

"I guess I was seven or eight. I thought that meant I didn't have power."

Laki barked a harsh laugh. "You gave up on your power when you were seven or eight?"

She nodded. "I was disappointed, but it was kind of a relief. I didn't have to try to be like my parents."

Laki shook his head, smiling. "They could have told you it rarely shows up by that age."

"Yours did."

"I'm strange. Jagryn, when did you suspect you might have magic in you?"

"I don't know. A year or so ago."

Laki gave Luskell a smug look and folded his arms. "See? I told you last night—you shine."

She hadn't understood him then—hadn't wanted to understand. But if it was true ...

"Why didn't they tell me? If you can see it, Mamam could, too."

"But do you listen to her?"

Luskell didn't answer. They had probably tried to tell her, but by then she didn't want to hear it. It was different to find out for herself.

"Remember what I said? I will teach you to fly," Laki said.

She looked from Laki to Jagryn and back again. "You'll teach *us*, then. No more fighting. Let's do what we came for. Let's learn some magic!"

Chapter 26

Luskell had power. No wonder she'd been so tired. It was a growth spurt, but not the physical kind. She had always assumed she didn't have any magic of her own, that she didn't want it, but now...

She wanted to try everything—the sooner, the better. She grabbed the book from Jagryn. "What else is in here?" She flipped through the next few pages, then slapped the book closed. "I know most of these already!" She grinned at the boys.

"You know the *words*," Laki said.

"How hard can it be? I'm going to try the fire spell again."

"Wait!" Jagryn took the book from her. She thought he meant only to protect it, but he opened it and read quickly. He held it open and showed her a page. "Is this the extinguishing spell?"

"Very funny. Yes, it is, but you won't need it."

She piled scrap lumber in the fireplace, then raised her arms dramatically and flung them at the wood as she said the spell. The woodbox erupted in flame, while the pile in the fireplace remained untouched. Jagryn extinguished the inferno, but not before an ember dropped onto the floor. Laki stamped it out.

Jagryn frowned at Luskell. "That's two scorch marks on my new floor." He pointed a finger at the unburned wood and said the fire spell. A small blaze crackled up. "There, you see?"

Vexed, she shouted the extinguishing spell. The fire went out, and frost coated the wood.

"Maybe we should try something else," Laki suggested.

Luskell cheered up immediately. "I know! Jagryn, get some pebbles. We can practice summoning them." Jagryn went out and returned with a handful of pebbles. He set one in the middle of the floor, and they all knelt around it. "I've seen Dadad do this one many times. It's a one-word charm. You point at the object you want, say the word, and it flies into your hand."

She concentrated on the pebble, pointed, and spoke. The rock flew right at her face. She ducked to the side as it buzzed past her ear and straight out the window behind her.

Jagryn quietly placed another pebble in the middle of the floor. "Good thing we didn't put the glass in yet."

He tried the spell, and the rock hopped into his hand. It took Laki two tries, but it worked for him, too. Luskell moved back and tried again. This time, she caught the flying stone. It stung enough to bring tears to her eyes, but she tried not to let on.

They stood up and practiced summoning stones from each other's hands and pockets until their palms were sore.

"Here's another good one—a repelling charm," Luskell announced. "Dadad taught it to Mamam when they first met." She shouted the charm and flung out one arm.

Jagryn staggered back and fell to the floor. "Hey!" He leaped up and copied her. She fell back, but Laki caught her. She smiled sweetly, then repelled him into the wall. He managed to repel Luskell and Jagryn at the same time. Soon they were all laughing too hard to continue.

Luskell sank to the floor, out of breath. "Ow. I'll have bruises from that. Let's do something else."

"We should teach Laki the lupine-and-butterfly illusion," Jagryn suggested. "No one will get hurt."

He explained the technique as well as the words. Laki got the knack of it almost immediately. His flowers even smelled good. Luskell was almost afraid to try, but to her delight, she produced the stem of lupine right away. Then her flowers burst into blue flame. She dropped the burning stem and stamped it out—the flowers were an illusion, but the fire was real. "I'm sorry, Jagryn. That's another scorch mark. Why didn't it work?"

"It's delicate," Jagryn explained. "You don't have to use all your power. You're making something beautiful, not trying to win a fight."

She tried again. This time, her stem of lupine exploded with a blast of butterflies that smashed into the walls and vanished. With a rueful chuckle, she sagged against the wall. "I don't know how to do delicate."

"Yes, you do. Think of dancing. Think of your silk dress."

Laki gave Jagryn a sharp look but said nothing.

Luskell recalled the boisterous, stomping dance she had done with Jagryn. That wouldn't do. She closed her eyes and imagined dancing with handsome Young Crane in her fine city dress. Smooth, soft fabric, tiny stitches, dainty details, intricate steps...A gentler heat spread down her arms as she breathed the magic words; the lupine appeared in her hand. She opened her eyes and finished the spell. Butterflies lifted away, light as air. Green butterflies, but it was an improvement.

Jagryn and Laki stared, open-mouthed. Then Jagryn grinned and applauded. "Perfect. How did you change the color?"

"I don't know—I guess by thinking about the dress." She turned and lit a small, controlled fire, in the hearth this time, and then extinguished it. "Teach us to fly, Laki."

He smiled up at her from his seat on the floor but shook his head. "On your first day? You might become—I don't know—a mountain lion and eat me!"

"Please?" she begged.

He shook his head. "Too much power. But we could try mind talking."

"I didn't know you could do that! Did Chamokat teach you?"

Laki nodded. "That's how I let him know I'm here. He has a real talent for it, and he says I'm not bad."

Luskell smiled. "Mamam must have taught him; Dadad isn't very good at it. What do we do?"

Mind talking did not require magic words, but intense concentration combined with natural ability. There was no way to test Laki's claim of speaking to Chamokat. Luskell and Jagryn needed to practice at a short distance first, so the three of them worked at it inside the house. Laki and Jagryn were soon exchanging good-natured insults, but Luskell had a harder time.

"I feel like my head is in a bag," she complained. "Nothing gets out."

"The first time is the hardest," Laki said. "You'll get it."

She didn't think so but closed her eyes and concentrated on sending a message to Jagryn. She felt muffled, smothered, closed in ... and then everything burst open. She opened her eyes. Jagryn was staring at her.

"You do?" he asked.

"I do what?"

"You want to kiss my brother?"

"That's not what I said!"

Jagryn frowned. "Why would I make up a thing like that?"

She felt her cheeks grow hot but forced herself to smile. "Anyway, I was joking. I said I would rather kiss him than either of you, as long as you keep being so mean to each other."

"That's not what I heard."

Laki stepped between them. "Sometimes the message is incomplete, especially when you're first learning. It will get clearer with practice."

"Now will you teach us to fly?" Luskell begged.

He stared at her. "Not today. Aren't you tired?"

"No," she lied. She was exhausted but didn't want to stop yet.

"I am," Jagryn said. "I can't do any more today."

Luskell wiped sweat from her brow and sighed. "Klamamam expects us back soon, anyway. Let's meet here again tomorrow." The boys nodded in agreement. "We should leave the book here, though. Jagryn can't take it home, and if Klamamam sees me with it, she'll ask questions."

Jagryn ran his hand through his dark hair. "I thought you said you already know everything in there."

"Not everything. We should make sure we've looked all the way through it before I give it back to Myn."

Jagryn nodded. "No one comes here but me and Uncle Jagree, and he hasn't since we finished the floor. Shove it in there, behind the woodbox. It should be safe enough."

Luskell slid the book into the dark space. It wasn't perfect but would serve to hide it from a casual glance. The three of them stepped outside.

Jagryn closed the door, then turned to the other two with a grin. "We're like a secret society, with our own meeting place."

Luskell grasped his hand, then Laki's. "The Magic Club."

Chapter 27

A chilly breeze blew as Luskell left Elika's old house with Jagryn and Laki. A few raindrops spattered down. As one splashed against Luskell's cheek, she turned uneasily. Something wasn't right.

Laki raised a hand to his face. "The rain says *danger*."

"I feel it, too," Jagryn said. Then he grinned. "It must mean I'm late and I'm about to get in trouble. I'll see you tomorrow."

He left them when they reached the Blue Heron. Luskell forgot her uneasiness when Klamamam emerged, smiling, from the kitchen. "Did you have a good afternoon?"

"Yes, I met Luskell's friends," Laki replied.

"Grynni and Greelit showed him their horse, and we—helped Jagryn repair Elika's house." Luskell longed to boast about her new-found power. But that would lead to inevitable questions of *how* she knew, or an I-told-you-so. Either would probably result in a ban on further book-borrowing. For now, she had to keep the news to herself.

Klamamam looked them over. "You're awfully clean."

Luskell smiled sheepishly. "Mostly, we kept him company."

Klamamam nodded. "I'm sure he appreciated it. Here, Luskell, a letter came for you. You can read it before you get to work. Laki, how are you with a knife?"

They went into the kitchen, Luskell lagging behind the other two. She unfolded the letter and read:

> *Dear Luskell,*
> *I write this before sunup. It has been too hot to sleep …*

She read the letter through, then slipped it into her pocket. It was a comfort to have a letter from her parents, even if it didn't say much. She was pleased about the fiddle they might bring her. From the sound of it, things were as dull in Eukard City as in Deep River.

"What does your father say?" Klamamam asked.

"Nothing much. It's hot in the city, but nothing's happening. They're still waiting for a meeting with the governor."

"Aren't you glad you came here? You'd have been bored and uncomfortable, *and* you would have missed Laki's visit."

Luskell agreed but didn't want to admit it. Another I-told-you-so. She shrugged, tied on her apron, and set out clean plates and mugs. Laki was adept with a knife, so Klamamam put him to work chopping meat and vegetables for a second pot of stew. The first one was already bubbling and fragrant over the fire, and they each had a plate before guests arrived. By the time Laki was done chopping, the first supper guests had joined the rider from Oxbow who had brought the letter. Luskell took Laki around and introduced him. Then he poured ale while she served the stew.

Once again, Foli and Rakkyn were eating together. Although Sulika did not join them this time, Young Crane and Bramynna came in and stopped at their table. A small gold loop gleamed on her earlobe.

"Do I see my baby sister with a courtship ring?" Rakkyn cried. He jumped up and hugged her. He smiled at Crane. "Were you waiting at the door while she had it done?"

"I wasn't about to let anyone else get there first."

Foli smiled, too. He shook Crane's hand. "Congratulations, young fellow. It's good to know what you want and go after it." He leaned across and kissed Bramynna on the cheek. "You didn't do so badly yourself, young lady."

She blushed. "It's only the first day." But she smiled happily. She and Crane took a table for themselves and barely looked at anyone else all evening.

Luskell was glad to see them together, though for an instant she wished herself into Bramynna's place. She supposed there would be time enough for that, with *someone*, later on. What surprised her was Foli's reaction. He didn't seem at all jealous. Bramynna was out of his reach, but he seemed perfectly content to spend his evening with Rakkyn. Maybe he was never interested in Bramynna at all. Or Sulika, for that matter.

Luskell was familiar with a few such pairings among magic folk in Eukard City, and one of Chamokat's friends, Atlatnak, had been living with another man for a few years. She couldn't even guess how they would be received in Deep River, but it looked like it could happen even here.

Luskell was so tired that night she could barely stay awake during stories. She had heard her parents talk about the effort magic required, and now she knew what they meant. She did her best to look alert so she wouldn't have to explain. Laki, on the other hand, sat on the edge of his chair, eager for each story Klamamam told. With strangers present, she didn't speak openly of Knot, but even the old, familiar tales were new to Laki.

Klamamam began one Luskell knew well about a wizard suspiciously like Knot. She drifted as she listened, eyes half-shut.

"... and so Luskell found her power ..."

No one else seemed to notice that Knot sat in Klamamam's rocker, staring straight at Luskell. "Congratulations, child."

She tried to answer and jerked awake with a snort. Klamamam gave her a funny look but continued her story to the end. "It's late, so good night, everyone."

After the guests had departed, Luskell intended to help gather dishes, but Klamamam stopped her. "You're half asleep already. Go to bed now."

"I will help clean up," Laki said.

"Thanks. See you in the morning." Luskell was fully alert after the vision of Knot—she hoped not too alert to sleep. She wanted to hurry to bed and try to resume the dream, but she pretended to drag her feet for Klamamam's benefit.

She undressed and lay down, already picturing the bright meadow and Knot's wild silver hair. Her heart pounded with excitement. He had tried to tell her about her power. That was why she could dream of him, and of Ketwyn, and of Elika. The dreams were real. Now she was too excited to sleep. She rolled over and tried to reclaim the exhaustion she had felt earlier. She thought of all the magic she'd practiced, how heavy her head felt, how her eyes wouldn't stay open...

"Luskell! Wake up!"

She was about to complain that she'd just gotten to sleep when she saw where she was—the bright, warm meadow where no sun shone.

Ketwyn bent over her. "Come, we must hurry!"

She got to her feet without effort and ran with Ketwyn. Sometimes it was difficult to run in a dream, but now she flew over the grass. Although they ran uphill, she felt no strain. Another figure ran downhill toward them, it seemed from a great distance, but then Knot was with them instantly. He folded his arms around her. His touch was heavier than Ketwyn's, warmer and more real. All too soon, he released her, and she looked into his eyes that were her eyes. His gaze was troubled.

"We don't have much time. I have to warn them, but they don't hear me."

"Have to warn who?" she asked.

"A man in Eukard City is using my name, but he is not me."

"Someone is calling himself Knot?"

"No, Yrae. The New Yrae."

Luskell shivered. That was familiar. "Walgyn said something about that. So it's true?"

"Yes. This New Yrae is dangerous."

"You say he's in Eukard City? Then it's all right! Dadad and Mamam are there."

"They're the ones in danger."

That didn't make any sense. Who could possibly harm those who could do anything?

Knot must have seen her confusion. "Listen to me. This fellow is no wizard, but he has some power and a lot of cleverness. He masks his presence, shields his intentions, so even my brilliant boy is unaware of the danger. With the help of this New Yrae, the governor plans to consolidate power over Eukard and the Aklaka. Together, they will rule a new kingdom."

To Luskell, that was politics, which paled in importance compared to the danger her parents were in. "But what can I do?"

Knot held her face between his hands. "Whatever it takes."

Chapter 28

After breakfast the next morning, Klamamam sent
Laki out to chop wood while Luskell washed the dishes.
There weren't many. The only overnight guest was the
rider from Oxbow, who had decided not to hurry back
after supper but stayed for stories and the night. While
she scrubbed, Knot's message filled Luskell's thoughts.
If Mamam and Dadad were in real danger, what could
she do to help them? Warn them, maybe. Send a letter?
That might take days to reach them, even if she sent it
with the rider when he left. But there was a faster way.

She had the ability to mind-talk. The one time she'd
used it, most of the message had been lost, and that
was with someone in the same room, but still ... Could

she send a warning all the way to Eukard City? That would be a challenge even for Mamam, who mind-talked over distance with practiced ease.

Luskell took a deep breath and closed her eyes. She pictured Eukard City and her mother's likely place in it. *Be careful of the New Yrae. He means you harm.*

Luskell didn't feel smothered this time. The message had gone somewhere, though she couldn't tell whether Mamam had received it. She waited a moment for a reply, but nothing came. There was no more she could do to warn them. *I'll go to Eukard City*, she decided. *I'll fight for them. I'll save them myself.*

"Luskell, what are you doing?"

"I—what?" She opened her eyes.

Klamamam watched her with a worried look. "I thought you'd fallen asleep over the dirty dishes. Do you feel all right?"

"Yes, I'm fine. I was—I was remembering a dream I had last night. I don't want to forget it."

"What did you dream about? Something good, I hope."

Luskell swallowed. She couldn't worry Klamamam with dire warnings. "I dreamed about Kladadad."

Klamamam's eyes widened, and she sank into a chair. "You did? About Knot?"

"I've been thinking about him a lot since I've been here. Maybe that's why."

"I suppose so. What did he have to say for himself?"

Luskell laughed uneasily. "It was a dream, so it didn't make much sense. He was glad you gave me the best room. He said it was his favorite."

"It was. I've probably told you that. How did he look?"

Luskell felt trapped in a deep hole. The wrong answer would give away everything. "He looked—the way everyone says he looked. He had hair and eyes like mine, and Dadad's face, if he was old. Old, but handsome."

Klamamam smiled. "Handsome. He was that." She sighed. "You've done enough for now. Take the rest of the day off—help the twins with their horse, or something." She didn't wait for Luskell's answer but went to her room and closed the door. Luskell heard her blow her nose. Luskell had promised to help train Kanala today, and she looked forward to it, but there was something else she wanted to do first. Dadad had once mentioned a book he'd studied called *Magical Combat*. That was where he first learned the repelling charm Luskell had shared with her friends the day before, but such a book had to contain even stronger spells. If she wanted to fight the New Yrae, that was the place to begin. She finished the dishes, then hurried to retrieve the first book from Elika's old house. They'd learned enough from that one.

The previous day's rain hadn't amounted to much. Thick clouds darkened the sky, but the air was hot and the ground as dry and dusty as ever. The door to Elika's house stood open. Luskell expected to find Jagryn working inside, but the house was empty. That was a relief; she hadn't decided whether to share *Magical Combat* with the others. They might not approve.

She looked between the woodbox and the wall where she had left the book, but the space was empty.

She searched the whole room, but there wasn't anywhere else it could be hidden. Jagryn must have taken it with him, after all. She hoped he wouldn't get caught. But Myn would probably let her take a second one, anyway. She had helped him, and they were her father's books. She made sure no one was watching, then pulled the door closed behind her and went to the Village Hall.

Myn was in the library, gazing out the window. He started when Luskell entered, then smiled. "Back so soon? I suppose you want another of your father's books."

"Yes, please. I can get it myself." She crouched in front of the lowest shelf.

He left the window. "One moment. Did you bring back the other one?"

"I—forgot it. May I have another, anyway? It's not like anyone is using them." She gave him what she hoped was a winning smile.

"It would be better if you brought it back first, rather than—I don't know—leaving it in a vacant house?" He produced the red book and laid it on the desktop. "Do you mind telling me what this was doing in Elika's old house?"

"I—It—you see—"

Myn's brow furrowed. "Jagryn has been working on that house, hasn't he? You know he's not supposed to have these."

Luskell's face grew hot. "No, it wasn't— What I mean is I didn't give it to him. I—wanted to try to learn magic myself." This was the last thing she wanted to tell anyone, but she wasn't a practiced liar. Telling something close to the truth was her best hope to get out of this without betraying Jagryn.

"I thought you had no power."

"How would I know if I didn't try? But I couldn't do it at the inn. I needed someplace private."

He nodded. Maybe he believed her. "And did you learn magic?"

She smiled and shook her head. "No. I don't have any power."

"Then why borrow another book?"

"I still need to check them for damage."

"Damage like this?" He opened the red book to the singed page. "This is new."

Luskell's heart plunged into her guts. "Fine. I lied. I do have some power. But I promise I'll be more careful with the next one." He didn't answer. She was sure he was about to deny her request when something else occurred to her. "What were *you* doing in Elika's house?"

Myn didn't say anything, but his face reddened. He sank into his chair behind the desk. For an instant, she saw Elika's house through Myn's eyes ... and Sulika, waiting for him.

Luskell rested her hands on the desk and leaned toward Myn. "I'll keep your secret if you keep mine." He met her gaze, rubbed his eyes, and nodded once. She grabbed *Magical Combat* before he could change his mind. If he knew what was in this book, he would stop her for sure *and* tell Klamamam. Then no one would save her parents.

"Be careful, Luskell," he said as she left.

She turned back in the doorway. "I could say the same. But maybe one of you should talk to Foli."

His expression grew pained. "What good would that do?"

She was tempted to reveal her suspicions and give him some hope, but they weren't based on anything solid. Why would anyone trust a fourteen-year-old girl on such a topic? "You won't know unless you try." She hurried away before he could say anything.

Luskell slid the book into her pocket and ran all the way back to the inn. She planned to shut herself up in her room with the spell book and see if she could learn anything useful before she met with Laki and Jagryn. This plan was foiled when Laki came in the back door just as she came in the front.

"The girls with the horse want us to help them," he said. "I couldn't find you, but I told them we would."

"I—had to go out," she panted. "But Klamamam gave us the day off, so we can help with Kanala if you want to. Let me change clothes first."

She hurried up to her room and closed the door behind her. She hid *Magical Combat* in her trunk, then changed into trousers as she usually did before working with the horse. Few girls were allowed to wear them, but Mamam always had a pair. They were more practical than skirts for hiking and other outdoor activities, so she had always allowed Luskell to wear them when it made sense. She pulled on a loose shirt and tucked it into the waist, but it was too hot for the overtunic.

She joined Laki and walked with him to the corral. She still hadn't made up her mind whether to tell him about *Magical Combat* when Grynni called to them. "Pa says we can sit on her today!"

Luskell smiled at this news. The horse was accustomed to all of them by now, except Laki. In recent sessions, she had begun to take the weight of a blanket or saddle to prepare her for the heavier weight of a rider.

"Some of you can," Uncle Jagree corrected. "I'm too big for her until she's older, and so is Laki, but the rest of you should be fine. Grynni, you're lightest—you first."

Kanala wore no tack except the loose loop of rope around her neck. To get her used to the weight of a rider, Uncle Jagree had Grynni lie across her back. The horse twitched her skin and craned her neck around to see what was on her. She seemed more curious than bothered. When it was clear she wouldn't buck or rear, Uncle Jagree helped Grynni sit astride. He led the horse at a walk around the corral. While Greelit took her turn, Jagryn joined them on the fence.

"You can go ahead of me," Luskell told him. "I may be bigger." She was nervous about riding bareback, even at a walk. The few times she had ridden, there had at least been something to hold on to. But her fears vanished once her turn came and she was seated on Kanala's back. She spoke quietly to the horse as she rode, and it almost seemed that Kanala answered. There was a connection between them; the horse would not let her fall.

While Luskell was still mounted, the rider from Oxbow approached and asked Uncle Jagree to ready his horse. "I usually go back the same night. I've let Stell's tales lure me before, but I think this is the first time I stayed for lunch!"

Uncle Jagree held Kanala's rope while Luskell dismounted. "This filly has probably had enough for now, anyway." He went to saddle the man's horse.

Luskell's stomach growled. She hadn't felt hungry until the rider mentioned lunch. Before she could ask Laki if he was hungry, too, a bright flash dazzled her eyes. A loud crack followed moments later. Kanala reared and whinnied. The others jumped back, but Luskell caught her rope and spoke to her until she calmed.

Uncle Jagree emerged from the stable, leading a saddled black horse. He opened the gate and peered into the distance. "That was close." He turned to the fellow from Oxbow. "Are you sure you want to leave right now?"

The man shook his head. "If a storm's coming on, I think I'll wait it out here."

"We should all get indoors," Uncle Jagree said just as lightning flashed again. Thunder cracked and rumbled behind it, but the rain held off.

Laki sniffed. "I smell smoke."

"It's been so dry the grass will burn quickly," Uncle Jagree said. "And the crops. At least it isn't windy."

As if it had been waiting for his words, a stiff breeze struck them. A thin plume of smoke was now visible to the northwest. Laki glanced at Luskell. "I may be able to stop it before it gets too large."

Before she could reply, he became a large falcon and sped away toward the smoke. The others watched, dumbstruck, but Luskell didn't want to stand around, waiting. She swung herself onto Kanala's back and grasped the creamy mane. "Come on, Kanala, let's help him."

Chapter 29

Once the rain started, it came down in the kind of soaking torrent usually reserved for late fall. No one ventured out who didn't have to. After their evening out, Ketty and Crane spent much of the day in bed, enjoying all that luxury at last. Ketty felt a twinge of guilt—she was usually a worker, a doer. But one day of leisure could do no harm.

By the following morning, the downpour had slackened to a drizzle. "Back to normal," Crane joked.

"We should go out," Ketty said. "We can be useful while we're waiting. Unless you don't want to get wet."

"Didn't I tell you once, I never get enough rain?"

She shook her head but couldn't hide her smile. She'd learned that about him the first time they met, decades ago, and lived with him long enough to know it was true. He'd grown up in a dry place; it made sense to love the rain.

After breakfast, they dug out their rain capes and set off in the direction of Balsam's House. About halfway there, Ketty jerked to a halt at the sound of a girl's voice right at her ear. But there was no one close to her except Crane. "Did you hear that?"

He gave her a puzzled look. Carts rumbled past and splashed through puddles as the drivers shouted to their animals. Merchants cried their wares, and residents called across to their neighbors from open windows and doorways. "Did I hear what?"

Ketty frowned. "It sounded like Luskell." She pressed her hand to her head, trying to hear more, but the voice was gone. "She said, 'Be careful.'"

"Mind-talking?" Now he seemed more interested.

"I don't know what else it could be, but how?"

"Maybe she's stopped denying her power. But could she progress from nothing to mind-talking in only two weeks? And all the way from Deep River?" He took Ketty's arm, and they began walking again. "Maybe you heard a mother calling down to a child."

She shook her head. "I don't think so. But it does seem more a mother's line; why would Luskell tell *me* to be careful? It's more likely *I* would tell *her*."

"That's your job," he agreed.

"What are mothers for? But I...." The puzzle of the voice in her head shrank in importance as she remembered something else. She had not been careful.

It had been such a joy, a relief, to touch again after so many sticky, uncomfortable days. In the delight of the moment, she simply forgot.

Crane looked at her in alarm. "What's wrong?"

She shook her head and forced a smile. "Nothing."

He studied her and raised an eyebrow as the truth dawned in her unshielded thoughts. "That seems like something to me."

"I can't keep a secret from you, can I? But what will we do?"

He drew her close and kissed her in spite of passersby. "We won't worry about it. Whatever happens, it'll be all right."

"Easy for you to say." She spoke crossly but couldn't help smiling. Perhaps nothing would come of her mistake. And if it did, Crane wouldn't run away like Knot had. He wouldn't treat her the way Walgyn had. They would face it together.

He squeezed her hand. "It's not like you to forget, but any of us can be forgiven a lapse or two between the weather and this New Yrae."

She sighed. "I haven't said this in a long time, but I'll be glad to get out of this city. It's felt wrong since we got here."

They walked on. "It was bad luck to be in town for the worst heat wave in decades. And I'm still not convinced the New Yrae is a real threat. Not that I wouldn't like to face him and put a stop to his tricks."

Ketty shivered. "With any luck, he's already wearied of them and moved on. Let's go to Balsam's House and find out."

There were no fresh victims of the New Yrae's cursed blade, but the first one was still there. He hurried to meet them almost as soon as they arrived. "Yrae," he rasped and touched his bandaged throat.

"We remember," Ketty said. "You look much better. Would you like me to check your wound?"

He nodded. "Please."

They escorted him into the room where she and Balsam had first treated him. It was spotlessly clean, with no sign of the bloody chaos of recent events. "Tell me your name." Ketty removed the bandage.

"Ettam."

"Well, Ettam, you're healing very well. You'll have a small scar here, but I've seen worse." Crane showed his disfigured hand, and Ettam recoiled. "Anyway, a scar like this could be useful. The story might be good for a drink at the tavern." She was trying to get Ettam to smile, but his expression remained anxious. "When do they say you can go home?"

He shook his head. "Yrae. Beware."

She frowned. "Are you afraid to go home? You don't need to be. The New Yrae hasn't been heard from in days, and he never killed anyone, so—"

"Didn't mean to kill," Ettam whispered. "Meant to scare."

Ketty grasped Ettam's shoulders. "Then you must show him you are not afraid."

"Not scare me. Scare you."

She drew back, but Crane chuckled. "I doubt he even knows who we are. If he did, he'd know we don't scare easily."

Ketty spoke healing words over the wound, especially the voice box. It wasn't badly damaged but still swollen, which made it difficult for Ettam to speak. The man had a terrible time making sense. She wrapped a fresh bandage around his neck and patted his shoulder encouragingly. "You're out of danger. Go home when Balsam says you can."

Ettam returned to the convalescents' common room. Ketty washed and dried her hands. "That was strange. He seemed to want to warn *us* when he was the one attacked."

"There's lot of fear flying around. He's probably warning everyone he meets."

"Maybe. But someone with Luskell's voice told me to be careful."

Crane smiled. "We should keep our eyes open, as always. But who could threaten us? No one can sneak up on you, and I have a sense for hidden things."

Ketty hugged him. "You're right. I don't know why I'm so jittery."

"Maybe because you have something to protect?"

"It's too soon to tell."

They spent the rest of the day there. Ketty found comfort in the routines and rhythms of healing. This was what she knew and was best at. She put her anxiety and Ettam's warning from her mind.

Although Crane was not primarily a healer, his skills had come a long way. He was especially helpful with children, who had always trusted him. Ketty smiled as she watched him persuade a little boy with a sore throat to open his mouth for a healer to examine. Her thoughts turned again to the possible second child.

Against her better judgment, she liked the idea of holding a baby again. Luskell had been a beautiful baby, good-tempered and easy to care for in the early months, a fascinating challenge as she grew older. Ketty would never forget Ketwyn, but Luskell's robust good health had tempered the loss of that first child. Another one would probably be as healthy. But what if it was as stubborn and headstrong as Luskell? What if it had as much power? Ketty shook her head. They would have their hands full.

The drizzle had stopped by the time Crane and Ketty left Balsam's House that afternoon. The sun broke through and dazzled off the wet pavement of the square. Crane squinted at the sudden brilliance.

"A day well spent," he said. "You'll make a healer of me yet."

Ketty smiled in a distracted way and glanced toward the Wizards' Hall. "Maybe we should share Ettam's warning with them."

"They already know about the New Yrae and these recent attacks. Ettam's warning doesn't add anything."

She frowned. "You're just like your father. He would never accept help, either."

Crane refused to be baited. "I don't need help. I'm not in any trouble."

She muttered something he couldn't hear. He assumed it was something along the lines of, "Men!"

Crane's thoughts had moved on to the governor's plan for the Aklaka. Snowabi wanted to settle them in permanent towns. Why? The simple answer seemed to be taxation—they would be easier to find and count. But there were no more than a thousand Aklaka in Eukard. He wouldn't receive much revenue from them, and if he meant to be a king, they didn't represent that many more subjects, or much of a threat to his power. It hardly seemed worth the trouble. There had to be some other reason.

As soon as they reached the house, he found Naliskat and Pataknan in their apartment. They were intent on a game of Baktat, an Aklaka strategy game played with stones on a board marked with a hundred squares. It was a popular way to pass the quiet winter days in Aku's Lap. Crane was familiar with the basics of the game but had never mastered its intricacies. A single round could go on for days and turn dramatically at the last moment. Pataknan was a skilled player, but Naliskat was nearly unbeatable. The only person to best him in recent years was his son, Nalaklak.

Crane watched the game in silence for a time. When Naliskat leaned forward to make a move, sunlight glinted off the knife in his belt and caught Crane's attention. "Liski, may I see your knife, please?"

Naliskat drew the knife without taking his eyes from the board and handed it to Crane, hilt first. It was a typical ceremonial knife carried by all Aklaka men—an obsidian blade set in a hilt of antler or bone, plain or decorated according to the owner's preference. As a rite of passage, boys of fifteen crafted such a knife with the help of their fathers or other men of the band and began wearing it at seventeen. Five golden nuggets decorated the hilt of Naliskat's knife.

"I haven't seen these on a knife before," Crane said. "Did you add them recently?"

Naliskat looked up from his game. "Yes, when Laki was making his knife. Pretty, aren't they?"

"Very. Where did they come from?"

"A couple of the streams above Aku's Lap are full them. They seem to wash right out of the mountain."

"You do know they're gold, don't you?" Crane asked. "That's probably at least a month's rent stuck on your knife handle."

Naliskat smiled. "To your people. To mine, it's decoration." He returned to his game. Pataknan was ahead, but this did not seem to unsettle Naliskat.

Crane turned the knife in his hands. "This feels important. If Governor Snowabi knows or suspects you've found gold, that could explain why he wants to move you out of the mountains."

With one move, the game turned completely, and Naliskat won. "He's welcome to it—if he can find it."

"I'm sure he will, if he has to destroy the forest to do so."

That got Naliskat's attention. "Destroy the forest?"

Crane nodded. "I wouldn't put it past him. He'll move all the Aklaka far away so they can't obstruct him. He'll beat you at a game you didn't know you were playing. You'll lose everything, and he'll win a great prize."

"And what is that?" Naliskat asked.

Crane drew up a chair as Pataknan put away the game board and stones. "This is just a hunch."

Naliskat smiled. "Your hunches tend to be right. Tell me."

"Snowabi wants to be king."

Naliskat and Pataknan exchanged a baffled glance. "Is that like Uklak?" Pataknan asked.

"Yes, in the sense of being hereditary and for life," Crane said. "But a king would rule over all of Eukard, not just a small band where he knew everyone personally. I doubt he would strive for consensus the way your Uklaks do. He could make law and take whatever he wanted."

Naliskat frowned. "But you haven't had a king in—how long?"

"Hundreds of years, and we haven't wanted one. But if someone could endear himself to the people, they might give him the crown. I think that's what Snowabi is trying to do, with some of these new measures he's put in place—increased guard patrols, feeding stations, free schools, and so on."

Pataknan's eyes widened. "Or he could—put a spell on them?"

Crane chuckled. "Snowabi's no wizard. And I didn't think he had a chance of winning them over with increased patrols or free schools, either. There's no sustainable way to pay for it all without raising taxes. People might be willing to pay for those things, but they wouldn't crown a king for the privilege. But with your gold—"

"It isn't *our* gold," Naliskat interrupted. "It is Aku's gold."

Crane nodded. "Fair enough. If Mother Aku gives up her gold, don't you think her children should benefit?"

Naliskat gave Crane a grim smile and thumped the table with his fist. "*All* her children, not just Snowabi. Let us make a plan."

Chapter 30

Kanala galloped through the open gate as if she had been waiting for this moment. Luskell heard Jagryn call, "Wait for me!" She chanced a look back and saw him on the black horse, right behind her.

She didn't know where they were going, but she clung to Kanala and directed her with words and thoughts toward the growing plume of smoke. Soon Luskell could see the fire. She had expected an isolated blaze, like a campfire, but this was a snaky line of flame. It spread quickly through the dry grass and had already blackened a large area. It advanced toward fields of ripening grain and a small farmstead. The old stone buildings of Deep River wouldn't have been in much danger from fire, but these buildings were newer, built of wood.

"Whoa, Kanala. Whoa." The horse stopped her wild gallop but pranced nervously.

Jagryn rode up beside Luskell. "That's Huvro's farm."

A man plowed a firebreak from a creek that crossed the farm, around the buildings, and back to the creek. A girl led two horses and a cow away from the barn to the far side of the creek. A calf followed its mother, bawling. Near the house, a boy drew water from the well to fill a washtub. A woman soaked heavy sacks in the tub.

"They should be able to protect the house and barn," Jagryn said. "And that field across the creek is probably safe. It might be too late for the other field."

A bird dove toward the earth near the growing wildfire. Then Laki's tall form became visible. Moments later, a section of the fire near him died down.

"We have to help him," Luskell said. "Come on, let's go!" She urged Kanala forward again, but the horse shied, nearly colliding with Jagryn's mount.

Jagryn backed away to give her space. "The horses are spooked by the fire. We should leave them with Ruvhonn." He gestured toward the girl leading the animals. He dismounted and led his horse across the stream. Luskell followed. The water was low enough that she didn't even get her boots wet, but maybe it would stop the fire if it got this far.

Luskell remembered Ruvhonn from the dance, though they hadn't spoken that night. She was Jagryn's age, and nearly his height, but with the kind of curvy figure Luskell could only dream of. Her cheeks burned red from effort, and her pale hair tried to escape from its two braids. She looked up from her animals in surprise. "Jagryn? What are you doing out here?"

"We're going to help fight the fire. Will you watch our horses?" Without waiting for an answer, he handed her his horse's reins and ran off toward the fire.

Luskell gave her a brief smile, spoke calming words to both horses, and ran to catch up with Jagryn. He ran around the edge of the wheat field on the other side of the house, rather than trample the crop they were trying to save.

"We all sensed danger yesterday," he panted as she came alongside him. "This must be it."

Luskell was about to agree, but a nagging sense told her this was only the beginning. That didn't mean they couldn't help here, though.

She was prepared for the heat of the fire as she neared it, but not the noise. It seemed to be in a roaring contest with the wind that fed it and pushed it toward the field. Laki had extinguished a small portion, but he would never stop it on his own.

"Laki!" Luskell cried. "Fly to the other end and work back this way. Jagryn, start at this end. I'll take the middle." As Laki became a falcon once more, Luskell ran again, almost as fast as in her dream. She threw down extinguishing spells as she went, with limited success. The fire raged on. When she was roughly halfway between the boys, she stopped and turned her full attention on the job.

She thought of something Jagryn had said the day before: "You don't have to use all your power. You're not trying to win a fight." Well, now she was. She drew on the depths of her power and threw everything she had at that wall of flame. It roared back at her. She screamed the extinguishing spell and swept her arm in a defiant gesture. A large section of flames fell back and died.

Luskell! She was startled to hear Laki's shout over the noise of wind and fire. With delight, she realized he was mind-talking. She grinned up the line and waved at him. He pointed at something. *Behind you!*

She spun to find the fire all around her. An ember had blown past her and set the grass behind her alight. The heat and noise were intense. This new fire raced toward the wheat field. On the far side of the field, Huvro and his wife and son beat out spot fires with wet sacks, but none of them were close enough to reach this one. Luskell extinguished it and returned her attention to the main fire, only to find it had raced up almost to her position. By force of will, she pushed it back onto ground that was already burned. Without fuel, it died on its own. And from either end, Laki and Jagryn moved toward her, gradually suppressing the line of flames.

When they reached her, the three of them stared around in amazement. Smoke filled the air, but the fire had stopped—right at the field's border. Exhausted and soot-blackened, they stumbled around the edge of the field. Huvro hurried to meet them.

"You've saved my crop, and I don't even know who you are!"

"It's Jagryn." His voice was hoarse from smoke. "These are my friends, Luskell and Laki."

Huvro stared. "Jagryn? Do you mean to say children saved my wheat? Boys?"

"No," Laki said. "Wizards."

"And one of us is a girl," Luskell added.

Huvro blinked. "I thought girls can't be wizards, but I thank you, whatever you may be. Come get cleaned up, and then I'm sure Honna can find you something to eat."

"Thank you," Luskell croaked. Between shouting and breathing smoke, she had little voice left. "We missed lunch."

A small group of men had arrived from Deep River and the surrounding farms to help fight the fire. Uncle Jagree was among them. He frowned at Luskell and left the group to confront her. "What were you thinking, galloping a horse that has barely learned to take weight?"

Luskell stared in shock. Uncle Jagree rarely showed anger. "I—I—she wanted to."

"She's too young to know what she wants. If you've hurt her—"

"I'm sorry. I'll let her walk back."

"You'd better. And as for you—" He turned on Jagryn, but before he could finish the scolding, the other men called for him to join them. He scowled, then turned away. They took wet sacks and shovels, and went to make sure all the fires and hot spots were out.

The three young people collapsed on a small patch of grass outside the farmhouse. Ruvhonn brought them clean water, washrags, and soap. She didn't say anything, but she was especially attentive to Jagryn. At first. Then her gaze settled on Laki. When he smiled at her, she blushed even pinker. Luskell glanced between them, first vexed with them for flirting, then with herself for caring. But as Laki scrubbed, and his familiar face emerged from the soot and grime, she noticed for the first time what a fine face it was.

Without warning, he turned and smiled at her. She immediately devoted herself to her own washing. The cool water felt wonderful, but one side of her face stung with a sharp pain when she scrubbed it.

Ruvhonn's mother Honna set down a tray of food. "You've burned your face!"

"I have?" Luskell touched the blistered place and winced. She had no idea when it had happened, whether all at once or over the whole time she was near the fire. She had been so caught up in fighting the fire she forgot about the danger to herself. But neither Laki nor Jagryn had burns.

Honna hurried to Luskell's side and gently dabbed her right cheek clean. "It doesn't look too bad. Hold a cool cloth on it for now and see Brynnit as soon as you get back to town."

She offered them bread, meat, and cheese. The food tasted good and satisfied Luskell's hunger, but she appreciated the mug of cold water even more. She had never been so thirsty and tired, as if she had run all the way from Oxbow.

While they were eating, it started to rain. "Better late than never," Huvro said. "You young folks should come inside until it stops."

"No, our families will be worried," Jagryn said. "We should go before it gets worse."

Luskell dragged herself to her feet. She was still exhausted, but Jagryn was right. Laki looked unsteady on his feet, too. When Ruvhonn's brother brought their horses, Jagryn insisted that Laki ride the black. "I didn't do as much," Jagryn said.

Luskell wanted to argue the point, but then she remembered Laki's transformation. That kind of magic took a lot out of a person, even when they weren't fighting fires. "You can ride Kanala," she offered. "You did as much as I did."

Jagryn smiled and shook his head. "You did much more. I can walk back."

With Jagryn's help, Luskell mounted Kanala and rested her head against the horse's neck. The cool rain felt good as they ambled back to town. They would be soaked, but they were in no hurry to explain where they'd been or what they'd done.

"No magic practice today," Jagryn said. "We did something real."

Laki chuckled. "The Magic Club is a good team. Not so secret anymore, but a good team."

Luskell was too tired even to smile in agreement. She was disappointed to put off learning magical combat, but she had nothing left. It would have to wait. But she had come to a decision. After they left the horses at the stable, she turned to Laki and Jagryn. "I have to tell you something." She drew a deep breath. "The danger we sensed was more than the fire. My parents are in trouble. I thought I had to save them. Now I think *we* have to."

Chapter 31

Jagryn and Laki insisted on escorting Luskell to have her burn treated.

"Why don't you boys go home?" Auntie Brynnit asked. "You need to change into dry clothes, and Jagryn, your parents must be worried sick. Laki, you could take word to Stell."

Laki crossed his arms. "I will stay with Luskell."

"Then so will I," Jagryn put in.

Auntie Brynnit shook her head but smiled. "Fine, just stay out of the way. Luskell, come over by the window so I can get a good look."

Jagryn and Laki moved through the open back door to the lean-to where a low fire burned in the stove. The warmth didn't reach Luskell. She shivered in her wet clothes as she sat in the chair Auntie Brynnit placed for her near the row of south-facing windows. Pots of herbs and flowers lined the broad shelf.

"Will I have a scar?" Luskell wasn't against the idea; Mamam had never allowed her childhood injuries to scar which meant she had nothing to show for her exploits.

"I doubt it. This doesn't look much worse than a bad sunburn. How did you get it? You must have been very close to the flames."

"In them," Laki said. "She is Aketnan's child."

Auntie Brynnit frowned at him, then returned her attention to Luskell. "If you were *in* them, your clothes would be burned. They're filthy with soot but not burned at all."

"I wasn't *in* the flames; it only looked that way to Laki. I was close, though. If I'd worn a dress, the skirt might have caught fire."

"What were you doing?" Luskell could hear the worry Auntie Brynnit tried to keep out of her voice.

"Um—fighting the fire."

Auntie Brynnit started. "Fighting it? Jagree thought you just went to watch. You're lucky you weren't hurt much worse, all three of you. What were you thinking?"

"That we could put it out," Jagryn said. "Like this, Auntie Brynnit." With a quiet word, he extinguished her cooking fire, then lit it again, as if he'd been practicing for years rather than only one day.

Auntie Brynnit stared at the flames, then turned to face Jagryn. "You were supposed to wait for Crane."

Jagryn shrugged. "I didn't."

Auntie Brynnit gazed at him, tight-lipped. "Your father will hear about this."

"Blame me—I talked him into it." Luskell was surprised Jagryn had the strength left for more magic. But he seemed to know how to ration his power. "Can you please do something for this? It hurts."

"I'm sorry, Luskell. Yes." Auntie Brynnit touched the burn so lightly Luskell barely felt it. She said a charm to reduce the pain and swelling and another to speed healing. Luskell had heard these words all her life, but now she understood them. The pain lessened immediately, though it didn't go away. "I don't have the power to make injuries disappear, the way your mother could, but it won't take long to heal." She dabbed on some good-smelling liquid and tied a bandage around Luskell's head. "That's lavender oil. It's wonderful for burns, and with so many blacksmiths in the family, I always keep it on hand."

Luskell nodded. "Mamam likes it, too."

Jagryn and Laki walked Luskell back to the Blue Heron. Klamamam was pacing and worrying out loud to Uncle Jelf and the rider from Oxbow. She ran to Luskell and hugged her tight. Luskell was so tired she could barely lift her arms to return the hug. "You're all right! You're—" Klamamam sniffed, pulled back, and stared at the bandage. "Lavender oil. A burn. Why did it have to be a burn?" She began to cry.

Luskell didn't have the energy to deal with a scene. She wanted only to get out of her clammy clothes and go to bed. "It's not that bad, Klamamam, not like Dadad's. I won't even have a scar."

"I promised to keep you safe," Klamamam fretted. "What will I tell your father?"

"Tell him his daughter may have as much power as he does," Jagryn said.

Klamamam frowned. "What?"

Luskell sighed and ripped the bandage from her head. She winced when it stuck to the burn. The pain was returning, in spite of the charm and the ointment. Klamamam recoiled at the sight, so it must have looked worse than it felt. Luskell gazed straight at Klamamam as she laid her fingers on the burn and drew on the remains of her power. As she spoke the words of healing, she felt a tingle in her hand, and then in her cheek as the charm took effect. Klamamam stared and opened her mouth to speak, but before she could form words, Luskell's strength left her. Black dots filled her vision. She swayed and fell.

Chapter 32

Luskell woke in her bed, dressed in a clean nightgown. Sunlight filled the room. She smelled smoke and sprang up in panic, then dropped back again in relief. There was no fire—it was her own hair she smelled. She rubbed absently at an itch on her face, and a patch of dead skin flaked away. Underneath, the burn was completely healed.

The door opened, and Klamamam looked in. On seeing Luskell awake, she smiled and came in. "Good to see your beautiful blue eyes again."

Luskell stretched. "I'm starving! How long did I sleep?"

"You missed supper and breakfast. I tried not to worry—your father was once out for almost three days. How do you feel?"

"Fine, now. My burn is healed, so I guess it was worth it." Luskell thought back to the last thing she remembered. "I fell, but I didn't hit the floor, did I?" She had no bumps or bruises, and she thought she remembered someone catching her. Probably Laki or Jagryn, though she fantasized it might have been Jagryn's handsome brother.

Klamamam smiled. "You were lucky Bron was right there."

"Who's Bron?"

"The rider who brings the mail. He and Laki carried you up here so I could put you to bed."

"That's nice," Luskell said. "Is he still here? I should thank him."

"No, he went home this morning."

Luskell looked around the room. "Were my clothes ruined?"

"They're fine. I washed them this morning. The rain stopped, so I hung them outside to dry. " Klamamam frowned. "You left your trunk open when you changed clothes yesterday. I found that book in it and returned it to Myn. I don't know what he was thinking, but you won't be borrowing any more spell books from him."

"They're not *his* books," Luskell protested.

"And they're not yours, either. Why would you need combat spells?" Klamamam shook her head and clucked at the idea.

Luskell thought about telling her why but changed her mind. If Klamamam thought there was danger in

Eukard City, she wouldn't let Luskell out of her sight. She tried to look as innocent as possible. "I hope I never need them. I was just—curious. When I learned what I could do..." She lowered her gaze. "I'm sorry I worried you. I guess I should get up and do my morning chores while it's still morning."

Klamamam laughed. "Laki and Jagryn did them already while they waited for you to wake up."

An idea sparked in Luskell's mind. "Are they here? May I see them?"

"For a moment. I'll send them up, but then you should come down to the kitchen and wash that smoke out of your hair."

Klamamam left. Luskell heard voices and then loud footsteps on the stairs. Jagryn and Laki burst in, their eyes full of worry and relief. Jagryn flung his arms around her. "I thought you were dead!"

"I'm fine. I just tried to do too much all at once."

Jagryn released her and backed away, his face red. Laki squeezed her shoulder. "I am glad you are well again."

"Me, too. Thanks for doing my chores." She lowered her voice. They had to leave the door open, but Klamamam wouldn't hear if they whispered. "We have to talk, and we don't have much time. Nobody will let us practice magic on our own now, so we have to save my parents with what we already know."

Laki frowned. "Why do you think *we* have to save them?"

"There's an evil somebody-or-other who calls himself the New Yrae. He's targeting them."

Jagryn smiled. "Either of them has more power than anyone. And the two of them together? He'll never touch them."

"That's what they think. It's what he wants them to think. He's able to hide himself somehow, so they won't recognize the danger until it's too late."

"But how do you know this?" Laki asked.

"Knot told me."

The boys exchanged a glance. Jagryn shook his head. "Knot is dead."

"Don't you think I know that!?" Luskell cried, then dropped her voice again. "I've been dreaming dead people for weeks. Ketwyn, Elika, Knot..."

"But how do you know they weren't just dreams?" Jagryn asked. "It seems natural you'd think about your brother and grandfather and wish you could meet them."

"Why would I dream about Elika, then? She's no kin to me."

"We visited the graveyard with what's-his-name, the fiddler. You saw her name on a stone. And we talked about her house."

Luskell frowned. "But she told me to tell Sulika she's marrying the wrong man."

Jagryn snorted. "That's no secret."

"Maybe not to *you*. But why would I even care about a thing like that? And when I dreamed of Ketwyn, he had bright blue eyes, exactly like Walgyn's. How would I know that?"

"I don't know. Maybe your mother—"

"No! Ketwyn died within hours of birth. If she even saw his eyes then, they were murky baby eyes. And she doesn't talk about Walgyn. I didn't know what he looked like until I saw him at the dance."

Jagryn sighed. "I'm not getting anywhere, Laki. You try."

Laki rubbed his chin and gazed at Luskell. "I think I believe her. Listeners often dream true, so why wouldn't magic folk? And we don't really know anything about what happens after death."

Luskell smiled at him. "Knot said they could talk to me because I had power, but I wasn't using it."

"Will the dreams stop now?" Jagryn asked.

"I don't know. I hope not. But I do know I have to help my parents, and I hope you two will help me."

The boys looked at each other and nodded. "We'll help," Laki said. "But how will we get to Eukard City?"

They fell silent as they considered this problem. It was about a week's journey on foot, but Luskell didn't want to take that long. Two days had already passed since Knot's warning. Even on horseback, it would probably take three or four days. And they didn't have horses.

"If we can get to Oxbow, it's only a day or two by coach," Jagryn said. "We'd have to pay for our seats, but I have some money from odd jobs."

"So do I," Luskell said.

Jagryn frowned. "I thought that was your fiddle fund."

"It was." She swallowed hard. "Dadad said they might bring me one. If not, I can start saving again later. But this is more important. We'll pool our funds and share them in common."

"But how do we get to Oxbow without anyone here noticing?" Jagryn asked.

Laki smiled. "I have no money, but I can still contribute. It's time you two learned to fly."

"You said it was too soon," Luskell objected. "You said we were beginners."

"No, I said it required too much power. But you're both rested now. I don't doubt you'll be able to transform. You have plenty of power, Luskell, and Jagryn is a natural."

"But we won't have time to practice. Klamamam will kick you both out any moment now."

Laki looked grim. "Then we won't practice. Jagryn, do you have a window in your bedroom?"

"Yes, but—"

"Good. When you go to bed tonight, make sure your window is open. Wait until everyone is asleep, then change into an owl and fly out the window. That way, no one should hear you go. Meet at Elika's house, then we'll fly to Oxbow before it gets light."

Luskell grinned. "Why not fly all the way to the city?"

He shook his head. "We'd have nothing left. It might even kill us, and then who would save Crane and Aketnan? But Oxbow is near enough. Bring your money, and a little food—whatever you can carry in your pockets. When you're ready to change, speak these words and imagine the owl. Understand it. Be it."

He had just enough time to tell them the spell before Klamamam appeared in the doorway. "All right, boys, time to go, before Luskell gets you into any more mischief!"

Luskell forced a laugh, and the others joined her. "See you later, Luskell," Jagryn said. "I'm glad you're feeling better." He smiled at Klamamam as he passed her.

Laki grinned in an uncharacteristic way and spoke in Aklaka. "Tonight we'll fly and be heroes."

Klamamam watched him go. "What did he say?"

"Roughly translated? 'See you later.'"

Laki didn't stay up for stories that night but went to his room soon after supper. Luskell hoped his tiredness was an act; otherwise, he'd miss their rescue effort. She had slept half the day, so she was wide awake even after the last story, but she rubbed her eyes and pretended to be sleepy as she helped clean up. She slipped half a loaf into her pocket and trudged upstairs.

As soon as her door closed behind her, she changed into her shirt and trousers again. The shirt was dry, but the trousers were still damp. It couldn't be helped; this was her most practical travel outfit. She opened her trunk and found the overtunic. They would arrive in Oxbow in the chill before sunrise, so an extra layer of clothing wouldn't go amiss. Luskell had been brought up so she wouldn't dream of going into the mountains without adequate footwear, so she also dug out and put on her sturdy boots.

There wasn't much else she could take—only what she was wearing or had in her pockets. She laid out a light cloak, which would help keep her warm and had a pocket big enough for the bread. She emptied her money bag and counted the coins: six silver duls and eighteen copper duleens, so a total of twelve duls. She hoped it was enough.

Luskell considered leaving a note for Klamamam, then decided against it. If she found it before they were well away, she might have time to stop them. A letter from Oxbow would be safer. Luskell blew out her lamp and waited in the dark for the rest of the inn to get quiet. Laki was silent in the next room. Then she heard the creak of a window and the soft hoot of an owl. She put on her cloak and opened her own window wide. She climbed up and crouched on the sill. She had no fear of heights, but the second floor window suddenly seemed awfully far from the ground. What kind of person willingly jumps out a window from a house that isn't on fire?

One who can fly, she reminded herself and turned her mind to owls. Not the little ones that lived in burrows around Deep River, but something with a large wingspan. A barn owl would not look out of place should anyone happen to see her. She formed as detailed an image as she could, grateful that her parents had taken pains to teach her about all the living things they'd encountered. She held the image in her mind and reviewed the spell. Her parents had often transformed where she could see them, but never where she could hear the spell. Now she understood why—they must have known she had latent power, and transformation was not something to play with or use lightly. But in their own way, they had prepared her for this moment.

Luskell whispered the words. The change was instantaneous, as if it had been waiting all her life. She spread her wings and floated away without a sound. What had been a shadowy, moonlit night seemed bright as day. The ground held no danger for her. A mouse froze as her shadow passed over. She was the danger now.

Elika's house, said her own voice in her mind. She let the mouse go and flapped to the empty house at the edge of town. A great horned owl and a spotted owl perched on the roof. Laki had arrived in Deep River as a spotted owl, so the other must be Jagryn. As she neared them, they joined her in the air. Together, the three of them circled the house just once for the pure pleasure of it, then turned north toward Oxbow.

Chapter 33

Stell's room was full of light. She thought at first she'd overslept, but the window was dark. She sat up and stared into the twilight-blue eyes of the man seated on the edge of her bed. She couldn't believe it, yet she wasn't surprised. He belonged there.

He smiled, an expression that had never failed to startle her with its warmth and sweetness. "I couldn't come to you in darkness."

She flung her arms around him and held him with all her strength. "Oh, Knot, where have you been?" She was sorry she hadn't seen him arrive; she never tired of watching his eagle form swoop through the window, then transform into the tall man she loved.

"I am never far from you."

She sat back and gazed at him again. His hair was white as she remembered, but his face looked younger. "How did you get in? I closed the window."

"I don't need to come in that way anymore."

She chuckled. How could she have forgotten? They were married, with no more need to sneak. He lived here now, and...No, that wasn't right, either. She frowned. There was a reason he'd been gone so long. "Have you come for me, then? Am I—"

He smiled and placed a finger to her lips. "Not yet, my love. You're much too strong. You are sleeping."

"Then this is only a dream." Her throat ached with disappointment.

"Don't say *only*. Where else could we meet?"

She had him lie down beside her and pressed against him. He was almost solid, not quite substantial, but his warmth surrounded her. The light dimmed to a gentle glow, brighter and warmer than the moonlight. "Why haven't we met before this? I've wanted to see you for so long. You used to send me dreams when you were living. Why did you stop?"

"Those dreams were magic, and my magic died with me. But if the dreamer has power, sometimes I can appear. It is more difficult with an ordinary person."

"Then how is it you're here?"

"Because you, my love, are not ordinary. I always knew it, but I had to remember. Your love is stronger than any magic."

She tried to answer but managed only a choked sob. She pressed her face against his shoulder.

He stroked her hair, a light, tingling touch. "I'm sorry, Stell. I didn't mean to make you cry. Have I ever given you anything but sorrow?"

She dried her eyes. "You gave me Crane. And he gave us a wonderful granddaughter."

He smiled, and the room brightened again. "Somehow, I never thought about grandchildren. Had I known Luskell was coming, I would have been more careful."

"More careful?"

"At the end. I wouldn't have thrown my strength away, if I'd known."

Stell's throat clenched as she recalled his final act, spending all his power on a complicated healing rather than wake Ketty after an exhausting day. It took a moment to master her emotions enough to speak. "You? Give up magic? Accept help? I don't believe it."

"For Luskell, I would have."

She sighed. "But not for me."

"For you, I *should* have. I learned too late. Can you forgive me?"

She pretended to think about it. She had never liked his heedlessness but had reconciled herself to it long before he made his last, fatal choice. It was his way, and she had accepted him with it, rather than not have him at all. And that last choice was an unselfish one, so he had changed some in those last months. He knew he was weakened and might live only a few more years, and then only if he refrained from magic. Instead, he gave it all away to an injured stranger, a woman with a child and everything to live for.

Stell had to clear her throat before she answered. "At least I knew you a little. Luskell wishes she could have met you, even once."

"In a way, she has."

Stell nodded. "She said she dreamed of you, but I don't think she knew it was real."

Knot grinned. "I'm sure she knew. She heeded my warning."

"Your—warning?"

He didn't answer right away. "Crane is in danger. Ketty, too. They're working too hard; they don't hear me. But Luskell was wide open—plenty of power, and she wasn't using any of it."

Stell sat up and stared at him. "What are you saying?"

"I told her what was happening, and she decided to help."

"Help?" she shouted. "Help how?"

"She tried to warn them."

"But how could she, when she's here, and they're in Eukard City? A letter would take too long, and could even Ketty mind-talk over that distance?"

"I think Luskell had the same thought. She and her friends are on their way to Eukard City right now."

"What? On their way to—Knot, what have you done?"

He sat up, too. "I couldn't let that imposter harm my boy."

"So you sent untrained children to save him?"

He looked hurt. "I didn't *send* them. It was their own choice, and they're not exactly children. They're young, but they have a lot of power. And the Aklaka boy has some skill."

"So one of them is trained, a bit. That solves everything. You never think, do you? You haven't changed at all." She crossed her arms and turned away.

"Would you want me to?" He waited for a response, which she did not give him. "It's too late for that. Only the living can change."

Those words cut Stell like a blade. In those last months when they were married, he had made all the changes he would ever make. He was dead now, and this visit was a gift. How could she spoil it by arguing? But how could he endanger their only grandchild?

He spoke as if he could hear her thoughts. "I had to tell someone they were in danger. There's so little I can do now, but I could do that. And I knew Luskell would hear me, though she surprised even me with her quick action."

Stell faced him again. She could never stay angry at him. He meant well, even if his actions almost always had unintended consequences. Luskell was so much like him, but she had youth as an excuse. "They'll get themselves killed," she whispered.

"Don't be so sure about that. Luskell has an alarming amount of power, and she's learning to control it. The boys aren't weak, either, and they'd do anything for her. The three of them will look after each other, while their enemy is working alone. And he doesn't expect them."

Against her better judgment, she let his confidence rub off on her. Maybe he was right. She had seen Luskell's power with her own eyes. Someone had said she was as powerful as Crane. Maybe it would all work out well. She lay down in Knot's arms. "It's never dull with you around. Can you stay?"

He kissed her, a weightless tingle against her lips. "I never left. You won't always see me, but I'll watch over you to the end of your days."

Luskell's swift, silent wings carried her through the moonlit night. The three owls flew above open fields, putting distance between themselves and Deep River with every flap. The thrill of flight had not yet worn off. Luskell thought they would have to stop and rest, but after hardly any time, they reached the main road. It couldn't be much farther now. She turned westward to follow the road toward the mountains. It was still dark when the moon gleamed off the surface of the oxbow lake that gave the town its name. The owls swooped into the shadowy pine woods outside of Oxbow and resumed their own forms. Laki immediately and deliberately lay down. Jagryn stumbled a few steps and collapsed. Luskell tried to stay on her feet, but it was impossible. She sank to the ground as if she had no bones.

Luskell hadn't felt the exhaustion and hunger while she was an owl. As she flew, she couldn't wait to talk about her first experience of transformation. Now that she had a mouth again, she wanted only to eat and rest. And do something about her hair. Neatly braided before she became an owl, it now hung loose and wild. All her clothes were dry, though, so it seemed a fair trade. Still, no wonder Mamam cut her hair short.

When they could sit upright, she passed the bread around, and Jagryn shared some cheese. They each had a drink from Laki's water flask. Only then did anyone feel like speaking.

"That was amazing!" Jagryn said. "I flew!" He grinned and shook his head in disbelief. "I never dreamed I'd begin my sixteenth birthday as an owl."

"Is it today?" Luskell did a quick count of days. "It is! Happy birthday!" She leaned over and gave him a squeeze.

"A fine celebration for an apprentice wizard," Laki said. "Are you a man now?"

Jagryn shook his head. "Two more years. But I see now why you didn't want to fly all the way to the city. I'm exhausted."

"Mamam and Dadad talk about it, but it was hard to imagine," Luskell agreed. She dragged her fingers through her hair and did her best to braid it into some semblance of order.

"That's why I wouldn't teach you when you were already tired," Laki said. "We should sleep now. Then we can walk into town and find the coach office."

Luskell did not expect to sleep well on the ground, but she was so tired the pine needles felt like a featherbed. She pulled her cloak around her, closed her eyes, and dropped off almost immediately. She dreamed of several vague presences that surrounded her. They didn't feel threatening, so she guessed Ketwyn or Knot might be among them, though they didn't give her a message or even show themselves clearly. She didn't know what it meant but chose to believe they were there to protect her. She didn't have the energy for more warnings.

Chapter 34

Stell woke in the morning, rested and more content than she'd felt in years. She couldn't recall her dreams beyond a general sense of warmth and well-being. She hummed to herself as she washed and dressed, built up the fire, and started breakfast for herself, Luskell, Jelf, and Laki. There were no guests this morning, now that Bron had ridden back to Oxbow.

She rapped on Jelf's door. He was usually an early riser but sometimes needed extra encouragement. "Good morning, Uncle! Are you up?"

"Just about," he replied.

Luskell often required more effort. Stell climbed the stairs and knocked at the best room. "Luskell? It's morning, and there's lots to do." There was no response, and Stell frowned. The girl had seemed fully recovered from the ordeal at the fire, but perhaps she still felt the effects. Stell was about to knock again when the front door flew open. Sunnea entered with Sulika right behind her.

"Is Jagryn here?" Sunnea called.

Stell leaned on the gallery railing. "No, I haven't seen him since yesterday."

Sunnea frowned. "He wasn't in his room when I called him for breakfast. Crane says he didn't hear him go out, but he's such a sound sleeper I wasn't surprised."

Jelf emerged from his room. "Jagryn doesn't seem the type to cause trouble." He felt for a chair and sat at the end of one of the long tables.

Sunnea wrung her hands. "It's our own fault. We were too harsh when we learned he'd been doing magic on his own. Elic told him not to leave the house without one of us, but what if he's run away? And on his birthday, of all days?"

Sulika put her arm around her mother. "You only wanted to keep him safe. He's probably sulking somewhere."

"Elic thought Jagryn might try to persuade Myn to give him another book," Sunnea said. "He's over there now."

"Myn doesn't get up this early," Sulika objected. Her mother gave her a puzzled frown, and she blushed. "I mean, he doesn't go to work this early."

"Luskell might know if Jagryn had plans today." Stell knocked again, but there was still no reply. She opened the door. "Luskell, do you—?" Luskell was not there, and the bed had not been slept in. Stell hurried to Luskell's trunk, which sat open at the foot of her bed. It wasn't obvious that anything was gone, but on closer inspection, she realized at least two things were missing: Luskell's traveling cloak and her money bag.

A breeze ruffled Stell's hair. She gazed at the open window, then left Luskell's room and flung open the door to Laki's. It was also empty, with the window wide open. That meant something, but what? She descended to the common room and sat next to Jelf. Sunnea and Sulika sat across from her.

Stell swallowed. "Luskell and Laki are also gone."

As she spoke, Myn and Elic came in. Sulika looked up and quickly away. "So he's not here?" Elic asked. Sunnea shook her head. Sulika moved down a seat so he could sit between them. He put his arm around Sunnea's shoulders. "He wasn't at Myn's, or Mam and Pap's. And Jagree hadn't seen him, either."

Myn remained standing a moment, then took a seat at the end of the table, next to Sulika. "I heard you say Luskell and Laki are missing, too. Do you think they're all gone together?"

"I know they are." Stell wasn't sure how she knew, but a tingle in her stomach told her she was right. "They've—gone to Eukard City."

"What?" Elic leaped to his feet. "Then we can still catch them. They didn't take horses, and they won't get far on foot."

Stell waved him back into his seat. "I don't think they're on foot."

Elic frowned. "What do you mean? All the horses are accounted for."

"Was Jagryn's window open?"

Elic and Sunnea exchanged a glance. They both nodded.

"So was Luskell's. So was Laki's."

"Is that so strange?" Elic said. "Crane and Jagryn always leave their window open on warm nights."

"So do I, but it was cool last night," Stell said. "I closed my window, but they all opened theirs." In her mind, she saw an open window and the silhouette of a man, an eagle; an eagle, a man. She drew a deep breath. "I think they changed into birds and flew away. Laki knew how, and he must have taught the others. We're too late to catch them."

Sunnea, Elic and Jelf all started talking at once. Although Sulika was usually above sentimental nonsense, she began to cry. Perhaps she made an exception for her young brother. "Jagryn's just a little boy! He thinks he's a wizard, but he doesn't know anything!"

Myn squeezed her shoulder. "Give him some credit. He's a capable, sensible young man. He'll be all right."

Sulika turned and looked at him, something she had avoided till now. Then she threw herself into his arms and cried on his shoulder. That silenced the rest of the group, though Stell hid a smile. Sulika's behavior had been odd all summer, but today she was full of surprises.

Loud voices outside the door broke the silence. "Rakkyn? What a surprise to meet you here!"

Sulika started at the sound of Foli's voice. She removed herself from Myn's embrace, but he reached out and gripped her hand. She didn't pull away.

"Good morning, Foli," said Rakkyn's voice, also unnaturally loud. "I was just going in to get some breakfast."

"What a coincidence! I was, too," Foli replied.

Stell shook her head. Those two had been eating together almost every evening lately. She was glad to see Foli with a friend. He'd been alone at the mill since his mother passed away, which had probably motivated him to find a wife. But a man needed friends, too, and Foli had never had many. He was a little too—sharp. Rakkyn was younger and more outgoing, but the two had clearly hit it off. In fact, the previous night, they had left together, and she had heard their conversation continue as they walked toward the mill. She began to have suspicions about this "accidental" breakfast meeting.

Foli and Rakkyn came in laughing but lost their smiles when they saw the crowd gathered. "Join the group," Stell said. She got up and headed for the kitchen. "We were about to have breakfast. Elic's family missed theirs."

Foli gave her a sickly smile and took the seat across from Sulika, on Myn's other side. He stared at their clasped hands. Rakkyn grinned and sat next to Foli. He slapped Foli's back. "Ever have one of those days where you get what you deserve?" Foli scowled at him but did not reply.

Stell hid a smile and went to dish up breakfast. She hadn't planned to feed eight, but it looked like there would be enough. As conversation picked up again, Elic looked in. "Can I give you a hand?"

"Yes, thank you. Carry that tray, please."

He lowered his voice. "How do you know they're going to Eukard City?"

"Knot told me." She clapped a hand over her mouth. The words had burst out of her, but she knew it was true. The dream came rushing back: Knot's disturbing message as well as his warmth. It was hard to share his confidence now. She swallowed. "They think they have to save Crane. Mine, not yours."

Elic's eyes widened. "Crane's in trouble? What kind?"

She was startled but pleased he didn't question her sanity. "I'm not sure. Knot spoke of an imposter who plans to harm Crane and Ketty. He couldn't warn them, so he came to Luskell. Apparently she talked Laki and Jagryn into helping her." She leaned on a chair. "Knot has great confidence in them. I wish I could share it, but they're so young. They're no better than Knot at seeing consequences."

Elic nodded. "At least they're not alone. You really think they changed into birds?"

"The open windows seem to say so."

He smiled. "I know I should be angry, but that's amazing! *My* boy can do a thing like that. Maybe they'll be all right."

"We can only hope so."

They carried the breakfast out to the common room. Conversation had died again. In front of Sulika and

Foli, two betrothal rings lay on the table. Elic set down his tray and looked from one to the other. "Sulika, what is the meaning of this?"

Sulika and Foli stared at each other, tight-lipped and silent.

Rakkyn got up and helped distribute the bowls of porridge. "It appears the wedding is off. Who wants breakfast?"

Chapter 35

When Luskell opened her eyes, the sun was high in the sky. Jagryn was already on his feet, and Laki crouched nearby. Luskell was hungry again, but they had eaten all the food before they slept.

"We could buy some in town," Jagryn said. He counted out his eight duls to add to Luskell's twelve.

"We'd better make sure we have enough for the coach first," she said. "Come on."

The coach office was easy to find, right next to the road. The man behind the counter stared at the three of them—or rather, at Laki. Though no longer legendary, Aklaka were still rarely seen in a place like this. "Good morning. What can I do for you?"

"Three seats on the morning coach to Eukard City, please," Luskell said.

The man continued to stare at Laki. "That'll be thirty duls for inside, twenty-four if you ride on top."

She made a show of counting out the money, though she knew it wasn't enough. "... eighteen, nineteen, twenty. Is that all? I'll count it again..."

"You seem to be short," the man said.

"We're all under eighteen," she said. It was a lie, but Laki wasn't much over. "Could you maybe...?" Her question died away as he shook his head. "It's important that we get to Eukard City. I have to find my parents there." She started when Laki drew his knife. She had never seen him use violence.

He laid it on the counter. "This must be worth something."

Luskell gasped. "You can't, Laki. You made that!" It was his ceremonial knife, a beautiful thing of obsidian, antler, and gold. The gold nuggets alone were worth far more than they needed, but it seemed wrong to part with it.

"I did not put in any coins."

The official shook his head. "I can't take that. There's a junk dealer down the road where travelers sometimes sell off their goods. He might give you something for it." Laki nodded and picked up the knife. He turned to leave the coach office, but the man called him back. "The junk dealer isn't too friendly with your kind. You should wait here while one of your friends sees what they can get."

Laki gazed at Luskell and held out the knife. "Will you?"

She sighed. "Fine, give it to me." She took it by the hilt.

"It'd be better if the boy did it," the official advised.

Jagryn held out his hand. "Maybe he's right."

Luskell kept her grip on the knife. "No. This trip was my idea. We're saving my parents. I should do it."

Jagryn walked along with her, anyway. There was no mistaking the junk dealer's shop. It was a shack near the road, surrounded outside with wagon wheels and other parts, and filled inside with mismatched dishes, furniture, clothing—anything migrants might sell in order to complete their trip over the mountains.

The junk dealer was shorter than Jagryn and three times as wide. He had a bland, pleasant face. "Buyin' or sellin'?"

"Selling." Luskell laid the knife on the counter.

He barked a laugh. "You're a girl! How old are you?"

"Almost fifteen."

He nodded, then picked up the knife and turned it over in his hands. "I'll give you five duls for it."

"Five?" Jagryn said. "That's no good. We won't take less than ten. Look, that's real gold."

"Fine. Why don't you step outside so your sister and I can negotiate." The junk dealer came around to their side of the counter. He smiled, revealing a gap where his front teeth should have been.

Jagryn's mouth dropped open. "My—?" He shook himself. "Forget it. We'll take the five."

With his free hand, the man grabbed Luskell's wrist. She tried to jerk away but he had a strong grip. He waved Laki's knife back and forth. "I wasn't asking permission."

As soon as the junk dealer touched her, Luskell caught a glimpse of his thoughts. She wished she'd lied and told him she was twelve, though he probably wouldn't have believed her. He wanted to take her into a cramped back room furnished with castoffs and *negotiate*, as he'd done with others before her. She tried to mind-talk to Jagryn, but she didn't know what to say and couldn't concentrate. She remembered her father's concern about boys, Klamamam's warning about strange men. She'd assumed her power would protect her, but she wasn't prepared for a man holding a weapon. The way he was waving it, she doubted he had any skill with knives. Was that more dangerous or less?

And then it flew from his hand straight at Jagryn. Not thrown; summoned. Jagryn caught it by the blade. The only color in his face came from his freckles.

Taking her chance, Luskell stamped on the junk dealer's foot with her heavy boot. He yelled and released her arm. She hit him with the repelling charm. He stumbled back, tripped over a cradle, and cracked his head against a heavy table. He slid to the floor, stunned.

"Is he dead?" Jagrn asked, his voice shaky.

"No." Luskell wasn't inclined to touch the man, but watched his chest rise and fall.

"Do you want him to be?" Jagryn's voice steadied and took on a hard tone as he stepped forward.

Luskell held him back. "Let's just go."

He nodded and turned in silence to leave. She followed, her heart racing. About halfway back to the coach office, she tugged on his sleeve.

"Wait." She paused, still shaking and breathing hard.

"Are you hurt?" As he spoke, she saw Jagryn's man face, serious and responsible like his father or his uncle. Like a wizard. Then, just as suddenly, he was a boy again. He looked as shaken as she felt.

"I think I'm fine, but look at your hand."

Jagryn stared at the knife as if surprised to see it. He unclenched his fingers and shifted it to his other hand. Blood welled where the blade had sliced across three fingers. "It didn't even hurt."

"Sharp blade."

He frowned. "Now it does. It's like trying to be a tailor all over again. I fail at everything."

"I don't think so. This shows you have a wizard in you. You hurt yourself later than most, but you don't have to have a scar." Luskell called up some power and traced her finger across the cuts. This healing required less effort than she had used for her burn; maybe because she wasn't hurt herself. "How's that?"

"Perfect." Jagryn pulled her close and kissed her. It caught her by surprise but it was nice, and she trusted him. At the same time, she was glad Laki couldn't see. Jagryn released her abruptly. "I'm sorry, I shouldn't—I mean, we—" He pulled a handkerchief from his pocket and wiped the blood from his hand and the knife blade.

Two mounted men in tall hats rode toward them from the west: a patrol of highway guards. It was their job to keep travelers safe from bandits and help people in trouble, though they were spread thin on the Dry Side. Luskell waved for them to stop.

"What can we for you, young fellow?" the older of the two asked.

"The junk dealer's unconscious," Luskell said. This wasn't the time to fuss about her gender.

"He can sober up on his own," the younger one said.

"Not drunk. Knocked out."

That got the older guard's attention. "Do you know how it happened?"

"Yeah, he finally crossed the wrong girl," Jagryn supplied.

The younger guard looked puzzled. The older one nodded. "About time. We'll take care of him. You two stay safe."

Luskell and Jagryn hurried back to the coach office. Jagryn handed the knife to Laki without a word.

The man behind the counter watched with interest. "He wouldn't give you anything for it?"

Luskell shook her head. "We decided not to deal with him. Or rather, we dealt with him and now the guards are taking care of him."

"I hope they lock him up," Jagryn growled.

The official started, then nodded slowly. "But what about your problem? Don't you need to get to Eukard City?"

"I'll go back home," Jagryn offered. "You have enough for two seats."

"No, we all go." Luskell turned to the official. "How much to go to Misty Pass?"

"For all three? Fifteen duls."

"Fine, we'll go there for now." She counted out the money. "Is there time to get something to eat before the coach arrives?"

"If you hurry. The cook at the inn can pack it to take with you."

She gave the rest of the money to Jagryn. "Can you take care of it?"

He gave her an understanding smile and left the coach office. He jogged off in the direction the official had pointed. Luskell moved out to the porch and sank down on a bench to wait. She rested her head in her hands.

Laki sat beside her. "What's wrong?"

She sighed. "I thought this would be the easy part."

"Riding the coach to Eukard City? Yes, it sounded simple."

"I didn't know I'd be fighting off junk dealers, or—"

"You what?" Laki asked. She looked up at him. His eyes blazed.

Luskell smiled and squeezed his shoulder. "Relax, I knocked him out. I'm my mother's daughter, after all. But if it's this difficult just to get there, how can we hope to fight the New Yrae?"

"We could go back."

She frowned. "No. We have to do it. There isn't anyone else."

Just then, the coach arrived. Luskell was afraid Jagryn wouldn't be back in time, but he returned before the fresh team of horses was hitched up. He held a large basket and grinned as he returned a handful of coins to Luskell. "One duleen for all this!" He lifted the covering napkin to reveal bread, meat, cheese, and fruit.

The sight of food improved her outlook. "But what do you two plan to eat?" She grinned as he replaced the napkin. She returned to the counter. "I need to send a note to Deep River right away. How much?"

"Two duleens, but the rider just got back from there. He won't make the trip again for a week."

She pushed one silver and two copper coins—a total of five duleens—across the counter. "Bron knows me. Will that get it delivered today?"

He nodded. She took the pen and paper he offered and wrote:

> Klamamam,
> Laki, Jagryn, and I are on our way to Eukard City. Knot says Mamam and Dadad need help. I trust his word and hope you do, too. We are all fine, and we'll be back as soon as we can.
>
> -Luskell

Luskell re-read the note. It was absurd to try to sum up their mission in so few words, but any more detail would only worry the home folks. It would have to do. She left the letter addressed to Stell and climbed into the coach with Laki and Jagryn.

Chapter 36

The lunch basket was empty before they reached Sweetwater. By then, they were into forest country—familiar to Luskell and Laki, but all new to Jagryn. The view out the window delighted him, and it seemed he would never tire of it. His excitement took Luskell's mind off her worries about her parents, and more immediately, how they would get to Eukard City.

The coach reached Misty Pass late in the afternoon and stopped at the Fogbank. Luskell's grandfather owned the inn, but she hurried away before anyone could recognize her.

Jagryn looked back. "Why don't we go in? Your grandpa might give us supper."

"I'm not supposed to be here. He'd either keep me here or send me straight back to Deep River. If we're going to Eukard City, he can't know we're in town. Let's stay at our place."

She led them to the far end of town and a short way into the forest. The path ended in an empty clearing.

Jagryn glanced all around. "Um—I suppose it'll be a nice night, but we're not equipped to camp out."

"Very funny. There's a house here."

"Where?" Laki stared into the clearing. "No, wait, I think I see something."

A glittering scrim hung across the end of the path, nearly invisible in the afternoon light. It could have been dust motes; Luskell knew it wasn't, though she saw it now for the first time. "Dadad puts a concealment spell on it when we're away, to protect from intruders."

"Can you lift it?" Jagryn asked.

"I don't have to." Luskell walked into the clearing. She knew where to look and made out the shape of the house behind the sparkle of the spell. Anyone without power would see nothing at all. Inside the spell stood a small log house with a green door. Luskell lifted the latch and went in. "This is Mamam's house. We stay here when we're in Misty Pass."

The single room was crowded with two beds, a table and chairs, and an assortment of chests and boxes. When the family wasn't living here, they used the house to store extra clothes, travel gear, and a supply of preserved food. Luskell rummaged in a chest and came up with dried meat and vegetables. She smiled at the boys. "See? We won't go hungry. I'll make soup."

"Do you know how to cook?" Jagryn asked.

"I've been learning. Besides, how hard can soup be?"

There was plenty of firewood stacked by the hearth. Luskell let Jagryn make a fire while she fetched water from the well out back. Late sunlight slanted through the trees. The air was warm and rich with forest scents. It would have been peaceful but for the echo of Knot's voice in her mind: *They're the ones in danger. Do whatever it takes.* She could not stay here long.

She heated water and crumbled the dried meat into the pot, then added the vegetables. While the soup simmered, she searched the house for enough coins to get them the rest of the way to Eukard City. No luck. They couldn't go by coach, and it was too far to fly. There had to be another way.

"What good does it do us, getting this far if we can't go on?" Jagryn asked. They sat around the table, eating the soup. The broth was weak, and the vegetables were still crunchy, but it was edible. "Maybe you could ask your grandpa for the money." He chewed a bit of meat that hadn't softened enough.

"No," Luskell said. "I have another idea. I know someone here who hauls timber and freight. If he's home, and if he's going that way, he might give us a ride."

"That's a lot of *ifs* and *mights*," Jagryn said.

"I'll go right after we eat."

"*We'll* go," Laki corrected her.

They cleaned up after supper and went out. It was still light, though the shadows grew long. Luskell took them back into the village to a big shed with the sign *Gratt and Son Hauling* over the door.

"Gratt?" Jagryn said uneasily. "I've heard of him. Are you sure about this?"

"Gratt's all right," Luskell said. "But if you'd rather, you can wait here." She left them by the shed and approached the house. She knocked at the door.

A broad-shouldered man opened it. He had blue eyes and black hair sprinkled with gray. "Yes? Oh, Luskell! I thought you went to Deep River. I didn't know you were back."

"I'm not," she said. "I need your help."

She told him what she needed, though she refrained from revealing that she'd received her information in a dream. From a dead man. That might be too much for someone who didn't encounter magic on a daily basis.

Gratt nodded. "If you can be ready early, Grall and I are taking a load of lumber down to Grass Flats in the morning. You could walk from there to Eukard City, easy."

"We'll be ready."

"Who's 'we?'" He peered into the shadows.

Luskell beckoned the boys over. "These are my friends, Jagryn and Laki. We're traveling together."

Gratt frowned. "Jagryn? Are you Jagree's son? Jagree and—Brynnit's?"

Jagryn shook his head. "Their nephew."

Gratt nodded. "Elic's son, then. I suppose you know he banned me from Deep River."

"I've heard the story. It was the day I was born—sixteen years ago today."

"A long time. You can tell your father I'm a solid citizen now." He swallowed. "Tell Brynnit I'm sorry."

Luskell knew the story, too. Back then, Gratt had been a young man with everything to prove. He'd been infatuated with Auntie Brynnit, only a girl then, no older than Luskell was now. Drunk one night, Gratt thought he could win her by force. Somehow, Jagree knew about it and showed up in time to fend Gratt off. There were hints of magic, but Luskell didn't know the truth of that; it might have simply been love. After the fight, Jagree delivered the concussed Gratt home, and Mayor Elic banned him from Deep River. Gratt moved to Misty Pass soon after, where he eventually met Crane and Ketty. The story had him giving them and Knot a ride to Deep River on a sled. Luskell wasn't sure she believed that part, considering the ban, but maybe; she'd only known Gratt as he was now.

It was odd, but Gratt, the grown man, seemed eager for Jagryn's good opinion, though he was still a youth. Jagryn's jaw was tight, his gaze hard. She laid her hand on his arm. "It's true, Jagryn. He has a family here, as well as a business. He's well-liked in town. And my parents trust him."

Jagryn glanced at her. The hard look softened. He nodded.

"Do you want to come in?" Gratt asked. "Have you had supper? I'm sure Alli would like to see you."

Any other time, Luskell would have been happy to see Gratt's wife Alli, a plain-faced woman with a kind heart, a beautiful smile, and real talent with supper. But not now. "Thank you, but we've already eaten, and the fewer people know we're here, the better."

They made arrangements for Gratt to pick them up early the next morning and returned to the house in the forest for the night. Jagryn and Laki shared the big bed; neither would fit in the trundle bed leftover from Luskell's early childhood. Why it was still in the house was beyond her, but it wasn't hurting anything, tucked away under her parents' bed. Luskell slept in her own bed. She didn't dream of Knot or Ketwyn but of flying over Eukard City. As she flew, she called out, "Be careful, Mamam! I'm coming, Dadad! I'm coming!"

Chapter 37

Stell spent all day expecting to see Luskell whenever she turned around. It was hard to accept that her granddaughter had left Deep River, harder still to accept Knot's message. During the years they were separated, she had often dreamed of Knot and sometimes turned her dreams into stories. But she had never received a message from the dead.

It was absurd! Crane *couldn't* be in danger, and Luskell *couldn't* be on her way to Eukard City, not as a bird or any other way. Why assume Luskell and her friends had flown away? Because of an open window? Luskell and Laki were both skilled climbers. They could have climbed out their windows and down the stone wall, met up with Jagryn, and found a secret place nearby to practice their magic—no wings required.

Elic had organized a search party, but even if the young people weren't found, Stell assumed they would come back on their own by suppertime. They had taken little or no food with them—half a loaf at most. Not enough for a journey.

But evening arrived without their return, or any promising report from the searchers. News had spread by this time, and every guest had a word of encouragement or advice. Stell didn't say so aloud, but the most helpful thing would have been for them to stay home. Instead the inn was busier than usual, and her helpers had all disappeared. It was too much.

Then Sulika walked into the kitchen and tied on an apron. "Don't worry, Auntie Stell. We'll help you."

"We?"

Myn, Foli, and Rakkyn followed Sulika in. Stell was too glad of the help to question their motives. Sulika had often helped serve in the past, and took it upon herself to show Myn and Foli what was required. They eyed each other with suspicion but listened quietly and did as they were told.

Rakkyn didn't need any training. Although he had never worked for Stell before, he was a natural host, greeting guests and conversing as he filled mugs and cleared plates. He smiled and laughed the whole time.

"I can't tell you how much it means to have you help tonight," Stell told him when he came into the kitchen for clean mugs. "I'm getting too old to run this place all on my own anymore."

"Aw, I wouldn't call you old." Rakkyn grinned. "But if you ever want to retire, let me know. I'd love to run a place like this."

"You would? What about your father's farm?"

He waved a dismissive hand. "I'm no farmer! Bramynna can have it. I'd rather live in town with—*like* Foli."

Stell pretended she hadn't heard the slip. She smiled and nodded. "So you want to be an innkeeper. I'll keep that in mind. I sometimes wonder what I'll do when this place gets to be too much for me. I can't expect Crane to come back and take it over. Do you cook?"

Rakkyn laughed. "Better than Bramynna." He glanced out the front window at the sound of hoofbeats. "Huh. What's he doing back?"

Stell looked out as Bron dismounted in front of the inn, and Jagree led his black horse to the stable. Stell had not expected to receive another mail delivery for at least a week. She met him at the door. "Come in and have a seat. Would no one give you supper in Oxbow?"

He laughed. "It does seem as though I just left, but somebody paid extra to have this delivered today." He handed over a letter. Her heart beat faster when she recognized Luskell's writing. "And this one came in from Eukard City this morning, so I brought it along." He gave her a second letter, addressed in Crane's writing to Luskell.

She fought to keep her voice calm. "You came all this way to bring two letters? Thank you."

He winked. "The supper will be worth it."

Stell hurried to the kitchen. Although it was a busy time, she couldn't bear to leave the letters until later. She unfolded the one from Luskell. It told her nothing, except to confirm Knot's report that they were on their way to Eukard City. She shivered. That much, she had dreamed true. Did that mean Crane really was in danger?

She opened the second letter, though it was addressed to Luskell.

Dear Luskell,

Dokral sold us a wonderful fiddle for you. I hope you will like it. I think he built it with you in mind. We may be here some time yet. We had our first meeting with the governor, but there are some sticky issues to resolve, and the next meeting has been delayed. At least the heat wave has ended, and we can sleep. We keep busy by helping at Balsam's House. Ellys and Ambug send their greetings.

-Love, Dadad and Mamam

Stell crumpled the letter in frustration, then smoothed it and put it in her apron pocket. Crane's letter told her even less than Luskell's. There was no hint of danger or difficulty. It seemed Luskell and her friends had made their trip for nothing.

Which would be better than looking for trouble, she reminded herself. *I only wish they hadn't gone at all.*

But Knot had said Crane was unaware of the danger. He was right about Luskell's destination. Much as she hated to, she was inclined to take his word for this, too. She sat at the table and rested her head in her hands.

"Auntie Stell? What's wrong?" Sulika set a stack of dirty plates in the dishpan. "Bad news?"

Stell showed her Luskell's letter. "I'm not sure. Luskell and the boys really are on their way to the city. If they were at the coach office this morning, they could be beyond Misty Pass by now."

Sulika squeezed Stell's shoulders. "It's good to know where they are. I'm sure there's nothing to worry about. They'll be safe once they reach Crane and Ketty."

Stell wasn't so sure, but she smiled and patted Sulika's hand. "How are you getting along? You and Foli caused some drama this morning. I was surprised he offered to work with you tonight."

"We called a truce while you need help, but I'm not sure he's sorry to break with me."

"And are you sorry?"

She frowned. "I don't know. It's hard to change all my plans, but—"

"You could still have a wedding."

Sulika reddened and hid a smile with her hand. "Maybe. What do you think I should do?"

Stell held up her hands. "I'm not sure I'm qualified to offer advice on marriage. I was a wife for all of five months, after seeing my man in secret for twenty-five years."

Sulika glanced out the door, then leaned close. "I've been seeing Myn in secret," she whispered.

"I wondered, when I saw you together this morning," Stell replied. "How long has that been going on?"

"A few days."

"Do you love him?"

"I don't know. I think so. Maybe. *He* loves *me*. He wrote me a poem."

"And Foli?"

Sulika shook her head. "Foli's no poet."

"You know that's not what I meant."

Sulika dropped into a chair and rested her hands on the tabletop, gazing at them as she spoke. "Foli—won me. I don't think he ever loved me. But we promised. Shouldn't that mean something?"

Stell tipped her head to one side and studied Sulika. "A promise is important, but it should be made and kept with honesty, not secrets. Now that the secrets are out, you have a chance to be honest and make a clean break. Isn't that better than keeping a mistaken promise and hurting each other later on?"

Sulika blinked rapidly and wiped her eyes. "I never loved Foli, but I liked him. I still do. I don't want him to be lonely."

Stell smiled. "I don't think he will be. There are many reasons to marry, but in my opinion, the best one is love. But don't rush into anything while you're confused."

"I won't. All plans are off until Jagryn is home safe."

"That's wise," Stell said. "Anyway, I thank all four of you for your help. I was just telling Rakkyn, I can't do it all myself anymore. What do you think he said?"

"That he wants to be an innkeeper?"

Stell stared. "How did you know?"

Sulika chuckled. "Rakkyn is my oldest friend. He's said that since he was six or seven. Make him your business partner, and you'll never want for laughs."

"We could both use a laugh tonight."

Stell remembered that later in the evening, when she sat in her rocker to tell tales. Her heart wasn't in it, and she was tempted to invite Rakkyn to entertain. But jokes didn't seem any more appropriate tonight than musty old stories. She sighed and looked around the gathering. Bron had returned to Oxbow after the meal. It was all local people tonight. These were her friends, her family. They were a comfort, not a burden.

"New stories are being written tonight," she began. "Lovers are finding each other, or losing each other." Shadows made it hard to see, but she thought Rakkyn rested an arm on Foli's back. Myn and Sulika sat near each other, not touching. "Some of our young people may be facing danger. My own kin may be in peril. On such a night, it's hard to have much interest in tales that are all told and finished. But it seems a story I thought had ended isn't quite finished, after all. So if you don't mind, I'll go on with that one."

Her listeners glanced at each other, some puzzled, others in anticipation of hearing something new. Sulika gave Myn a shy smile. His hand crept nearer hers.

"Most of you have heard the earlier parts of the true story of Yrae—how he placed Deep River under a spell, how Crane sought him, how I gave him a new name. I called him Knot in an attempt to bind him to me. It wasn't enough. The very next day, Knot and Crane both left me again. I am always saying goodbye!" She paused as her throat tightened. She hadn't expected to be so moved by her own story. "But Knot wasn't lost to me. He visited as often as he could, and when he couldn't come in person, he sent me sweet dreams. I wished we could meet openly, but he wasn't ready for that. What if someone discovered he was Yrae? He regretted what he'd done to Deep River, but there was no undoing it. Those eighteen years were gone. So for seven years, I settled for secret meetings and the promise of 'someday.'"

Stell chuckled to herself. "That may have been for the best. It gave me time to learn that he would be a difficult man to live with. His way was always to act without a thought of consequences, then regret it later. But he was an astute judge of character."

"That's obvious," Elic said. "He chose you, didn't he?"

She smiled at him. "And he trusted you with our secret." She turned to the rest of the group. "Knot chose to reveal himself to Elic early on, even his old identity as Yrae. And the secret was safe until there was no need for it anymore." She thought for a moment. "Knot's last secret visit was sixteen years ago today, the night Jagryn was born."

Elic gave her a tight smile and squeezed Sunnea's shoulders. They both looked exhausted. At least he wouldn't have to continue the search come morning, now that they knew where Jagryn and the others were.

"Before Knot left the next morning, he told me he would come back to stay. I waited, but I didn't see him or hear from him for three months, and I thought I had lost him for good. It seems he was in the worst danger of his life, turned to stone at the brink of a cliff. He was calling for help in the only way available to him, in broken, mysterious dreams. Some came to me, some to Crane, some to Ketty. Brynnit had one, and even our friend Laki, who was only three years old. I couldn't help Knot, but I knew who could: our son. I didn't know where Crane was, so I asked Ketty to find him. The two of them rescued Knot and brought him back to me again, this time to stay. We were married, after twenty-five years of sneaking around. I got to see Knot every day for the rest of his life—too short a time, but he died to save another. This was really the end—the secret meetings, the dreams, our life together—all over, nothing but memories. Nothing but story."

Stell smiled to herself as she looked at her audience. Myn's hand lay over Sulika's, and she rested her head on his shoulder. Foli and Rakkyn were gone, but everyone else had stayed. Most of them looked puzzled or dissatisfied. It wasn't much of an ending to a story— where was the drama, the triumph, the surprise?

She took a deep breath and sat up straighter. "Or so I thought. Last night, I met Knot again." Somebody gasped. The sleepier listeners shook themselves to alertness. "He came to me in a dream and told me things I couldn't know. It seems I never lost him, though I couldn't see him. That story won't end until mine does. Perhaps not even then."

Stell paused to wipe away a tear and blow her nose. She laughed a little. "I apologize for telling such a quiet tale, but I've shared it for a reason. We can't know how things will end, but even now Knot watches over Luskell and her friends. He can't help them, but he believes in them, as he believed in Crane, in Ketty, in Elic...in me. I have no choice but to believe with him."

Chapter 38

The New Yrae was not sorry when his employer directed him to end Eukard City's heat wave. It had been an effective distraction, but less so as people acclimated to it. The heat also increased the effort required for shielding and concealment at a time when the New Yrae had to call upon those powers almost constantly. Sheer exhaustion helped him sleep, though his sleep was troubled by dreams. He couldn't remember them when he woke. All that remained was a sense of disapproval.

His carefully planned "random" attacks hadn't succeeded as well as he'd hoped either. They had shocked and frightened the populace, but the wizard

Crane and his healer friends had worked out the countercurse with ridiculous ease. They refused to be drawn off into a pointless search for an invisible attacker. The New Yrae couldn't help a grudging admiration for such clear-headedness and skill, but his employer's plan depended on the Aklaka coming under Eukardian control. Based on Crane's advice, their diplomatic party had flatly refused the governor's proposal.

If only they didn't have such a fluent translator! An imperfect understanding of the demand might have led to agreement. By the time they knew what was being asked of them, it would be too late. But now they had a clear understanding.

The most expedient solution was to get rid of the translator. With Crane out of the picture, the Aklaka would be adrift. Diplomacy would, of necessity, be at an end. The Aklaka people would be brought under Eukardian control for their own protection—by force, if necessary.

And then the next stage of the plan could begin. But first, the New Yrae had a new role to play.

A knock sounded as Crane finished his morning cup of byttyr. Ketty didn't care for the drink and had already gone to dress for the day, but Crane liked to linger. Their only plan today was a walk in the countryside. Now that it wasn't too hot, they might get as far as Grass Flats, a small farm village to the east of the city. He hoped the caller wasn't on some official business that would conflict with this simple pleasure. He answered the door.

A page in the governor's livery inclined his head. "Good morning, sir. Governor Snowabi invites you to dine with him this evening." He held out a letter.

Crane took the letter and scanned it. "On the rooftop terrace? I don't think I've ever been up there."

"It is a beautiful spot, and tonight promises to be a fine evening. What shall I tell the governor?"

"Tell him thank you. We accept. Shall I convey the invitation to the Aklaka ambassador?"

"That—won't be necessary. The ambassador's invitation was issued separately."

Crane puzzled over this. Naliskat usually insisted that Crane translate. But he understood and spoke enough Eukardian to accept or reject an invitation to supper. Perhaps this page had less trouble with Naliskat's accent than did the governor. He smiled at the page. "You're—Trenn, am I right? Excuse me for asking, but I heard you were related to the governor. Is that true?"

"Yes, he is my uncle. But don't believe the rumors. Low as it is, I've had to earn my post."

"You do it well. I'm sure we'll see you tonight."

"Perhaps." With another slight bow, Trenn turned and departed.

Crane closed the door and went to find Ketty. "The governor has invited us to supper at the mansion."

She frowned. "What do you suppose he's after?"

Crane chuckled at her suspicion. "Why does he have to be *after* anything? Besides, this might give us a chance to read him more clearly."

"Maybe, but I don't trust politicians."

"I didn't actively read the messenger, but he wasn't giving off any sense of an ulterior motive."

"What was he giving off?"

"Nothing but polished manners. These political types are very controlled."

"I'll say! I don't think they feel anything." She sat down and pulled on her good walking boots. "This won't interfere with our walk, will it?"

He smiled. "No reason it should—we've got all day. If we leave now, we can have lunch in Grass Flats."

She looked happier about that. He picked up his staff and took her hand. They walked out into a beautiful summer's day.

Luskell lay on her back on top of the load of lumber. It rose high above the wagon box, and she and her friends rode on top. It was well tied down but swayed with the motion of the horses. Jagryn sat at the front with his feet on the back of Gratt's seat while Laki sat cross-legged farther back. Luskell felt safer lying down.

She shielded her eyes with her arm and let the sun's warmth soak into her. Gratt had picked them up at first light. Mountain mornings were cold, even in summer. Thankful for her cloak, she had huddled with Jagryn and Laki in the empty wagon and longed for a hot breakfast—something more satisfying than cold travel rations. Gratt had stopped a short way outside Misty Pass and picked up the lumber at a sawmill, and now they were on their way down to Grass Flats.

The warmth and motion lulled Luskell into a half doze. As she lay there, she became aware of the feelings of everyone around her, like a cloud surrounding the wagon. She had inherited a touch of her mother's empathy, which pleased her more than she would have predicted. With not much effort, she found she could connect the emotions with the people. Gratt: content, pleased with the weather and the trip. Grall: happy to go along on a longer delivery than usual, a real partner in the business. Jagryn: a little apprehensive, excited over the journey, guilty over feeling excited when people were in danger. And intertwined with all of these was a strong current of affection.

She tried to read his thoughts as she had done accidentally with the junk dealer. At first, she thought she had failed—the thought of the junk dealer brought back a memory of the road in front of his shop. But this was not her memory. Jagryn was remembering holding her, kissing her...

She quickly withdrew from his mind and turned her attention to Laki. He was much calmer than Jagryn. There was an undercurrent of worry, but it was controlled. He was Listening. She didn't overhear a message from the trees or earth, but he didn't seem distressed by anything he'd learned. After a while, Listening turned to daydreaming. He flew over the forest, high in the mountains, to a remote, windswept cliff—the place where Aku's keepers calmed the volcano's anger. Now Luskell saw herself in the daydream. She and Laki stood together, dressed in some kind of Aklaka ceremonial regalia.

"Stop that." Laki spoke softly, in Aklaka.

Luskell sat up. "S-stop what?"

He smiled. "It isn't polite to spy on a man's private thoughts."

She stared at him, then smiled sheepishly. "I'm sorry. I just discovered I could do it. I didn't mean to pry." An awful thought hit her. "Can you do it, too? Read my thoughts?"

He shook his head. "I could feel you lurking in my mind, that's all. But I've never tried. There are so many other things to Listen to that are less complicated."

They both laughed, and Jagryn turned around. "Are you two telling secrets back there?"

"No," Laki said in Eukardian. "But you should learn to guard your thoughts before Luskell reads them."

Jagryn grinned. "I don't think I have any secrets from her anymore." He moved back to sit with them. "Crane reads thoughts, doesn't he?"

"Yes, that's how he knows when someone is using magic, or has the ability. He can't see it the way Laki and Mamam do, and neither can I."

"So you're your father's daughter?" Jagryn said.

"I guess I'm like both of them, because I also detect feelings. I think Mamam's more sensitive than I am. She described it as an assault that she had to protect herself from. Dadad says he had to keep his feelings in check for a long time."

Laki wore a thoughtful look. "How does this New Yrae hide himself from such people?"

Luskell sighed. "I don't know." She had forgotten her worries and been happy for a short time, but now he had reminded her of the reason for their journey. "Maybe they haven't come near him. But if he intends to actually harm them, he'll have to be close."

Before they could solve this puzzle, Gratt pulled the wagon off the road, and the five of them shared the generous lunch Alli had packed.

"We should reach Grass Flats late this afternoon," Gratt said. "Grall and I plan to spend the night there and return to Misty Pass in the morning. You might want to stay there tonight, too, and go into Eukard City tomorrow."

Luskell shook her head. "It's light late. We'll have plenty of time."

"Do you know where your parents are staying?" Jagryn asked.

"Embassy House, in the same apartment we had last time. I hope to have supper with them tonight, but if it gets too late, we can find something on the way. We have a few coins left." The three duls left in her moneybag seemed like hardly anything; everything was more expensive in the city. But it should be enough for a meal.

They packed up the lunch basket and resumed their journey. For a long time, the road wound down from the mountains. At last, they came around a final curve. From there, the road ran almost straight through farmland to the city. Jagryn stared ahead at a blurry, gray smudge on the horizon. "Is that it? Is that Eukard City?"

Luskell laughed at his excitement. "Yes. It doesn't look like much from here, does it?"

They continued down to the fertile river bottom and the village of Grass Flats. The land rose again on the other side of the village, so by the time they arrived there, the city was no longer visible. But it was close enough to reach by nightfall.

Chapter 39

Ketty and Crane walked a trail in the hills above the city. A few fluffy clouds floated in the bright blue sky. The day was warm but not hot, the air scented with flowers and moist earth. She sighed happily, glad to be outside the city. It had felt wrong all summer, oppressive in a way that reminded her of—something. The precise memory eluded her. More pleasant feelings chased this vague apprehension away.

The trail headed down the other side of the ridge to the village of Grass Flats. They bought lunch at the inn there and carried it to a peaceful spot beside a stream.

"I've been thinking about Luskell today," Ketty said.

"Me, too," Crane replied. "I'll be glad when we're finished here. I didn't know I'd miss her this much."

"Maybe we shouldn't have left her in Deep River." Ketty frowned. "It's strange, though. I almost feel like she *is* with us. I kept expecting her to pass me on the trail."

Crane laughed. "Wasn't that a great day, when her legs grew longer than yours? No more complaints that we walked too fast!"

Ketty chuckled in agreement. "Soon I'll be the one asking you two to slow down."

"You're always welcome to borrow my staff." He held it out.

She waved it away with a smile. She didn't need anything to lean on for such a gentle hike. "I wish we could stay here all day. Or even camp out!"

"We don't have to hurry back, but you know we can't stay all night. Besides, I thought you hated camping out."

"I don't like it in winter. It's all right in summer, with you."

They stayed out as long as they could, but late in the afternoon, they finally headed back. They had misjudged the time and returned to Embassy House later than expected. They met Naliskat and Pataknan on the front steps.

"Shall we wait for you?" Liski asked.

"No, go ahead. We'll see you there," Crane replied.

Ketty and Crane hurried inside to change their clothes for supper with the governor. She had laid out her best dress before they left, a gown of pale blue silk with a delicate lace jacket. She'd worn a dark blue velvet wrap to last winter's Governor's Ball, but this was the first time she'd worn the summer jacket. The fine dress was an extravagant luxury beyond anything she would usually buy, but Luskell's green dress had persuaded Ketty she needed something equally nice. Occasions such as this supper with the Governor called for it; if she wore it rarely, that meant it would last longer. As a final touch, an illusion made her short hair look like an elegant knot, with fetching curls around her face.

"Maybe we should stay in," Crane said when he saw her.

She smiled. They both liked how the cut of this dress flattered her figure. "Later."

As they headed for the door, Crane glanced at his staff. "I've had this in my hand all day, but I don't suppose I'll need it at supper."

Ketty had almost forgotten the strange, oppressive feeling, but now it returned. "No, bring it."

He peered at her. "Is something wrong?"

She shook her head. "Bring it. I'll feel better."

"Goodbye, Gratt. Goodbye, Grall," Luskell said. "Thank you for the ride."

"You're welcome, but I still think you should stay here tonight and go on in the morning," Gratt said.

She laughed. "It's still early. We have lots of time."

She and her friends waved goodbye and made their way to the footpath that cut across the hillside west of the village. The gentle slope was an easy climb, especially now that the heat of the day had passed. It had been a few years since Luskell had walked this path, but she remembered it connected to a trail that ran along the top of the ridge. When they reached it, she called a rest and let the boys have their first clear view of Eukard City. It lay spread out below them, ablaze in late sunlight.

Jagryn shaded his eyes and stared. "It's even bigger than I thought! How do you find anything?"

"You learn your way around," Luskell said. "Dadad knew it well by the time I came along, so I had a good guide. Now I'll guide you."

Many paths and roads ran from the trail down into the city proper. She chose one that led to the Garden District, a familiar neighborhood. The low sun shone between buildings and cast long shadows over the roadway.

Jagryn looked with wide eyes at the closely-packed buildings and crowds of people, and he wrinkled his nose. She felt his unease without trying. "It stinks!" he said.

"No, it doesn't." Luskell breathed the combined odors of cooking, garbage, and many people. She hadn't smelled it in a long time. "Well, maybe it does, a little. You'll get used to it."

"Are you sure we're safe here?" he asked.

"As long as we stay together and try not to look like visitors from the country. Now come on, we still have a long way to go."

"You mean there's more?"

Laki hadn't been to the city before, either, but he managed to conceal his awe. He was more likely to draw stares himself, but no one bothered them. He tried Listening. "Odd. I can't hear anything. Too many people, perhaps, or not enough trees."

Luskell thought about taking them to Braffin's Garden. It wasn't far, and there were plenty of trees there. She was inclined to stop at the Osprey for some supper. It had been a long time since lunch. But now that they were here, she was eager to know her parents were safe.

They reached Embassy House before sunset. Luskell hurried to the apartment they had occupied in the past. She tried the door, but it was locked. When she knocked, no one answered. Jagryn looked worried. "It doesn't mean anything," she assured him, though she fought down rising panic. "Laki, let's see if your father is home."

He rapped on the door across the hall. After a moment, Pataknan opened it. He gaped a moment, then shouted and threw his arms around Laki. "Liski, look who's here!" he called in Aklaka. "Your son is here, and Luskell, and . . .?" He cocked his head at Jagryn.

"Takni, this is our friend Jagryn, from Deep River," Luskell said. "May we come in?"

"Yes, of course. Crane never said you were coming."

They went into the apartment and closed the door as Naliskat emerged from another room. He stared, then grinned and bounded across the room. "Laki, you rascal! Does your mother know you're here?"

"No," Laki replied. "I let Chamokat know I went to Deep River, but not that I came to the city."

Naliskat nodded. "A little adventure never hurt a boy, but what are you doing here?"

"We're looking for my parents," Luskell said. "They aren't home. Do you know where they are?"

"No, I don't. They were out all day. Takni and I went out before supper and met them as they returned. Crane said he'd see us 'there.' I'm not sure what he meant, but they'd gone out again by the time we got back." Naliskat frowned. "They didn't send for you?"

Luskell shook her head. "They're in danger and don't know it."

Naliskat looked skeptical. "That seems—unlikely. Think who you're talking about!"

"It's true," she insisted. "And we came to rescue them."

"I hope we're not late," Ketty said. They had reached the Governor's Mansion.

Crane glanced at her. That dress of hers still left him breathless. "If we are, Snowabi will look at you and forgive anything."

He showed their invitation to the guard at the door who directed them to an outside staircase. Another guard stood aside and gestured for them to go up. The sun cast long shadows ahead of them as they climbed.

They reached the terrace. A table had been set with the finest dishes and utensils, but no food had been put out yet, and no servants or other guests were in evidence. "You see, Ketty? We're not late at all. I think we may be early." Crane walked to the low parapet and shaded his eyes to gaze at the view. A few stripes of cloud lay along the horizon. The sunset would be spectacular. It was an ideal evening for a rooftop supper.

"Maybe we are," Ketty said. "But where are Liski and Takni? They were on their way before we even changed clothes."

"I don't know. It isn't like them to get lost, but they hadn't been here on their own before."

"I don't like it. It feels like a—"

"Like a what?" There was a thud, and Crane turned from the view. Ketty lay on her back, a look of terror on her face. Her mouth worked, but no sound came out. Blood gushed from a slash across her chest. Crane hurried toward her. How had it happened? She was impossible to sneak up on.

Before he could reach her, a powerful force ripped the staff from his hand and drove him backward, right to the parapet. It meant to fling him over. He tried to change into something with wings, but he didn't have the required focus. Someone was trying to kill him. Ketty might already be dead. And there was nothing he could do about it.

Chapter 40

"Have you eaten?" Naliskat asked. Luskell and her friends followed him to the dining room and sat at the table. "There's plenty—we thought Crane and Aketnan would join us."

Luskell took a plate and ate a few bites, though worry had stolen her appetite. She only half-listened as the three Aklaka conversed in their own language. None of them seemed worried about her parents. Laki told them about his time in Deep River, and Naliskat praised him again for taking charge of his own life.

Luskell didn't feel like translating the whole conversation for Jagryn. "It's nothing you don't already know," she assured him, but she was vexed at their lack of urgency. When she could bear it no longer, she interrupted in Eukardian. "It feels like a trap."

Laki and the other Aklaka stared at her.

"What does?" Jagryn asked.

"Wherever Mamam and Dadad went. He said he would see Naliskat 'there,' as if they were expected somewhere together."

"He probably planned to meet us here later but was delayed," Pataknan said in Aklaka. "There's no reason to believe they're in trouble."

Luskell kicked the table leg in frustration. Dishes rattled, and Naliskat's drink splashed onto the table. "But what if it was a trick to get them by themselves?"

Naliskat frowned as he steadied his mug. "Who would do such a thing?" He had switched to Eukardian now, too.

"The New Yrae. According to Knot, he's working with the Governor."

Naliskat's eyes widened. "According to Knot? Since when do you receive messages from the dead?"

Luskell shook her head and closed her eyes. "You have no idea. Knot says they believe that, with Mamam and Dadad out of the way, you will not be able to communicate, and the governor can do whatever he wants with the Aklaka."

Naliskat nodded. "Your father thinks Snowabi wants to be a king."

"Knot thinks so, too. I don't care about that. If my parents are in danger, I have to find them."

"*We* have to," Laki corrected her. "But how?"

She considered the problem. They had no idea where her parents had gone, and the city was a big place. It was still light now, but the sun would set soon, making the search even more difficult. And with the New Yrae shielding himself—

"I've got it!" she cried. "Laki, you had trouble Listening, didn't you?" He nodded and translated for Pataknan, whose eyes widened in recognition. "I think the New Yrae is interfering somehow. So if you Listen for the spot where there is the *least* to hear, maybe you'll find him. I can try the same with thoughts and feelings."

Jagryn nodded. "Search for the blank spot. But it's still an awfully big city."

"We'll start with the government and diplomatic buildings, then work outward if we have to," she said. "I doubt they've gone far. They were on foot, and if it was an official invitation—"

"So, owls again?" Jagryn asked

"The search will go faster if we fly," Laki agreed.

The three of them stood and headed for the door. Naliskat grabbed Laki's arm. "Wait. You've done enough. Let me handle it from here."

Laki patted his father's hand. "It will take too long. I'll send word to Takni when we find something."

The young people hurried outside before anyone could prevent them. The sun rested on the horizon now, turning Eukard Sound to fire. Luskell pictured the biggest, fiercest bird she had ever seen and changed into a golden eagle. Jagryn was an owl again, and Laki became a falcon.

They circled the neighborhood, feeling for absence. It was harder than it sounded, like seeking the one silent person in a noisy crowd. Every house and shop seemed to be full of people spewing thoughts and emotions. Not one was shielded, as far as Luskell could tell. She hoped she would see her parents returning so they could call off the search. What was she even doing here? She was still discovering her power and knew nothing of rescue or fighting. It wasn't fair.

You should have thought of that before you left Deep River, she told herself. No, it wasn't fair, but she had listened to Knot and made her own choice. She would have to see it through.

She widened the circle and swooped low past the Governor's Mansion. It, too, was awash with thoughts and feelings. Luskell thought she picked up a spurt of fear, but it was gone before she could place it. For all she knew, it was a kitchen girl who had broken a plate. She flew on to the Legislative Council Hall, which seemed more promising—a large blank. She perched on the roof, and the other two joined her. She hoped this was the place. She was running out of ideas, and if they stayed in bird form much longer, they would pay for it later.

She reached with her mind into the building. She was aware of Laki and Jagryn near her. They were uneasy, puzzled, afraid. But there was nothing else—no thoughts, no emotions, no life. She ruffled her feathers in disgust. The Council Hall wasn't shielded; it was empty. Everyone had gone home already.

This wasn't working, but it was the only idea she had. And it *should* work. Luskell calmed herself and reached out once more, trying to sense emptiness. This time, she not only felt it but saw something, too.

She had flown too low to notice before, but there was activity on the roof of the Governor's Mansion, and her eagle eyes saw it clearly. A tall figure struggled against an invisible force that pushed him backward. Only a low parapet kept him from falling to the courtyard below. Suddenly another figure appeared as if from nowhere, and the struggling man flew onto the parapet. By some miracle, he didn't fall. She couldn't imagine anyone but her father maintaining balance up there. Without another thought, she launched herself into the air.

Crane pressed his hands against the parapet to keep from falling over the edge. He searched the terrace for his attacker and finally detected the telltale sparkle of a concealment charm. To a person with no power, even that would be invisible, but Crane could see the spell itself and a distorted image behind it. Then his assailant moved and became visible. Maintaining concealment while moving was a challenge even for Crane, but this villain didn't need it anymore. Crane couldn't fight back; it was all he could do to hold his ground. He recognized the man but didn't believe his own eyes.

How had this assassin managed to get so close without either of them noticing? The pressure relented for a moment, and he had a flash of hope. Then it surged stronger and lifted him onto the parapet. He fought for balance, but it would all be over soon. *Goodbye, Ketty. Goodbye, Luskell. Forgive me.*

Loud wingbeats drummed past Crane's ear. The biggest eagle he had ever seen soared over the wall. With a high-pitched cry, it flared its wings and raked its talons into the face of his attacker. The great bird clung to the man, clawing and flapping as he he tried to protect his eyes. Blood spattered out in the breeze of those mighty wings. The force that had been driving Crane backward abruptly ceased. He fell onto his hands and knees. The impact stung, but he stayed down only long enough to catch his breath. He scooped up his staff and leaped to his feet.

The eagle had disappeared, but a falcon and an owl flew onto the terrace and became boys who looked like Laki and Jagryn. Crane rubbed his eyes and looked again. They cast repelling charms at his attacker until the man crashed into the table. Dishes flew off and shattered. The New Yrae struggled to his feet to continue the fight. Crane performed a quick binding spell, then took a deep breath, pointed his staff, and cast another, more powerful spell. His enemy slumped unconscious across the table, drained of power and vitality.

Crane felt only a moment of triumph. He turned in grief to where Ketty lay. Could she have survived? Another boy knelt by her. Crane blinked. Or not a boy. He knew those springy brown curls.

Chapter 41

Ketty climbed a grassy hillside. It was bright and warm, though she couldn't find the sun in the sky. The place seemed vaguely familiar, like something she'd seen in a dream. But this wasn't a dream. She was here for real.

Without warning, a group of three people blocked her way. She thought she recognized two—a tall, red-haired boy and a young woman with dark chestnut hair—and knew the third for certain. He was Knot. Ketty couldn't remember why she had thought she would never see him again.

"Where have you been? I'm so glad to see you!" She hugged him close. He was warm but not quite solid.

"Ketty," he murmured. "I've missed you, too, but you can't stay here."

"Please? I just got here."

"It isn't time yet."

She released him and glanced at the other two. "Who—?" She shivered. The boy had bright blue eyes and no freckles. "Ketwyn?"

He smiled his father's smile. "Look, Mama, you're older than Grandma Lukett now."

The young woman stepped forward and opened her arms. Ketty stared. Of course she looked familiar; it was her own mother, as she'd looked before the illness that took her life. She was so young. Ketty stepped into her embrace, and Ketwyn hugged both of them.

"There's no more time," Knot said. "You must go back."

Ketty frowned. "Back?" She looked over the way she had come. Impossibly far away but perfectly clear to see was the rooftop terrace of the Governor's Mansion in Eukard City. Her own body lay bleeding. She turned to her mother. She didn't want to lose her again.

Lukett smiled gently. "Go. Luskell needs you. Crane needs you."

Luskell? Crane! Everything rushed back, right up to the moment she was attacked. "I have to go! They need me!"

Crane hurried to where Ketty lay. The wild-haired youth crouched over her. "Luskell? Is that you?"

She turned to him, her face wet with tears. "Something's wrong with the wound, Dadad. Why can't I stop the bleeding?"

He kissed and hugged her as best he could with her hands pressed to the wound. "Are you a healer now?"

"I'm—everything now, but I have a lot to learn."

There was a story there, but it would have to wait. "The wound is cursed, but I know the counter to it." He laid his hands on top of hers and spoke the words he and Balsam had discovered. The bleeding stopped. The wound closed.

Ketty lay without moving, her freckles more prominent than usual on her pallid face. The illusion of an elegant hairstyle had vanished. Crane felt for a pulse, afraid it was already too late. The wound wasn't deep enough to strike any vital organs, but it was long, and the curse had kept it bleeding freely all the time he'd struggled not to fall. Then he felt a beat, faint but steady. He kissed her. "It's over, Ketty. You're safe now. Please wake up."

She stirred. "Mama?"

"No." Crane nearly choked on tears of joy. "It's Crane and Luskell."

She blinked and opened her eyes. "Crane! Is it really you?" She struggled to sit up. He slipped his arm around her, and she clung to him. "Mama said you needed me."

"I did. I do. Always." This wasn't the time to ask how her long-dead mother came into it. "I'm sorry,

Ketty. I should have listened to you. I couldn't believe we were in any danger."

"You're just like your father." She shuddered. "I—need to lie down. What happened to me?" As he eased her back, she frowned at her ruined dress, then gazed around at the other faces. "Luskell, why are you wearing your hiking clothes? What are you even doing here? And is that Jagryn? And Laki?"

"Don't be too hard on them, Ketty. They saved our lives."

Luskell slumped down next to her mother, exhausted. She couldn't imagine doing any more magic for a week. Dadad took cushions from the dining chairs and placed them under Mamam's legs to prevent shock. Mamam shivered, though it was a warm evening.

"Luskell, give her your cloak," Dadad said.

Luskell had forgotten she was still wearing it. She'd had it on since they left Misty Pass in the morning; it was easier to wear it than carry it. She unfastened it and tucked it around her mother. She shuddered at the sight of the wound, a slash from Mamam's left collarbone almost to her right hip. It would leave an ugly scar, but at least the bleeding had stopped.

Mamam was asleep or unconscious again and didn't appear to notice when Luskell covered her. That was understandable—she had lost a lot of blood—but

Luskell wished her mother could see who was taking care of her.

As if she had heard the thought, Mamam's eyes flickered open, and she stared at Luskell's hands. "Luskell, you're hurt!" She tried to sit up. Dadad gently laid her back down.

"I'm not hurt, Mamam. I'm fine." Luskell smiled to reassure her.

"But your hands—so much blood—" Mamam winced and pressed a hand to her wound. "Is it—my blood?"

"Don't worry," Dadad said. "We'll take care of you. You'll be all right now."

You have to be. Luskell couldn't believe she had ever been angry at her mother.

A guard appeared at the top of the outdoor stairway. At the same moment, the door to an inner access flew open. The governor burst onto the terrace, accompanied by three more guards, including one with a fancier hat. "I heard a noise! What is going on here?"

Dadad went to meet him. "I was hoping you could explain. I received this invitation." He held out a letter.

I was right, Luskell thought with horror. *It was a trap.*

Snowabi's face turned red. "I—I know nothing about this."

Dadad kept his suspicion hidden, though Luskell caught a hint of it. "Then it seems your page has undiscovered talents."

"My—what?" The governor looked past Dadad at the unconscious man who still lay across the table. Luskell frowned. What did he mean, page?

"Yes, your nephew, Trenn, brought the invitation this morning. It seems he was laying a trap."

"A trap? Why would he do such a thing?"

"I don't know. Are you saying you didn't know he had magical abilities?"

Snowabi opened his mouth, then closed it again without answering.

Dadad went on. "Yes, it turns out the villain who calls himself the New Yrae was your nephew and page. He tried to assassinate us tonight and very nearly succeeded." He glanced at Luskell and smiled. She returned a weak grin. They had barely arrived in time. A moment more would have been too late. She squeezed Mamam's hand.

Footsteps pounded on the outdoor staircase, and Naliskat and Pataknan appeared. When the guard tried to bar their way, Naliskat shoved him aside and walked right up to Snowabi. He glared down at the governor. "Your plans are at an end," he growled.

The governor looked helplessly at Dadad for translation, though Naliskat had spoken in Eukardian.

"Allow me." Laki stepped in next to his father and turned to the governor with a polite smile. "The ambassador says your plans for the Aklaka are at an end." He also spoke in Eukardian, but with only a hint of an accent. "They are unacceptable. If you want our gold, that is one thing. But we will not be imprisoned, and you will not be a king."

Snowabi huffed and looked everywhere but at Laki. "Who are you?"

"I am Nalaklak, the ambassador's son. And also the Uklak's son. Someday I will lead the Aklaka. And as you can hear, I speak for myself. You can't murder your way out of dealing with us."

The governor frowned. "I understand you, but I don't know what you are talking about. What is this about gold, or a king, or murder?"

Dadad approached the unconscious Trenn. "Let's revive your nephew and ask him."

Chapter 42

With Naliskat's help, Crane hefted the unconscious young man into a chair and conjured more magical bonds to hold him upright. The light was going, but at a word from Crane, all the lanterns flared up. Something on the floor reflected a dull gleam—Trenn's weapon. He must have dropped it in the struggle with Laki and Jagryn. Crane picked it up with care and laid it on the table. It didn't look like much—a plain wooden hilt with a dark iron blade no longer than Crane's middle finger. It had a sharp edge, but the real danger was its curse. After things were settled here, he would have to render it harmless. First things first. He spoke a reviving charm.

Trenn's eyes flew open, then squeezed shut again. "My head," he groaned. He strained against his bonds, then muttered the unbinding spell. Crane held his breath. This was basic magic, one of the first spells he had learned himself. It didn't require much power, but nothing happened. Trenn stared at Crane. "What have you done to me?"

"I disarmed you." At Trenn's blank look, Crane explained further. "I drained your power."

"Can you—give it back?"

"No." Crane almost apologized. Helpless and pleading, Trenn seemed little older than Luskell. But Crane hadn't used the spell lightly. He had too many people on this rooftop to protect from whatever Trenn might attempt if he weren't rendered harmless. "You'll feel weak and sick for a few days. You should recover with no permanent damage, if my own experience holds true."

"Your own—how could you, if you know how it feels?"

"It hollows you out, doesn't it?" Crane swallowed a lump in his throat as he recalled his own loss of power, many years ago—at the hands of his own father, no less. A thing like that was hard to forgive.

"How did you learn such strong magic?"

Crane raised an eyebrow. "From Yrae."

Trenn's eyes widened. "You knew him?"

Crane had to smile, though the lump was back. "Nobody *knew* him, but I suppose I came close. I learned a lot from him."

"He was your master?" Trenn frowned. "That doesn't fit his reputation, and neither do you. You're supposed to be a do-gooder."

"Thank you. I try. Tell me why you borrowed that name when you had never met the man."

"To instill fear."

Crane nodded. That was what the original Yrae had used it for. "It worked on some people, but if you wanted to scare me, you chose the wrong name."

"But his reputation—"

Crane shook his head. "A reputation he cooked up for himself. He made mistakes—big ones—but he never killed. He went to great lengths to protect those he loved."

"Loved? Yrae?" Trenn scoffed.

"I know. At one time, I shared your skepticism." Crane drew another chair up and sat facing the young man. "But enough about me. Why don't you tell us what this is all about?"

Trenn's face was a sickly green, but he maintained a dignified expression. "I work for the governor. Ask him."

"I did. He denies any knowledge of tonight's event. He may not even know that you have power."

Trenn jerked around to glare at Snowabi. At this sudden movement, his dignity was swamped by obvious nausea. He regained control and locked eyes with Crane again. "He lies."

Crane kept his expression mild, but his heart raced. He reached out to Snowabi's mind and found it racing, as well, with blame, plots, alternative plans—too much to untangle now but defensive enough to persuade Crane that Trenn spoke the truth.

The three guards and their captain closed ranks around the governor, who was almost as pale as his nephew. They seemed content to let Crane question Trenn, but he knew he was on treacherous ground, interrogating the governor's kin. He would have to proceed with care.

For the first time, Crane noticed Ganyk, the council member who had attended the diplomatic meeting. He must have come out with the governor, though now he stood apart from that group. Crane wasn't sure what this meant, but he assumed more officials made things more complicated. He couldn't allow further harm to Ketty, and Luskell was profoundly weakened. They both needed protection.

Jagryn? Laki? Stay close to Luskell and Ketty. Take Liski and Takni with you.

Jagryn looked startled, then nodded. Laki murmured something to the other Aklaka in their language. All four quietly moved and took up positions around Luskell and Ketty.

Crane glanced once more at the governor, then nodded to Trenn. "Go on."

Luskell watched without much interest as Dadad began to question the young man. She knew this was important, but it seemed to take place at a great distance. She had done her part and wished it over so she could rest. She would be fine after a good sleep, but there was little chance of that on this stone-flagged terrace.

Mamam had recovered enough to recline against one of the cushions. She hugged Luskell's cloak to her as if she were still cold. She pressed her hand to her chest and whimpered.

"Does your wound hurt?" Luskell asked.

Mamam shook her head. She stared at Trenn. "He is in pain."

Luskell was about to argue that Mamam must be confused; she was the one who had been injured. Then Luskell felt it, too—an ache of loss, an almost physical anguish.

Mamam continued to watch. "Strange. His feelings were completely shielded before." Her eyes widened. "Crane, how could you?"

"Dadad? He didn't do anything except bind him."

"No, he drained his power. I'm sure of it. Trenn must feel he's lost his soul. The poor boy!"

"How can you feel sorry for him?" Luskell asked. "He tried to kill you. He doesn't have a soul!"

Mamam turned her gaze to Luskell. Her eyes were filled with tears. "I can't help it. I'm too weak to shield myself. And I know how it feels. So does your father."

Luskell stared at her mother. Through no fault of her own, she was suffering. She seemed to blame Dadad, but Luskell laid the blame on Trenn. She got to her feet. "I'll end his misery."

Jagryn and the three Aklaka stood around Luskell and her mother, a protective barrier maybe, but Luskell didn't want protection. She pushed past Jagryn.

He clutched her shoulder. "You should stay here."

"I have unfinished business." She shook him off and strode to the wrecked dining table where the cursed blade lay. Before her fingers touched the handle, Dadad raised his left hand, palm out. An unseen force struck her squarely and stopped her progress. Even without the words, she recognized the repelling charm she'd practiced with Jagryn and Laki. Dadad had never before used his considerable power against Luskell; the experience gave her a whole new respect for him. But it was a controlled force; it didn't knock her down or even drive her back. But she couldn't move forward.

"No, Luskell. That isn't the way." Dadad's voice was calm, even gentle, but the pressure did not abate.

"He tried to kill you and Mamam! He should pay." Luskell scowled at Trenn. She had to admit he didn't look like much of a threat now. He looked sick, and, for some reason, his face was bloody.

"He is. He will. But we do not attack the defenseless." Dadad turned and gazed at her, pleading but firm. "We find what is lost, heal the sick, make the broken whole. We do not curse."

Luskell frowned. "Knot did."

"That wasn't a curse. It was an enchantment." They exchanged a wry smile over this family joke. Luskell stepped away from the table, her hands raised. She expected Dadad to send her back to Mamam, but he stood and beckoned her over. When she reached his side, he put his arm around her shoulders and drew her close. He felt warm and strong, and she leaned against him. "Look at Trenn's face. You already left your mark on him."

She looked more closely at the wounds on his face, scratches and gouges—from an eagle's talons. "And I'd do it again."

Trenn glared at them. "What do you mean, *she* did this? I thought that eagle might be Yrae himself."

"Oh, he would have been so proud, but no, the eagle wasn't Yrae. It was Yrae's granddaughter."

"Granddaughter?" Trenn's eyes widened. "Then you are..."

"Yes. His son. Do you see now? You may have borrowed Yrae's name, but you were no match for his family."

Crane held Luskell close to his side. He wanted, more than anything, to keep her safe, but she didn't seem to need his protection. He was proud of her and frightened for her, but he knew Knot would have been delighted.

Trenn still looked sick, but he spoke firmly. "If my uncle told you he didn't know about tonight, he lied. It was my idea, but he gave his blessing."

Crane pulled his attention back to the interrogation. "And he knew you were the New Yrae?"

"Of course he knew! Do you think he would have given me a job if I didn't have useful skills?"

Crane frowned. "I thought that was a favor to your mother."

Trenn snorted. "He let her believe that, but he always looked down on us. My father wasn't good enough for him."

"Did your father have power, too? Was he a wizard?"

"He had some minor talent, but he never earned a staff. Neither did I, but I had enough power to show Snowabi it was useful to have a magic user in the family."

While Trenn talked, Crane examined the younger man's mind. He saw the father performing illusions in the market for a few coins and dying of a common illness when Trenn was still a boy. There was resentment against Snowabi's grudging support and great pride in a gift for magic. Yet he resisted his early teachers at the Wizards' Hall. They refused to teach him the kinds of magic he craved, either because he wasn't ready or the spells were too dark. They encouraged him to develop his natural ability for shielding and stealth, but he wanted more. He learned in secret, from books, a practice Crane wouldn't recommend but for which he had sympathy. Trenn also met in secret with shady characters down by the docks, picking up curses and unsubtle weather spells. His talent for shielding kept these habits from his mother's eye and remained his greatest power. The draining spell was the only reason Crane had access to his mind now. He had great ambition, out of proportion with his abilities, but it seemed to be the only thing that kept him going. He wanted to be somebody—not so different from Crane's father at that age.

"My uncle wanted to be more than governor," Trenn continued. "He wanted to be king, and I was going to help him."

So ambition runs in the family, Crane thought. "Eukard hasn't had a king in centuries. What made Snowabi think he could be one?"

Trenn rolled his eyes, and Crane didn't even have to read the thought behind it. They agreed about Snowabi's outsized opinion of himself. "You've probably guessed by now I can shield myself and those around me. I was to hide Snowabi's thoughts, keep anyone from suspecting the plan, while the governor gained as many allies as possible on the Legislative Council and among the Governor's Guard. I can also bend thoughts toward or away from a particular subject. Anyone he couldn't charm or coerce I was to bewitch into trusting him."

"Now see here!" Snowabi objected.

Ganyk squeezed the governor's shoulder. "You'll have a chance to tell your side, Governor. Let's hear the young man out."

Crane returned his attention to Trenn. "You aimed to bewitch the entire nation?" This idea had an eerie familiarity.

Trenn shrugged. "Maybe just the city. I heard Yrae did something like that once."

Crane couldn't help but smile. "Yes, he did, though on a much smaller town than Eukard City. I grew up under that spell. I knew something felt familiar this summer, but I couldn't place it."

"I managed to enchant small pockets of the city for a day or so," Trenn said. "That wasn't our focus yet. Snowabi was more concerned about a population of unknown numbers not under his rule. If he could bring the Aklaka under his control...and there were rumors of gold."

Crane thought of the gold nuggets on Naliskat's knife hilt. He had been right so far. "Gold—to enrich the national treasury?"

"And Snowabi's own pocket. The Aklaka are sitting on a fortune they don't care about. If he could organize them into settlements, he would have control of their society and their riches. But we couldn't accomplish that if his true goal came out too soon. So I had the job of shielding his thoughts from someone like you." Trenn gave Crane a respectful nod. The gesture was weakened by the impotent fury he couldn't hide. His power was all he had. Losing it, even temporarily, was utter humiliation. Crane sympathized, but it was too late now.

"I don't know why I didn't see it before. Things were always strangely quiet when you were with us in meetings," Crane said. "I suppose you were responsible for the heat wave, too. But why the random attacks on people in the street?"

"The Aklaka ambassador resisted our proposal. The governor asked me to do more—distract you, throw you off balance, send a warning. So I bought a cheap blade, cursed it and..." He waved toward Ketty.

Crane resisted the urge to punch Trenn. In some ways, he was like Yrae. He acted without a thought for consequences. But Yrae had never killed anyone. Then again, neither had Trenn—yet.

"In the end, it seemed the only way to act on the Aklaka problem was to get rid of the translator," Trenn said. "The governor asked me to take care of it as privately as possible, so I organized this little supper party—where you would be tragically killed by a mysterious, unseen assailant. I was going to sustain a wound myself in my heroic effort to save you."

"And you failed!" Snowabi exclaimed. "You were defeated by children! Now I'll never be king!"

Trenn sneered at his uncle. "You would have worn the crown, but I would have been the real power. You were my puppet, and I was your heir! I would have been king one day. But you had to rush things."

The various guards had gathered behind the governor with Ganyk. They spoke in low voices for a moment. Then their captain tapped Snowabi on the shoulder. "Sir?"

He sighed and turned. "Yes?"

"You're—under arrest."

"On what charge?"

Ganyk stepped forward. "You swore to uphold the constitution of Eukard, which states that no leader may reinstate the monarchy without the approval of three-fourths of the people. Attempting to make yourself king is treason."

From the other side of the terrace, someone let out a quiet whoop. Crane thought it was Jagryn, but he didn't turn to look. His attention was still on Trenn. "I think we can assume you will be arrested, too. It's lucky you didn't kill anyone. You'll be free again one day, and you're young. What do you plan to do with your life?"

Trenn shook his head, then winced. "I have no skills. Without my power, I'm nothing."

"It should return."

Two guards marched the governor away. The other two approached Trenn. Crane unbound him and helped him to stand. Luskell moved out of the way and stumbled against the supper table. She seemed exhausted, but that was understandable after all the magic she'd done. She would recover quickly with rest.

Crane returned his attention to the guards. "He needs a healer. Could he perhaps go to Balsam's House for a few days?"

The Captain of the Guard shook his head. "We can bring a healer to the prison to care for him."

Trenn turned toward the guards and held out his arms for the manacles. Then, without warning, he jerked away and staggered to the table. He grabbed Luskell with one hand and the cursed knife with the other. He pressed the blade to her throat. "I won't go to prison."

Chapter 43

Trenn held the girl tightly, the cursed blade to her throat. He was glad she knew enough not to struggle; he preferred not to hurt her and lacked the strength for a fight. He trembled with fatigue, fear, failure. He couldn't pretend to be the New Yrae anymore. It was over.

How had everything fallen apart? Now Snowabi would never be king, and Trenn's only hope of worldly power was snuffed out. Without his magic, he had nothing. He would be nobody again. Except in prison, he would be worse than nobody. No one would fear him there.

The girl couldn't have been even fifteen, but already she had more power than he could dream of. Already, she used it well. She had risked her life to save others from an unknown adversary. Trenn couldn't think of anyone he would put himself at risk for—not without promise of payment.

She had everything he wanted. She was kin to wizards—to Yrae! What must it be like to have a father like hers, power like hers? Trenn didn't want to hurt her. He wanted to *be* her.

Not possible, of course. She could change, but he never would. The only power he had left was in the blade he held. Her father, for all his might, was wise enough to fear it. The girl knew better than to struggle near that cursed edge. For now, he had everyone's attention. He could pretend it was respect. Whatever happened, he would not be remembered as a nobody.

His trembling increased, and the emptiness inside became a physical ache. He longed for relief, for rest. For the end.

Luskell wanted to scream her fury to the darkening sky, but she kept still. How could this have happened *again*? Why did every horrible man want to pull a knife on her? But this blade was more than sharp, and Trenn had already shown he wasn't afraid to use it. She locked eyes with Dadad and tried to be strong. Either he would rescue her, or she would save herself. She refused to imagine the alternative.

She didn't fight Trenn as he backed away from the guards. His emotions nearly overwhelmed her—anguish at the loss of his power, anger at his uncle's betrayal, and fear. Of what? Of prison? She was too muddled to try to read his thoughts, but she knew he was more frightened than she was. The knife shook in his hand. He reminded her of Kanala on that first day, trembling and skittish. She began to croon the Aklaka lullaby, the song that calmed mountains.

No one moved. Luskell sang, and Trenn ceased his trembling. The knife moved away from her throat, not much, but enough. As with the junk dealer, she stamped her heavy boot on his instep and dropped out of his grasp. He howled as she flung herself away from him to the safety of her father's arms.

"My baby, my brave girl." Dadad stroked her hair. He shook and wept as much as she did.

Trenn leaned against the parapet and stared at them. The guards approached him with the shackles but halted when he brandished the knife. He climbed onto the parapet. He continued to point the knife at the guards. Then he held it to his own throat.

"I won't go to prison, and I won't live without power."

He drew the cursed blade across his throat and plunged backward off the parapet.

"No!" Luskell screamed and sprang forward.

"Don't look, Luskell." Dadad tried to hold her back.

She had to see for herself. She broke away and leaned over the parapet. Trenn lay face up in the courtyard below. Something dark pooled around him. "We need to get down there! You could still save him, Dadad. Couldn't you? If we hurried?"

He shook his head and drew her away. "Why didn't he believe me?"

A memory of emptiness washed off him, a hollowness from the loss of his power. Luskell had discovered her own power so recently, she had never considered what it might feel like to lose it. Based on these echoes, she didn't want to know. But her parents did. Had they wanted to die? Luskell cried for them ... and for Trenn. She had hated him enough to kill him herself, but now she felt only pity. He was an ambitious young man with a unique talent. How could he have nothing to live for?

Dadad held Luskell while she cried. When he talked to other people, she felt his voice as a comforting buzz but didn't hear the words. After awhile, she dried her eyes. Her tears changed nothing, except that she felt even more exhausted. "The governor was arrested, and Trenn is dead. There's no one left to interrogate. Can we go now?"

"Not yet," Dadad said. "Get comfortable. The Captain of the Guard still has to collect statements from everyone for the official report. And Ganyk has just taken word to Klanya about what must be an unexpected promotion. We should wait for her."

These names were only vaguely familiar to Luskell. She sat with Mamam again to wait. Jagryn stood close by while they gave their statements. Mamam briefly lifted the cloak that covered her to show the bloody rag of her best dress. When Luskell related how she'd seen what was happening from the roof of the Legislative Council Hall, she saw disbelief in the Captain's eyes.

"That building is closed this time of night," he objected. "How could you get to the roof? Fly?"

"Yes, as a matter of fact. I changed into an eagle."

He scratched his head. "Trenn said something about an eagle, but I wasn't sure what he was talking about."

"That was Luskell," Jagryn said. "She flew right into his face and saved Crane from going over the edge."

"I wish I'd seen it," the Captain said. "Could you change again now?"

Luskell sighed and shook her head. "No. I'm too worn out."

"I might have something left." Jagryn concentrated and, for a moment, became an owl again. Then he turned back. "We can all do it, as long as we're rested."

The Captain of the Guard stared with his mouth open. He closed his mouth and made a note, then went to Laki.

Jagryn slid down to sit, leaned back against the parapet and closed his eyes. It seemed like a good idea, so Luskell closed her eyes, too. But when she did, she saw Trenn's broken body again, staring up at her from a pool of blood. She shuddered and resolved to keep her eyes open.

On the opposite side of the terrace, Laki had finished giving his statement and was deep in conversation with his father, but they were too far away for Luskell to hear. Somebody brought food, and she ate without tasting. She was hungry, but she had never felt so tired in her life. It helped to see Mamam looking better. She was still too weak to get up, but her color had improved, and she ate with a good appetite.

"Do you still—dream about Ketwyn?"

Luskell looked at Mamam with surprise. They hadn't talked about Ketwyn since the night they arrived in Deep River. "Yes. At least, I saw him a few times. I hope I will again."

Mamam nodded. "I think I saw him, too, when I was...*bleeding*. I was in a beautiful meadow, light and warm without any sun."

Luskell shivered to think what this meant. Before she could say anything, Mamam continued. "My mother was there, too, and Knot. They told me I couldn't stay. But I was most interested in Ketwyn. He wasn't a baby, but a young man, with red hair and no freckles and blue eyes like—"

"—like his father's. I know."

Now it was Mamam's turn to look surprised. "How would you know that?"

"I met Walgyn at the dance in Deep River."

Mamam frowned. "I should have told Stell to keep you home that night."

"I'm glad you didn't. I had such a good time, and Walgyn is a talented fiddler."

"Exactly the problem. Did he know who you were?"

"Not until I introduced myself. Then he said there was a resemblance." Luskell took a deep breath and continued. "He asked about you."

"And what did you tell him?" Mamam's voice was tight, but she didn't sound angry.

"That you weren't there. That you'd married a great wizard." Mamam smiled at that, which gave Luskell courage. "I said I'd ask you to write to him."

Mamam huffed and turned away. "Why would I do that?"

"To give him a chance to apologize?" Luskell offered. Mamam glanced at her but didn't say anything. "He asked about Ketwyn, so I showed him the grave. Walgyn played a tune for him."

Before either of them could say more, the door into the mansion opened, and the man Dadad had called Ganyk emerged with a tall woman. Her silver hair looked like it had been arranged in a hurry, and she'd put on a simple, loose dress such as Luskell or her mother might wear to the market. But she moved with authority. The Captain of the Guard spoke to her with obvious respect.

"Who is that woman?" Luskell whispered.

"Lieutenant Gov—no, *Governor* Klanya." Mamam wore a satisfied smile.

The Captain consulted his notes as he reported what had happened. When Klanya glanced in her direction, Luskell grew hot and looked away. She wanted to impress this woman, but she was sure her part of the story sounded ridiculous. She didn't know where to look when the new governor approached.

"I am very sorry about your injuries," she said to Mamam. "I will personally see that you receive all the care you need." She turned to Luskell and Jagryn with a stern look. "You young people were very foolish to intervene in such a dangerous situation." She smiled.

"Foolish but brave. You probably saved at least two lives, and foiled a devious plot."

"You believe our story?" Luskell asked.

"Is there any reason I shouldn't? Now then, I understand the Aklaka ambassador is here. I would very much like to meet him. We were never properly introduced."

Dadad signaled Naliskat to come over. Laki and Pataknan followed. "Governor, this is Ambassador Naliskat and his—entourage."

"I am happy to meet all of you," she said.

Naliskat narrowed his eyes. "I *will* be happy to meet you if you do not insist we move into towns."

He had spoken in Eukardian, but Dadad began to translate. Klanya held up her hand to stop him. "I understand. We will arrange new talks, but I can assure you that I have no interest in moving anyone who doesn't wish to move."

Laki rushed forward and grasped Klanya's hand. Naliskat smiled. "Governor, this is my son, Nalaklak."

"I promised Luskell I would meet the governor," Laki explained. "I thought it would be years from now."

She shook his hand warmly and smiled. "I am pleased to meet you, Nalaklak. You speak even more clearly than your father."

He grinned. "Beginning tonight, I will serve as his apprentice and translator." He looked at Dadad. "If Crane is willing, that is."

Dadad nodded. "Yes. It is time you spoke for yourselves."

Luskell stared at Laki. "What do you mean, apprentice?"

"I might not be Uklak for many years," he explained. "The ambassador also does important work, and it will be good training."

"And a new challenge."

He smiled. "Just what I need."

Near midnight, the Governor's Guard provided a carriage to take everyone back to Embassy House. Dadad carried Mamam into the apartment and settled her in the big, luxurious bed. Luskell helped him remove the ruined dress and apply a proper dressing to the scabbed wound. Mamam instructed them at first, but by the time they'd put a nightgown on her, she was asleep.

Rather than make up a separate bed for Luskell, Dadad insisted she sleep with Mamam.

"Are you sure?" Luskell asked. "You must be tired."

He smiled and kissed the top of her head. "Not as tired as you. You saved my life tonight. Let me watch over you and pretend you're still my little girl."

She hugged him. "That's not going to change." There was no one she would rather have guard her. He stepped out while she undressed and climbed into bed, then he pulled a chair close to the bedside and extinguished the lamp.

It had been a long, strange day. Luskell was so exhausted she could barely move, but she was still afraid to close her eyes. She stared into the darkness and listened to Dadad's steady breathing.

"When can we go home?" she asked.

"I'm not sure. Where is home, for you?"

"With you," she murmured without hesitation.

"Ah. For now, at least. But where do you want to go?"

"Deep River."

"I do, too. After a day like we've had, I long for a place where nothing happens." His chair creaked as he shifted position. "I thought you liked the city."

"I do, but—I don't know. It's different. I saw a man die." Her throat clenched, and she drew a sobbing breath. "Why did he do it, Dadad?"

He took her hand and held it tight. "I don't know. Maybe his power was all he had to live for." He sighed. "I told him it would return, but did he have any reason to believe me? Maybe I shouldn't have—"

"You did the right thing."

He didn't answer right away. "I hope so," he murmured at last. "I try to think about consequences before I act, but there wasn't time."

Luskell closed her eyes. "Klamamam says Knot never considered consequences. He would act and regret it later."

Dadad made a noise between a laugh and a sob. "He never learned. But he found a kind of redemption in the end. I wanted that for Trenn. I don't think he was a bad man."

"He was—afraid." Luskell could barely open her mouth, she was so tired. "Alone. No—love."

She let sleep take her. Once again, she had a vague sense of Knot and Ketwyn nearby. She was glad they could still visit her dreams, even though she was using her power now. They didn't speak to her, but she felt their pride.

She tried to get to them. It was like pushing with tired limbs against a heavy curtain, and she feared the effort would wake her, but at last she found herself in the bright, warm meadow. Elika was there, too, tending a bewildered young man.

Knot smiled at Luskell. "He just arrived."

"I know," she said. "He wanted to be like Yrae."

He raised an eyebrow. "Then he got his wish."

"Will you take care of him? He made some mistakes."

"I know something about that."

Ketwyn joined them. "Mama was here."

"I know," Luskell said. "Thank you for sending her back."

"That was more your doing than ours," Knot said.

"Dadad was the one who knew the countercurse," Luskell objected.

"And who saved his life? Without you they would both have been lost. But yes, we did send her back. Children need their mother."

"I don't feel like a child anymore."

Knot nodded. "Perhaps not. But I stand by my words."

Chapter 44

Luskell woke to sunshine streaming into the room. She couldn't believe the whole night had passed, but it was close to noon.

She rolled over to find Balsam examining her mother. "Good morning, Luskell. Any hurts I should know about?"

"All I needed was sleep. How's Mamam?"

"Excellent, considering she should be dead. It's a good thing we worked out the countercurse." She studied the entire length of the wound. "Yes, this is healing well already. But you always did heal quickly, didn't you, Ketty?"

"No thanks to me this time." Mamam's voice was weak, but she managed a smile. "I think it was mostly Luskell. She got to me first."

Balsam started, then winked at Luskell. "In that case, you can come work for me anytime." She continued to gently probe the wound. "It's too late to prevent scarring, but you can reduce it when you get your strength back. Get Luskell to help you. She—" Balsam paused with her hands over Mamam's abdomen. "Ketty, you never told me you were expecting!"

"I—what?" Mamam stared.

"Don't tell me you didn't know!"

Mamam paled, then pinked up again. "I—didn't. I mean, I knew I might be, but with everything that was happening...Are you sure?"

Balsam smiled. "Fairly sure. Once you've recovered, you'll know for certain."

Luskell sank back weakly against her pillow. She remembered what Knot had said—*Children need their mother.*

Not a *child. Children.* He must have known. Things would be changing. Luskell would no longer have her parents to herself. But she liked having a brother—at least in her dreams.

After Balsam left, Mamam drifted back to sleep. Luskell got out of bed and put her travel clothes back on. She joined Dadad in the dining room.

"I saved you some breakfast," he said. "Although I suppose it's more like lunch now."

She sat at the table and filled a plate with fruit and bread. "You never answered me last night. When can we leave?"

"We must be patient. Your mother has to regain her strength first, and I still have work to do here."

"What work? Laki will translate for Naliskat now."

"True, but I'll sit in on the first meetings with Klanya until Laki knows what's expected of him. And I should talk to Bardin at the Wizards' Hall. How did Trenn manage to learn the wrong kinds of magic, completely undetected by anyone who might have stopped him? I don't want another 'New Yrae' to rise with no plan for how to stop him."

"Makes sense, I guess," Luskell admitted. "How long will all that take?"

Dadad chuckled, but he wasn't laughing at her. His hazel eyes were full of sympathy. She hadn't thought about it before, but they were like Klamamam's eyes. "A week should do it. We'll plan on a couple of days in Misty Pass. I'll write and let Mama know to expect us in ten days' time."

Luskell sighed. "A week." It seemed a long time, but she guessed it could have been worse. "I'll need some clothes, then. These are all I have with me." She indicated her trousers and shirt.

Dadad raised one eyebrow. "Funny you should mention that." He went into the sitting room and returned with a large, paper-wrapped parcel. "This came for you this morning."

Luskell untied the strings and folded back the paper. Inside were three simple summer dresses, one green, one blue, and one brown, as well as a nightdress and underthings. The dresses were slightly faded but clean, and when she held one up, it was long enough. She met Dadad's smiling gaze. "Who—? How—?"

"Last night, I told Governor Klanya how you three must have traveled with only what you could wear or fit in your pockets. I think she understood what that might mean for a girl."

Luskell sank into her chair, stunned. "The *Governor* sent these?"

"She must have felt she could spare them. And she is about your height."

Luskell smiled. "I feel better about the future of Eukard."

Dadad squeezed her shoulders. "So do I. Now, if you're all set, I need to go out soon. I should take Jagryn with me to the Wizards' Hall so he can meet Dalmer and some of the other apprentices. It's a disadvantage for a young wizard not to know any others."

"You didn't, and you turned out fine."

He smiled. "Thank you, but you know I've never been quite at ease around the others. It's better to be comfortable with every kind of people, including those with power."

"Should I come, too, then?"

"You already know everyone there. Besides, one of us should be here when your mother wakes up." He kissed her on the top of her head, took his staff, and went to fetch Jagryn from Naliskat's apartment.

Luskell sat down, at a loss. When she was in Deep River, she had wanted only to be here in the city, with her parents and her friends. Now she was here, and

Mamam was sleeping while Dadad was planning to spend more time with Laki and Jagryn than with her. And she couldn't even go out and find her other friends. She might as well not have come.

She closed her eyes and saw Trenn again, staring at her from a pool of blood. She had saved Mamam and Dadad from that fate. Her visit here was not wasted. She was the hero.

She reached for her new fiddle, which she had not yet played. She plucked a string and smiled. Already, she liked the sound. She tuned it and began to play a song Dokral had taught her. She hadn't played in weeks, but it sounded better than before. Maybe Dadad was right—Dokral had made this instrument with her in mind.

"That sounds lovely." Mamam stood in the doorway. She clung to the jamb, but at least she was on her feet.

Luskell lowered her bow. "I'm sorry; I didn't mean to wake you."

"No, I was ready to get up." Mamam made her way to the table and the remains of breakfast. "Where's your father?"

"He said something about taking Jagryn to the Wizards' Hall." Luskell drew a deep breath and let it out before plunging ahead. "Was Balsam right? About—a baby?"

Mamam smiled and nodded. "I'm certain now. You saved both of us."

"Boy or girl?"

"It's too soon to tell. All we know is you'll be a sister next spring."

"How did that happen?"

"Luskell, we've had that conversation. You know very well how it happens."

Luskell blushed. "That's not what I meant. Why didn't you know already?"

"I've been—distracted. But the timing is good. We can go to Deep River and stay until after the baby is born. And you can help Brynnit when the time comes. It will be excellent training for you, now that we know what you can do."

"Dadad says we'll go to Deep River in a week. He's writing to Klamamam."

"Well, in that case, I have a letter to write, too." Mamam finished her breakfast and went to the writing desk. Luskell assumed she was writing to Grandpa Eslo in Misty Pass to let him know they would be stopping there.

The seven days passed quickly, with plenty of fiddle practice and instruction in healing. Luskell was happy to learn, though she didn't have much natural aptitude for it. She didn't see Dadad or the boys as much as she would have liked, but it was time well spent for all of them. The city seemed less haunted with each day. But at the end of the week, she was ready to leave.

The day arrived at last. Jagryn, the eager apprentice, had volunteered to go with Dadad to hire a cart to take them and their luggage to the coach office. Luskell waited with Laki on the front steps of Embassy House.

"It feels strange, leaving you here." She had known he would be working with his father now, but it hadn't sunk in until now that this meant he would stay in the city. She would have to say goodbye. "Was this the adventure you expected?"

He grinned. "I don't know what I expected, but I'll never forget it. I wish we didn't have to break up our Magic Club."

She nodded. "I know. We were just getting started. But it's not like we'll never see each other again."

"You'll stay in Deep River with your parents?"

"Yes, at least until the baby's born—after Spring Balance, Mamam says. She's teaching me healing, and she wants me to help Brynnit when the time comes."

"We all have new responsibilities. Will you come to the city again next summer? I know I'll be here."

"I don't know." Luskell's family had always spent at least part of the summer in Eukard City because they had to, but now that obligation was past. "I think Mamam wants to spend more time in Misty Pass after the baby comes. She grew up there, and it's pleasant in summer—not as hot as Deep River. But Balsam invited me to work with her here. I wonder if they'd let me come by myself."

"You've done it once already," Laki pointed out. "What about next winter? Will you come to Aku's Lap?"

"I doubt it, not with a new baby."

"Maybe you could come there by yourself. It isn't far if you fly from Misty Pass." He glanced around and spoke in a softer voice. "Will you think about what I said? About—someday having a daughter like you?"

"No. I won't." She couldn't look at him as she answered, but sneaked a glance after the words were out. His look of disappointment was hard to bear.

"Why not? Is it Jagryn?"

The question shocked her into silence, and she found she couldn't answer directly. "Laki, you're old enough to think about these things, but I'm not. Ask me again when I'm—I don't know, when I'm twenty—and maybe I'll consider it." He nodded, and she knew the matter was settled, at least for now. He deserved more than only a goodbye. "I owe you something." She took his face between her hands and pressed her lips to his. He pulled back and stared at her. Then he drew her close and kissed her in earnest. Kissing Jagryn had been exciting and comforting at once. This was wilder, like riding Kanala bareback at top speed. She withdrew, thrilled but dizzy.

He was grinning again. "I think you owe me one more."

Just then, Jagryn and Dadad arrived with the cart and driver. Luskell was glad neither of them had seen her kiss Laki. She gave him a peck on the cheek. "Goodbye, Laki. Maybe I'll see you next summer, or in Aku's Lap. Or you could run away to Deep River again."

He laughed heartily. "I'm an adult now. No more running away. But listen for my voice in your mind."

She listened for him all the way to Misty Pass but heard nothing. She was distracted from this pursuit by Grandpa Eslo's look of surprise when they descended from the coach. It was obvious he hadn't received a letter alerting him to their arrival. But he was delighted to see them. He put them all up at the Fogbank for two nights, rather than let Mamam trek back and forth from the cabin at mealtimes "in her condition." She laughed and swore she was fine but didn't seem to mind the pampering.

The truth of Mamam's letter was not revealed until they continued their journey. The coach made a late-morning rest stop in Sweetwater, and everyone got out to stretch. Luskell stared as Walgyn's lanky figure unfolded from a bench in front of the coach office.

He grinned at Mamam, then dropped his gaze to the ground. "You cut your hair."

"And what business is that of yours?" Her tone was sharp, but her voice quavered.

"None, I guess. It looks good on you." He glanced at her and smiled again. "I could hardly believe it when I got your letter, after all this time."

Her expression softened. "Life is too short to cling to old wrongs."

He nodded and cleared his throat. "I'm sorry, Ketty. About sending you away. When I sobered up, I tried to find you, but no one saw which way you went. And I'm sorry about Ketwyn. "

"You couldn't have saved him."

"No. At least now I know where he is." He smiled at Luskell. "Thank you. I—think I dreamed about him."

"I thought only magic folk—"

"He thought so, too, but someone called Knot told him that creativity and love are almost as strong." He stared at the case in her hands, and his eyes lit up. "Fiddle?"

"Yes, I just got it."

"Do you know 'The Blacksmith's Courtship?'"

She grinned. This was the rollicking tune she had danced with Jagryn. "I can play the second part."

He turned to where his fiddle case lay on the bench and opened it. "Then I'll take lead."

They tuned up and began to play. The other passengers clapped and stomped, and a pair of them even danced, until the driver called for them to return to their seats.

"Will I see you again?" Walgyn asked as Mamam climbed back into the coach.

"We'll be staying in Deep River for about a year," she said. "I imagine we'll see you at the Summer Dance."

"By then, I'll know if I have a brother or a sister," Luskell put in.

Mamam frowned at her, but Dadad smiled. "Ketty will know long before that."

Walgyn reached through the window to shake his hand. "Your daughter says you're a great man. I don't know whether that's true, but you're a lucky one."

Luskell's face warmed when Dadad smiled across at her and said, "You don't have to tell me that."

Chapter 45

Late that afternoon, Luskell and Jagryn sat up in the back of Uncle Jagree's wagon on the road from Oxbow to Deep River. Dadad rode up front, and Mamam reclined in the back with her eyes closed, not quite sleeping.

"It'll be good to stay in Deep River awhile," Mamam murmured. She had recovered from her wound, but her new pregnancy made her tired. "Are Sulika and Foli still waiting for us? When's the wedding?"

Uncle Jagree chuckled. "Hm. No. Sulika and Foli aren't waiting for anyone now."

"What? Did they get married already? Or do you mean the wedding's off?"

He glanced back and winked at Luskell. "That one is. There may well be another. But nobody's waiting anymore."

Luskell had almost forgotten that drama but was proud of the small part she'd played. She grinned at Jagryn. He looked down, red-faced and shaking with suppressed laughter.

Mamam smiled but didn't open her eyes. "Sounds like there's a story waiting."

Uncle Jagree nodded. "Ask Stell when you get there. Or Rakkyn. He has an interesting perspective."

Perspective. Luskell liked his understated way of putting that. Maybe her own perspective would seem interesting, too. She'd never before paid attention to how grown folks related to each other. She'd seen a lot this summer of what could go wrong—or right. She felt closer to being grown folks herself, what with her power. And Jagryn's wizard face. And Laki's kiss; she couldn't forget that if she tried.

They rolled on in companionable quiet. Mamam dozed. No one spoke until a blackened pasture came into view.

"Is this the place?" Dadad asked. Luskell had told him all about fighting the wildfire. "You were right, it is close to the field." He held up his thumb and forefinger almost touching. "You were this close to the crop going up in flames."

"Considering we barely knew what we were doing..."

"That won't be true for long. You will begin formal instruction tomorrow morning."

Luskell glanced at Jagryn. "Both of us?"

"Of course, both of you! I can't leave so much power untrained. Besides, I'm curious to see what you can do."

Luskell felt warm all over. Dadad had always planned to come back and teach magic to Jagryn, but she never figured she'd be included. "I wish Laki could be with us, too."

"He'll be learning plenty on his own," Dadad replied. "I imagine you'll have much to share when you meet again."

"We will." But some of the warmth had gone out of the day. She still hadn't heard from Laki, and now she was probably too far away. She leaned her elbows on the tailgate and watched the scorched pasture recede.

"You miss him, don't you?" Jagryn's voice was quiet, just audible over the squeak and rumble of the wagon.

Luskell's face grew hot. Laki would be good at his new job, she was sure, but it could be more than a year before she saw him again. By then, everything might be different. She didn't look at Jagryn as she answered. "Yes. I miss him."

"I do, too. I wish he could have come back with us, even for a short time."

"I'm glad you two are friends now. I wasn't so sure at first."

Jagryn laughed. "Laki's a good fellow. I'd choose him, too, if I were you."

Luskell started. "I haven't *chosen* anyone."

Jagryn raised his eyebrows and grinned hopefully.

Luskell smiled and shook her head at his eagerness. She glanced around at Mamam, resting again with her eyes closed, and at Dadad sitting tall and straight on the seat up front. Luskell was the daughter of magic. And its granddaughter, but so much more. She could dream her own dreams and follow her own path wherever her power led. In time, she might let someone join her on that journey. Magic users were hard to live with, but her parents showed it could be done. Would it be Laki or Jagryn? Or someone she hadn't even met yet?

She turned back to Jagryn. "Maybe I never will choose." A sprig of lupine appeared in her hand, the blossoms changing to purple and green butterflies that burst into fireworks. "Let's learn some magic."

The End

About the Author

Karen Eisenbrey lives in Seattle, WA, where she leads a quiet, orderly life and invents stories to make up for it. Although she intended to be a writer from an early age, until her mid-30s she had nothing to say. A little bit of free time and a vivid dream about a wizard changed all that. Karen writes fantasy and science fiction novels, as well as short fiction in a variety of genres and the occasional song or poem if it insists. She also sings in a church choir and plays drums in a garage band. She shares her life with her husband, two young adult sons, and one elderly cat.

Special Thanks

... to Benjamin Gorman for starting the little publishing-company-that-could and inspiring me to pull this manuscript out of my hard drive and into the world; and to Brionna Poppitz and Sydney Culpepper for their mad editing skills.

...to Michaela Thorn for the beautiful, powerful cover art.

... to Angelika, Nan, and Yvonne, my invaluable beta readers. Your comments and suggestions turned an OK draft into a book.

... to Amy and Tim, my writers' support group who have patiently listened to me read chapters, not necessarily in order; and posthumous thanks to Anne, who read the earliest draft of this book, the last thing I finished before she passed away.

... to Steve Scribner for help with the map of Eukard.

... to Keith Eisenbrey, my example for doing the creative work that needs to be done in spite of everything else. He has read countless drafts (of this and other projects), listened to me fuss over ideas, welcomed the host of fictional people who live in my head, and kept a roof over our heads all these years. I couldn't do any of it without him.

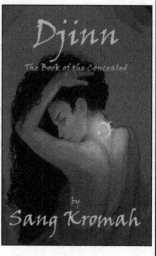

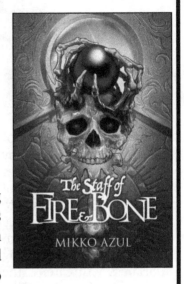